TO LIVE AGAIN

To Live Again

by

Ailene Blair Stanley

Printed by CreateSpace,
An Amazon.com Company
2017

First printed: 2017

ISBN-13: 978-1976452475

ISBN-10: 1976452473

Printed by CreateSpace, An Amazon.Com Company

Contents

Author

Ailene Stanley has published this, her debut novel, after much research into the historical aspects of her stories. It became more than an interest for her and for several years has taken up time and given much pleasure.

Although Scottish and Canadian Ailene lives on the south coast of Devon, as close as possible to France she says. Her great loves are her library, which reflects her eclectic choices, and also the study of language.

Travel has been a life-long delight spanning many years and many places in Europe, North America and China. Her writing encompasses her interests in different places in different times and incorporates her understanding and affinity with the feline of the species.

Her trip to the Canadian High Arctic inspired a series of articles but her favourite experience was walking in the wilds of British Columbia with two wolves. Sailing across the English Channel and into the French canals with her husband and family are also memorable experiences in Ailene's life.

Her five children have left the nest and live mostly in Canada. Now living alone she enjoys the opportunity to write freely.

Acknowledgements

There is no measure of my gratitude to my writing friends who have patiently and so very kindly walked the path of this novel along with me over too long a period of time. My Writing Mentor, Leo Wilson, herself a writer of several novels under the name of Leo Debs, has painstakingly taught, advised and encouraged throughout my journey. My fellow writers who have shared their time and their own literary contributions with me have become friends of a select kind, the never-to-be-forgotten or ever-taken-for-granted kind: Hilary Leavens, Sue Chalkley, Michael McLarnon who writes as Michael Trelissik and John E Clarke. I must make special mention of the late Roger Johnson, formerly part of our group, whose wit and intelligence entertained us for many years and who gave me encouragement that will always stay with me despite his sad departure.

At the end of this road I have a new friend to thank for the assistance given to me in the publishing of this novel, David J Richards, also Barry J Stanley my former husband whose support and positive influence helped bring this interest of mine to fruition.

I am also grateful for the technological advances available to writers today which have enabled me to see the final outcome of my research and imagination in print.

The Call

A canopy above of branch and leaf.
Inquisitive, we nine run beneath.
My eyes are wide, forward strains my ear.
I am cat, I am small, I am brave, I feel fear.

What is this night through which I race?
I do not know. What is this place?
What beings are these that run with me?
Where is the light? I cannot see.

Large and small I sense them all.
Sleek and furry, short and tall.
Oh that great one defies belief.
He looks at me. I see his teeth!

We pause. We wash, a feline trait.
Then onwards rush to meet our fate.
All nine of us, we flee, we flee,
A Smilodon in front of me.

Is this jungle moving past?
Can ferns and creepers move this fast?
The darkness closes in behind.
A backwards road I'll never find.

Our path is blocked. A tall cliff face.
Captives in this strange new place.
We stop as one and gather round.
I cringe. I shrink. What is this sound?

A voice I hear, but in my head.
Says 'Share your birth, the life you led,
The world you knew in joy and pain.
The call has come to live again.'

I won't be first. I won't be last.
It might be good to share my past.
But I'll let that big one go ahead.
My name is Wutki. I'm no longer dead.

The moon, I see the moon. It's really bright.
Other eyes shining in their flight.
The shadows lift. We choose the best.
A ledge for each. A place to rest.

'You children of the feline race.
You walked the world in light and grace.
Tonight your stories will be revealed.
Your onwards journey will then be sealed.'

Then appeared the gentlest glow.
It came from nowhere and fell below.
The largest cat was bathed in light.
He stepped in front in aura bright.

A new voice spoke, both deep and bold.
Wutki watched the scene unfold.
Past life images were seen.
All eight cats settled. Was this a dream?

The Call

Present Day

One by one they emerged from the darkness, fearless, their tails streaming behind them, ears pricked forward, nostrils testing the unseen. As a group they paused to take in the presence of the others. With some amazement they surveyed their fellow felines.

Standing tall in their midst was a rare sight that none of the other eight had ever seen during their mortal lives. Sarval was the largest, his muscular body was covered in a golden sleek coat and his huge head was adorned with a pair of long teeth protruding from his large mouth. He was a Smilodon, the sabre-toothed cat.

Respectfully the others passed a short distance from him. They arranged themselves at random to allow him his space. As if on command some of the cats started the ritual washing while still keeping a close eye on their nearest neighbours. They waited in stillness. Then they leapt as one into the undergrowth.

The little female Maine Coon, Wutki, tried to stay in the middle of the group of cats rushing through the foliage. She neither wanted to be first in line nor last. She was experiencing a strange excitement. Her earth life was over. It had been for some time now and she had been waiting for this summons. Tonight she had been called forth from the great mass of her species living in the other world. Now a new beginning awaited her. It was a leap into the unknown for all nine of tonight's selection. What lay ahead, none of them knew.

Sabre-toothed Sarval naturally took the lead, his massive front legs trampling the foliage and creating a pathway which the others could follow. None of the group was a follower by nature but somehow this night-time summons required an unfamiliar response. No one flinched at the task of keeping up with the streaming tail in front of them. Smilodon was never designed for long runs, his body being too heavy for such exertion, but that belonged to another lifetime. No thoughts of prey, the hunt and the kill were uppermost in any of their minds. The long fronds of ferns growing out of tree stumps, taller creeper-covered trees, the canopy of leaves and branches high above them, all was sensed rather than seen. It formed an illusion of a moving jungle rushing past them out of darkness and into the blackness closing in behind them.

Bringing up the rear was an intrepid traveller, a fearless, happy individual whose earth life had taken him from the Old World to the New. Vidarr was a large cat raised in the forests of Norway. This jungle caused him no trepidation.

Without warning, Vidarr veered to one side as his predecessor on the path skidded to a halt. They had run an inestimable distance through the jungle to a natural impasse flanked on three sides by a wall of solid rock. It was broken only by ledges linked by pathways more suited to mountain goats than large claw-footed mammals like Sarval. All the cats had managed to stop their headlong rush in time to avoid collisions and had grouped themselves around the flat caked earth at the foot of the cliff. They glanced curiously at one another, attempting to discern the others' thoughts by their reactions. All except Smilodon exhibited the same uneasy curiosity. Sarval was busy licking a massive forepaw as if all of this was a daily occurrence. The others began to suspect this may not be the first time he had received the summons or perhaps his simpler form of intellect lacked the highly developed curiosity of the more evolved felines.

At first nothing happened but soon the sensitive animals began to realise that they were under scrutiny. Vidarr placidly sat in his place in the irregular little circle while Wutki crouched hoping to make herself smaller and less visible, if that was possible. Sarval appeared to be totally unconcerned. After all he did have the largest eye teeth in the entire cat kingdom. A pervasive gentleness settled on them all. The Scottish Wild Cat settled down with a domesticated style miaow and started to purr in such a way that she even surprised herself. The others took their cue from the Smilodon and from the Forest Cat and a stillness settled upon the entire nine beasts.

The darkness gave way as if the moon had emerged from behind a cloud but there was no moon above the high cliff. With the rocky impasse before them and the solid jungle behind them almost no sky was visible. Using their powerful ability to see in the near dark they searched the shadows but all they saw was the base of the rock.

A voice was heard, no, not actually heard, rather it was perceived in the depths of their minds. None of the cats could have ignored this voice or even turned away. Wutki sat up straight, all thought of cringing lost in the wonder of this strong compelling sound.

'Please take your places that you may be given your onwards assignments. There will be the opportunity for questions later.

Sarval, you are the oldest and perhaps the bravest of our group. Be the first to approach. Come to this ledge which will be shown to you and await further instructions.' The huge cat leapt agilely onto a large lower ledge which was temporarily illuminated. One by one the cats were called by name and allocated a niche on the cliff face. Some had to scramble up paths but sure-footedly they all reached their allotted positions. A stone coloured tom looked over at his nearest neighbour who was only slightly below him, a grey tabby. She in turn peered over her ledge at Vidarr while Wutki nestled against the cliff face.

A small tremulous voice spoke from a lower ledge. It was the little Maine Coon, 'May we see you?' she politely addressed the thin air in front of her, talking to the disembodied voice in her head. Unknowingly she was voicing the thoughts of all the cats.

'Perhaps you will in time, small cat. Have patience. For now we have much to accomplish before the night is through.

You nine cats, children of the great race of felines which have populated this world down through the ages, have been selected this night. Your stories will be told, whether it be an account of all of your life, or a single incident, whether it be of your birth or your death or of your offspring. It matters not. Based on these accounts of the lives you have led you will be reassigned. No more information about this will be given to you at this time so save your questions. Sarval, Great-one, the time is now yours.' and to the amazement of all the other eight cats a deep and rumbling voice was heard in their minds. The images to go with it began to unfold as if they were present and witnessing the events in life.

Sarval the Smilodon

11,000 years ago

It was dark in the den beneath the pile of rocks strewn haphazardly across the rolling hills. Sarval stretched his full length and unsheathed his treacherous claws, long, curved and deadly.

Summers were mild in the future Rancho La Brea. Despite this, Sarval could feel the early morning chill penetrating his sleek golden coat which had lost its winter fullness.

Slowly, belying his capacity for speed, he stepped out into the rays of the rising sun. He lifted his tawny head and sniffed the scents on the breeze. He yawned, fully revealing the chilling sight of two massive fangs. He had lived many summers here in this area which in the far distant future would become known as the Los Angeles Basin. Now he barely noticed the characteristic smell of the sticky asphalt which oozed to the surface of the earth.

Through the magical aura lent by the inevitable coastal fog Sarval's keen hearing detected the cries of a condor, the great fish-eagle of the Pacific coastline. This was no bird in flight. It was the piercing screams of a bird in panic, trapped by its talons in one of the leaf and dust coated pools of cleverly disguised molten asphalt. The cries died away quickly as once the tail feathers and wing tips of the condor touched the black tar, the bird was unable to struggle free. Yet another victim was sucked below the surface, swallowed alive, its skeleton preserved for future excavations. Sarval knew the bird's cause was lost and was diverted by an odour and unmistakable sounds.

He could smell her. The warmth of the promise of future oestrus wafted up the hillside accompanied by the high pitched squeaks and hoarse roars of the cubs, his offspring. He knew to give them a wide berth unless bearing meat from a kill to share with the females and growing cubs. An old male was not welcome in the cat nursery. The knowledge that his sabre-toothed progeny was thriving satisfied him.

Later, just before sunset, Sarval was strolling along the ridge which dropped steeply down to the river. Not far upstream was the sound of falling water where the river crashed over a turbulent waterfall. He was not driven by hunger but was patrolling the perimeter of his territory and was enjoying the last of the evening warmth on his neck. It was quiet. The hunting activities of that day were over. Animals and birds were starting to settle for the night in their dens, pastures and perches. The upper slopes were turning pink. Sarval paused to peer down into the chasm at the gathering shadows. At this point the sides of the ravine were unscaleable. One lone pine clung precariously to a barely existent ledge, rooted in a crevice too small to be seen.

The spray from the waterfall rose into the air. It created a curtain of mist full of illusionary shapes and animal phantoms. Watching this pantomime of nature, Sarval's attention was distracted by a sound on the opposite side of the ravine. He noticed the smallest of movements from a shape almost concealed in a shrub. Sarval froze, crouched, and lay concealed on the rocky ridge. He listened intently for sounds of movement or attack.

After a period of silence except for the crashing of water, Sarval cautiously raised his head and looked across the gap. The creature was still there in the same location but was now peering over the top of the shrub at him. Their eyes locked. Sarval instinctively remained motionless, searching for indication of a threat. The distance from the lip of one side of the ravine to the other was too far for any Smilodon to leap and Sarval had not noted *Homo sapiens* as being either speedy or capable of long leaps. The pair eyed one another. Neither blinked. Man and beast took the measure of the other.

Sarval flexed his giant claws ready for fight or flight and the human gripped his spear with his right hand. For what seemed like a long time the two were locked in eye to eye contact. Both were tense and unsure. Then the skin-clad creature stepped out from behind the shrubbery, sat down on the rim of the canyon, placed his spear at his side and proceeded to watch Sarval with no sign of fear. At that point Sarval almost ran away but he couldn't help but notice that this was a very small human, a juvenile in fact, and whether out of interest or ignorance the boy was prepared to remain on his side of the divide without any menace towards him. Sarval, surprised, sat down also and proceeded to clean his forepaws while watching the boy out of the corner of his eye. He seemed content to observe the big cat in the gathering dusk and before darkness fell totally they both rose and retreated on their respective sides of the river. An owl, drab in its summer coat, hooted as it spotted a struggling mammal trapped at the edge of a rapidly solidifying tar pit. It swooped over the camp of the humans and over the head of the sabre-toothed Smilodon, as it descended to eat the struggling hare.

The following morning, emerging from his rocky shelter, Sarval roared his appreciation of life into the valley. Its huskiness reverberated over the bone-filled tar pits and the lush vegetation along the river banks. The warming sun aided in burning off the sea-fog. Sarval was aware. Deep down, almost on a subconscious level, he could sense a change in the Rancho La Brea. He looked over this unstable area which he had seen buckle and split asunder more than twice in his twenty two years of life. His daily route straddled the meeting place of two of the earth's vast geological plates. His great paws constantly crossed back and forth over this fault line. As he surveyed the scene he noted that the notorious tar pits continued to claim their victims. Another bird had been trapped. It was extra food for his kind and for the scavengers who pulled the remains of the trapped creatures out of the pits. Sometimes they lost their own lives in the process. Such was the cycle of life and death in which he existed and survived.

He stood upon ancient rock which spanned the cracks and folds far beneath him in the darkness of the earth's crust. Unseen by his eyes, molten oil was slowly rising through fissures from petroleum-rich layers below. It was the source of both life and death to many and had been for thousands of years.

Now, as the sun rose higher, it was the time of day to stalk at the pools. Sarval had not hunted the night before as he knew from experience that no easy prey was available after sundown when the surface of the land cooled. Sarval had often watched the smaller nocturnal mammals, the skunks, raccoons and the weasels drink with impunity from the surface water which now lay over a solidified pool of tar. Despite the darkness of these nights Sarval's night vision showed him these small mammals which he could have hunted if he wished. His preference was for the larger herbivores which roamed by day and were engulfed along with the birds, the insects and even the plants. They were all simply seeking water to drink.

As the air warmed, Sarval smelled the evaporating light oil. That was his signal to go down into the valley to feed. Hunger drove him rapidly towards his favourite spots. He passed the remains of the sea-eagle's feathers but the carcass was gone, retrieved and transported to the den of the huge dire wolves, a small meal for their ever hungry pups. Sarval drank carefully at the edge of the pool. It looked exactly like a harmless pool of water, sky and cloud reflected, leaves and feathers floating on the calm surface but Sarval knew better. He avoided placing his weight in the shallows of the pool which masked its lethal potential. He bounded along, confident in his familiarity of the area. He hoped to find animals strange to the region. They were at most risk, also the migrant herds of giant bison, camels, horses and perhaps a mammoth or mastodon on the move north. All of these animals had lost their kind to the tar pits where, layer upon layer, century upon century, lay their remains.

Sarval detected the roars of his fellow Smilodon coming from the lower end of the valley where the rocky hillside flattened out into the grassland favoured by their large mammalian prey. A hunt was in progress. With leaps and strides Sarval covered the distance to see what the roars signified. It wasn't as large a herd of bison as once there used to be. Before the days of Sarval, his kind inhabited a much colder region with ice which extended from the top of the world all the way south over the entire continent. The bison felt the earth warm beneath their hooves. They saw the thinning of their grasslands which up till now had provided adequately for their needs. One by one the great herds were travelling northwards, pursuing the ice as it retreated once more to the top of the world.

Sarval's stocky powerful body burst from the valley into the waving sea of grass. With each leap he could see the heads of his Smilodon pride bobbing up and down above the stocks of the grass. The chase was in full swing. Sarval joined his family group. A female had cut off a young bison from the herd which was fleeing in panic. She leapt onto its back and stabbed the juvenile in the neck with a ferocious slashing action of her teeth. She wasn't heavy enough to bring the animal down as she lacked the necessary weight in her body despite her muscular forelegs. Neither did she have the physical strength in her bite despite her fangs. In seconds all the females without cubs and those not burdened with the weight of imminent young were on the bison, biting and slashing viciously. They were joined by several young males not yet mature enough to move out alone and still running with the pride. Their concentrated charge knocked the wind out of the animal and all clung to the weakening prey with claws of steel. No vital organ had been pierced by the sabre teeth but the blood loss was bringing the animal down. Fiercely the big cats clung on to whatever part of the body they could access. Their jaws opened to an incredible extent, unhinged it seemed, as they continued to slash. Arteries punctured, the bison could run no more and within a dozen paces collapsed.

The whole pride advanced on the kill, males in front, the females right behind, when, with a roar, Sarval burst through their ranks. He stood over the kill, holding the others at bay. Sarval, as the senior male, ate first. Then the other hunters ate next. Always there was meat left over from an animal as large as the bison. Sarval supervised the hauling of chunks of fresh kill which were given to the waiting cubs back at the nursery area. With aggressive roars and slashing feints Sarval held off the mothers while the cubs ate. Then it was the turn of the mothers and after they were satisfied an old female with a massive infection in her leg bone, the cartilage destroyed, came to eat. She dragged one of her rear limbs uselessly. Another younger female approached awkwardly to take her share, her back damaged by heavy prey in a hunt. Sarval watched from a distance the infirm members of his pride eat unmolested. One of the adolescent males sidled up to the food again but was deterred by a rumbling growl from his leader.

Led by instinct inherited through genes down through the ages he saw other creatures leave their wounded to die. Without the feeding and nurturing of the sick and wounded the size and strength of the pride would be reduced. Wounds which were not fatal could heal if the animals could be kept alive until fit to hunt once more. Sarval presided over it all.

The abandoned carcass in the grass was quickly preyed upon by the scavengers of the plains. Vultures and large stork-like birds competed shoulder to shoulder amidst much squawking and fierce growling from the menacing dire wolf pack. Sarval left them undisturbed. All were necessary. All were welcome.

The summer evenings were lengthening in the Rancho La Brea. A balmy, almost heady air hung at the end of the day. Several times now as Sarval took his final evening stroll he caught glimpses of the same human on the opposite shore. The scents from their camp were becoming familiar to him and the human sounds would sometimes float on the inshore breeze over the river valley.

The bison herd normally slowed its migration at this time of year to benefit from the maturing pasture. This summer they were strangely restless.

The big cats witnessed them repeatedly stampeding inland, leaving behind their lush coastal vegetation in favour of the scrubland of sage, ragweed, thistle and juniper.

Sarval and his pride stayed clear of the herds when they were moving in panic like this as the danger to themselves was not worth the risk. If trodden on by a giant bison there was no hope of survival and the hooves of the wild horses were equally deadly. Camels, llamas, pronghorns, all were determined to distance themselves from the coastline. Only the previous day, Sarval and his hunting band found themselves fleeing from the valley floor, scrambling upwards over loose rocks and rough steep terrain in a terrified bid to avoid being trampled by the largest group of mastodon that Sarval had ever witnessed. The stench of their musth floated upwards in the clouds of dust in the wake of the charging herd.

Sarval's hunters turned their attention to the giant sloths which inhabited the live oaks, the walnut trees and also the giant redwoods in the sheltered canyons. As they descended to drink, their stalkers pounced. Without a fight the pride was kept in fresh meat although the muscle of the sloth was stringy and sinewy and they tended to have bony lumps under their skin. The dire wolves were better equipped to eat sloth as they had strong teeth, much stronger than the brittle teeth of the Smilodon. They were not the feast of fat and blood-filled flesh provided by the other herbivores. Nothing tasted as wholesome as a newly killed young bison to the sabre-toothed tribe.

In search of fresh hunting grounds Sarval crossed the river upstream and headed back down towards the valley on the other side. The wind was blowing from the sea and it was gaining momentum with every passing hour. Sarval's fur was flattened on his face and the hot air on his nostrils and mouth was making him thirsty. His ears were against his skull and the roaring of the wind and water made it difficult to hear. He was high above the river bed now and descent to the water to drink was not feasible. He was turning his head from side to side contemplating his situation when, from downwind behind him, the earth trembled with a sudden rumble of hooves. Sarval burst into speed. A glance behind him told him he was running for his life. An enormous mixed herd of bison and horses, antelope and elk was almost upon him. They were in full stampede. He knew he would never outrun them over a distance as their stamina was incomparable. He either had to find shelter or outflank them. For the moment neither seemed to be an option so he ran as never before!

The ravine was deepening on one side of him so a leap into the canyon was not an option. Suddenly, on his right flank, a small rocky outcrop came into view. Sarval veered towards it. He was panting hard and his legs were aching. He felt his heart thudding, crushed in his ribcage. The pounding hooves were almost upon him when, with a massive effort, he leapt towards the steep side of the cliff face. It would be his only retreat from certain death.

His claws clutched at the broken rock surface but the impetus of his jump was too great. He slipped downwards, his claws scraping agonisingly over the rock face as he desperately tried to get a hold. The charging animals were now directly below him. As he hit the ground the strangest sensation overcame him. Instead of slamming his body onto the rock-strewn earth he felt himself continue to fall. He seemed to fall a long way. The animals were now above him and passing safely over this newly revealed pit with their long strides and huge leaps.

Sarval had no option but to sit it out in the darkness and seclusion of the den that contained him. There was no way to count the size of the herd or to measure the length of time before the earth ceased to vibrate and the dust settled. Night had fallen and Sarval was trapped. The pit had been cleverly designed to prevent escape. The sides were sheer and leant inwards. No leap could bring him up onto the surface and no amount of scraping with his now bleeding claws could enable him to climb out. Exhausted from his flight and futile attempts to free himself from his prison Sarval settled with his head on his front paws but he was not asleep. He was listening, resting and recovering, and contemplating his next move.

The sun was well risen the next morning when its rays finally penetrated to the floor of the pit. Several stakes had been strategically placed upright into the floor. Sarval's smaller size and sheer luck had thrown him clear of the pointed wooden tips designed to impale a larger catch. Now Sarval could see clearly and his situation did not seem to have improved with day break. He heard footsteps above and he crouched with a snarl. As he looked towards the sound, the familiar face of the boy was looking over the lip of the pit. The boy's eyes widened in shock. Sarval's snarl died in his throat. He stood up looking intently at the human face he recognised. Without a sound the face disappeared. A short time later he reappeared, chattered something at Sarval in his human language. He waved an arm at him to back off and dropped a huge leafy branch down into the pit. Sarval leapt clear. It took the rest of the morning but log by log, branch by branch, the boy created a ramp which eventually Sarval was able to mount. As the boy rolled yet another limb from the tree over the lip, Sarval burst from his captivity. The boy felt the warm roughness of the big cat's fur on his bare leg as Sarval paused. Once more he stared the boy in the eye but this time there was no protecting ravine between human and feline. Before the boy could move a step, Sarval passed him, making sure of his freedom.

The next day the routines of the inhabitants of the basin were in chaos. Those who could run were stampeding. Those who could trumpet and roar were filling the air with their warning cries. Birds were in flight with much shrieking and cawing. Laden with their tools and possessions, the humans had packed up their camp and were moving quickly inland in a long straggling line. Then the two plates supporting the land mass at the rim of the planet's greatest ocean began to slip and grind together with a terrifying sound. Even the fearless predators took to the hills.

Dire wolves, coyotes, grey foxes and short faced bears moved in unison up the trails to higher ground. The maneless cave lions, pumas and jaguars, all elusive members of the big cat families, crossed paths with Sarval and his pride. They ran unsteadily away, led by instinct and driven by an invisible threat.

The animals moved more swiftly up the slopes away from the sea. They overtook the humans who were toiling up the same animal tracks. Sarval leapt agilely over the rocky outcrops. Travelling quickly upwards, his familiarity with the high spots enabled him to travel off the beaten tracks. The herbivores and mastodon were restricted by their lack of claws, their cumbersome weight and also by the large groups in which they travelled.

As Sarval reached the top of one of the tallest rock piles almost at the summit of the highest hill, he was riveted to the spot by a hissing sound which filled the entire region. The creatures paused in their flight. Even the birds in the air were silenced. Sarval turned towards the sea. Many eyes witnessed the impossible. The sea itself was in retreat. The beaches were left high and dry. The shallows revealed their rock pools. Sandy shoals never before seen were above water and the tide line was barely visible. The sea was still in retreat from the shore.

Sarval shook his head and roared. This was the signal for all the animals to shout their panic and dismay. Then there was silence once more. The sea had ceased its hissing departure but now a new sound was faintly heard. It rumbled in the distance and a shadow appeared far out to where the sea must now be. The rumble increased in volume and vibration. The shadow darkened and swelled. Every living creature stared in dumb wonder, then in horrified realisation. Still rooted to the spot every eye watched as the sea rose up before them and fell upon the land in a solid wall of water, higher than ever any wave before.

The panic before was nothing in comparison to what took place now. The water crashed its way over the shore and across the coastal plain. It swept trees and bushes and rubble before it, levelling everything in its path. It picked up logs and vegetation which it used as an ever stronger battering ram.

Sarval leapt the short remaining distance to the top of the hill and the wave continued its path upwards towards him. The agile climbers, the felines, the birds, all were driven ahead of the danger but many of the creatures of the Rancho La Brea were battered and consumed by the tsunami.

Sarval's claws dug deeply into the loose rock. The wave swept past him only the distance of one leap below him. The giant wave was losing momentum and all kinds of shapes and figures swirled below him. Nothing in all his previous years had prepared Sarval for desecration on this scale. He felt overcome with numbness due to the shock and the horror of the scene before him. Such destruction was unprecedented.

Sarval waited and wondered if the waters would retreat. As he watched he saw a familiar head bob into view. The boy! Sarval was instantly on his feet and slipping and sliding down the wet rocky hillside towards where he had seen the boy in the water. He had been floating backwards with all the mass of broken vegetation. Sarval ran alongside the flow until he saw his opportunity and with a great spurt he sped out onto a small promontory. As the boy was swept underneath a giant claw caught hold of the skin belt he wore around his waist and up over his shoulder. With one powerful heave the boy was out of the flood and onto the hillside. He lay face down. He was still. The Smilodon stood over him. He sniffed at the boy's legs. He carefully ran his great sabre teeth down his back and he nudged him gently, then more insistently and finally quite forcefully. The pressure on the boy's back was rewarded with a spluttering cough and he vomited up the foul sea water from his lungs.

When the boy sat up finally and rubbed his eyes he was alone on the rock. All around him were animals, singly or in groups making their way inland. In the distance he thought he caught a glimpse of a family of sabre-toothed cats heading east towards the tar pits but then he saw his own kind going in the opposite direction, south to safety, and he struggled to join them.

The boy grew to manhood, destined to lead his tribe. He never saw Sarval again. For as long as he lived, he defended the right of the big cats to have their own territory and to hunt freely.

Sarval and the remnant of his family group lived out the remainder of their days without realising that they were the last of their kind. Many of their bones fell into the pits as they had done for thirty million years, only to be discovered over ten thousand years later. Sarval died peacefully at a great age, not in a tar pit, but lying proudly on the rocks above his den. He did not know that the existence of the Smilodon would be discovered by *Homo sapiens,* descendents of a boy who had saved his life and whose life he gave back to him.

From Sarval to Rasui

The sound of a great Smilodon sigh brought all of the cats back to the present, to the cliff face in the dark. Sarval, his story told, settled down with his head on his paws but his eyes remained open and alert.

None of the others dared speak. The sights and sounds of a lifetime lived before history began had hushed them all into a state of reverent silence. Their reverie was interrupted as the incorporeal voice spoke. 'Thank you Sarval. Your story has been a fitting start to tonight's proceedings. Let us continue our enlightenment with our brother the Egyptian Mau.'

At that moment the gentle light faded from Sarval's place and a small glimmer of light emerged from one of the more recessed niches in the rock face. All heads turned in that direction and as the light strengthened an indistinct shape became gradually visible in the dark alcove. A small, smooth head was just visible atop a slender elegant body and Wutki was heard to gasp and wonder aloud at where this cat had appeared from. Had no one observed this mysterious being running through the forest together with all the others at the start of this night?

'Will you please step forward now,' said the voice. The light shone brightly on the lithe figure as he descended almost snake like to the centre of the clearing. All eyes were riveted on the apparent newcomer.

'In the ancient land of Egypt, where you come from, cats were not given a name according to the custom of those people but *we* have always thought of you as Rasui meaning "the dream" and so you were known in that land,' and at that his head lifted suddenly as if in recognition of the name. A pair of green eyes shone and as the mesmerised cats saw into their shining depth the scene before their eyes changed to an early morning sunrise in another time and in another place.

One Summer in Egypt

600 BC

The cat lay deep in the rushes. A clump of tall papyrus hid him from view from the river. The water flowed silently past, still grey in the early morning. The cry of the night birds and the rustle of the nocturnal dwellers on the river bank were ebbing away as Rasui waited for the Sun Gods to usher in a new day. Khepri, the sacred Scarab Beetle, was rolling the sun around one more time and the pink tinge on the horizon announced his arrival.

A dark shape slid into view only a short distance from the bank where Rasui lay. Only a pair of watchful eyes and a bump of a snout were above the surface. Nothing else revealed his presence except for a gentle swirling of the water behind his long reptilian tail. Rasui held his breath and stilled the motion of his own tail. No feline experienced in the ways of the delta would permit a ferocious predator like the Nile crocodile to discern his presence. The silent shape continued its progress northwards, deeper into the delta. There the river split into smaller streams before seeping into the Mediterranean Sea.

This black land of the flood plain had been home to Rasui and to the generations of the Mau before him. The river had slashed the desert of North Africa with a strip of fertile land nourished each year by its flood waters. It had been good to this family of cats. They were African in origin but

Egyptian in ways beyond the understanding of all other cats.

Many miles away to the south, the early rays of the sun were rising on the river bank, illuminating a series of burrows. It wasn't long before a set of twitching whiskers cautiously emerged from the darkness of a hole, followed by a pair of sharp black eyes. The big male rat extended his forelegs and dipped his back in a stretch which looked like a greeting of acquiescence to the Sun God. Behind him lay his mate with a squirming, squeaking brood, nursing, before emerging into the morning.

But further south, things were not as they should be. In the Ethiopian Highlands the monsoon rains had failed to arrive. During the winter almost no snow had capped the mountain tops and filled the high valleys. The Blue Nile and the White Nile had next to nothing to contribute to the great River Nile. What were normally vast torrents combining forces at Khartoum were nothing more than a trickle of barely usable water.

Back in the land of Egypt farmers and fishermen awaited the annual coming of their God Hapi. He was the God of the Inundation. He flooded the river banks with fertile silt, making up for the lack of rainfall in their desert climate. Without this inundation, Egypt starved.

Now in the dawn light Rasui slipped through the reeds and headed for the city, Per Bast, the perfect place for a cat to live out its life. The Cat Goddess, Bastet, reigned in Per Bast and the magnificent statue to her was housed in a beautifully laid out and well-kept temple. It was home to countless sacred cats and kittens, so many of them that no one had ever been able to accurately number them. There they luxuriated in peace and adoration.

Rasui had been born behind a pillar in the main courtyard of the temple quite a few years before. His mother and father before him had been temple cats. His offspring lived and thrived amongst the hordes of resident cats and they also were impossible to count. Yes, generation after generation of the Egyptian Mau had found a life of plenty and tranquillity here within the temple.

He was dark and long and lean. His head stretched royally to his small but graceful body. He walked with a dignity and a litheness giving him a hauteur which only an Egyptian Mau could display. At this time every morning Rasui headed for the brick and mud walled house on one of the side streets leading to the temple. 'There you are my precious,' Amisi greeted Rasui as he picked his way across the courtyard skirting her grandfather's reed and papyrus nets, lead weights, poles, baskets and sundry fishing equipment. Since the death of her mother when she was a little girl, Amisi had lived in the home of her grandparents, Khenti and Halima, along with her father, Shalam, a temple scribe. Rasui gave her ankles an affectionate rub with his powerful head in contrast to his regal demeanour then followed her as she headed for the temple. She was laden with baskets which smelled delectable to a hungry cat.

Amisi, a slender and dark-haired temple maiden, was entrusted with the sacred duty of feeding the protected cats of Bastet within the temple compound twice a day. Rasui was never far from Amisi's side as she made her way along the edge of the tree-lined canal towards the tall pillars of the temple entrance. Always there were cats straying along the pathway awaiting their breakfast. By the time Amisi had passed the massive statues set in the towering gateway she was engulfed in a parade of cats of all sizes and colours. The entourage entered the shaded area within the low walls. The square temple was at the centre and within was the effigy of the Queen of Cats, the Goddess Bastet with the body of a woman adorned by a feline head. She shone like crystal in the morning light and also in the evening candle light. The cult of the worship of Bastet was one of the most popular in Lower Egypt and drew crowds of hundreds of thousands to worship and honour the Goddess in her festivals.

Amisi positioned her baskets in different spots and the temple cats gathered each day at the same places as if assigned. The baskets were opened and after the initial swarming and scrabbling each cat retreated with its own fish, a Nile carp or perch or maybe even a tiny catfish.

Rasui did not always participate in the ritual feeding at the temple. Amisi's grandfather, a fisherman when he was not acting as a temple priest for three months of the year, gave Rasui his pick of any fish he wanted from his catch.

Rasui followed Amisi into the outer rooms of the courtyard. One of the senior priests assigned to the morning rituals greeted her with clasped hands and a short bow. 'Good morning Little Flower and how are your charges today?'

'Well, Master, thank you. We have many new arrivals expected in the coming weeks. The females seem to be eating for many growing young.'

'It is good my child. And I see your special one is looking particularly well this morning,' he said gently rubbing Rasui's ears. 'Will your father be here today?'

'He is coming along shortly I believe.'

'Good. I have many tasks for his pen today.'

Amisi smiled. 'At home Father has been knee deep in papyrus pith and reeds for a week. He has been rolling many new scrolls and cutting a set of reed pens which he is anxious to use so he will be happy to be kept busy.'

Amisi moved into the woman's quarters and washed and changed from her homespun robe into the pure white linen dress of the temple maiden. She wore a belt made of beads and shells strung tightly into a thick rope. Having brushed out her long thick hair she went to assist the priests with guiding and advising the daily worshippers.

The cats were sprawled everywhere. No area was off limits to these precious animals. Hundreds of cats found sunny spots to bask in. All the ledges were occupied by warm, lazy bodies. Architectural features were adorned with preening females and door lintels were guarded by large males. Pregnant queens gathered in clusters under the trees and shrubs in the garden and for now all was well in the cat paradise on the Nile. Rasui selected a suitable spot and joined the cats sleeping in the sun.

Back on the river bank, far away to the south, the burrows were once more occupied. The rat population preferred to feed at dawn and at dusk but now the situation warranted feeding at any available hour. The female rat had managed to find a few kernels of grain to sustain her and more importantly to provide her milk for the young but her mate had gone hungry yet again. Where was all the plentiful supply of food that they were used to finding around the villages and settlements? And more significantly, where was the rain? The river had usually swelled with the new rain and winter snow-melt by this time. The grain stores should be replenished by the farmers but nothing was happening. If the rats were going hungry then the humans must be in dire straits.

At midday Amisi's duties in the temple courtyard and gardens were finished until she fed the cats again in the evening. Rasui stayed in his comfortable spot having joined the others in the shade. He knew she would return with the supper in the cool of the evening. Rasui retreated further under a shrub as the air felt very heavy. Several times he raised his head and pricked his ears as he thought he could hear a distant rumble from the red lands beyond the Nile but it was too far away to be of immediate concern.

Amisi met her father Shalam and his father Khenti coming through the portals as she was leaving. Her father had his arms full of his writing materials. Amisi laughed at the not unexpected sight. He smiled at her. 'The Master will be pleased to see you have come prepared,' Amisi said and asked Khenti 'What duties do you have today?'

He looked solemn as he replied. 'I have the most sacred of all duties assigned to me for the next three moons. I will be in the mortuary. I have finally been called to be an apprentice embalmer. At my age!' he added with a proud smile.

'Well let's hope you are not kept too busy there. Our cats are well nourished and with that and the protection of Bastet you are not likely to have many in the mortuary.'

Khenti laughed roughly and said 'And who do you think keeps them well nourished then?' and Amisi danced off laughing also.

When she got home Amisi washed outside in the courtyard of the house. She was covered in a layer of fine dust being carried in on the breeze. The wind felt pleasant and somewhat cooling but it was spoiled by the dry powdery feel of the almost invisible dust. 'Is that you Granddaughter?' called a small voice from one of the bedrooms on the balcony above the courtyard. Amisi ran up the brick steps and found Halima sitting up on her bed with her feet up.

'Are you alright Grandma?' Amisi questioned in alarm.

'I am fine my little lovely. How are your temple-children today?'

'Happy and lazy as usual,' Amisi replied. 'But why are you in bed?'

'I am not actually in bed as you can see but just resting a little as I have one of my storm headaches coming on. Pass me that jug of water, would you dear?'

'Oh, a storm headache! Does that mean the floods are coming now?'

'I wish it did but no, it's quite the opposite.'

'What do you mean Grandma?'

'It's not water that's coming. It's sand.'

Amisi gasped and jumped up. 'I must get back to the temple and warn them.'

'No need Granddaughter. They will know by now when they see there is not a cat in sight. They have the best alarm system possible. No, stay here and help me shut all these windows and cover the doorways.' Halima struggled up and together they went to attach all the solid shutters designed to keep out the desert, if that could ever be possible.

Rasui had been asleep. He twitched and squeaked a little as he dreamt. His paws quivered and his whiskers rose as he ran like the wind over the temple masonry but then he sneezed. He opened his eyes but closed them once more as something was not right. He opened them again and blinked a few times but there it was, a fine layer of dust, falling like the rain they seldom saw. It settled on everything including his nose. He stood up, shook his head and arched his back. The heat had reached an unbearable point. He felt listless but all the cats were on the move. The ones highest on the buildings and the walls were scampering down. The females with their kittens were leading them from the courtyards. The flow of cats through the garden told Rasui he'd better move, and move now. He pushed his way through the steadily moving throng. There was no panic but he could feel a hot wind reaching its tendrils into Per Bast. In the distance was an opaque orange curtain which stretched from one side of the horizon to the other in an unbroken, menacing mass.

Rasui joined the leaders at the head of the procession of Bastet's sacred temple cats and led them down towards the canals then around to the back of the temple. There, several low entrances led down flights of stairs into a nether world, created by the hand of man to honour the God. The cats flowed down into the permanent coolness and stillness of the ossuary in an almost unending stream where there was room for all the living as well as the dead.

Rasui and the countless others of his kind were in the catacombs. They spread throughout the different levels of underground passages and along the galleries. There must have been many hundreds of live cats down under the Temple of Bastet now but there were even more dead cats, thousands, maybe a million, all perfectly preserved and wrapped in linen, mummified for eternity. Rasui felt perfectly at home in the presence of his ancestors, as did all of the cats who happily stretched out on the earthen floors in front of those who had gone before. They washed and rested while listening to the desert storm as it progressed above.

The painted eyes of those whose bodies had been preserved as offerings after their natural lives had come to an end, and who had been greatly mourned in their passing, silently and steadily stared at their descendents with neither judgement nor comment.

The cats listened. The wind howled, screamed, rose and barely fell. Nothing reached the cats below except the roar. The desert dust, as light as ground grain, danced ahead on the lighter breezes driven along by the body of the storm. The unrelenting heat of the sun on the Sahara had baked the earth, desiccating the sand and pulverising it into dust and grit. No moist air from the bare snowless mountain peaks tempered the all encompassing dryness of the desert. The anticyclonic wind freely lifted the surface of the land. It fed on itself as it circled over the earth, gaining in strength and density as it travelled towards the delta.

A darkness descended as the towering wall of sand steadily approached the city. All of the residents took cover and sheltered their animals with them. The temple priests had no fear for their cats as they knew where they would be and that they were safe in the long seemingly endless underground galleries. Shalam and Khenti took cover inside the temple with the priests and worshippers. The broad gates were closed and barred.

Then it hit. The very ground seemed to vibrate. After the fine powder came the lighter grains of sand which choked, followed by the stinging grit which blinded and forced all creatures off their feet. Larger chunks bombarded all beneath it indiscriminately.

Rasui listened intently but went on washing as if nothing at all was wrong. He knew that in a few hours, probably three or four, eight at most, the danger would pass and when he led the cats back up to the surface the world would be changed but not permanently. The flood would come and wash the world clean again. The wind which normally funnelled down the river valley would take the rest of the dirt away.

Rasui was first to extend a twitching nose up onto the surface. All was silent. The wind from the desert had come, and gone, and wreaked its havoc in the process. Later a wide trail of paw prints appeared in the dust and led back to the temple courtyard. The cats had emerged in time for their evening meal before the sun set over the western desert. The Nile glowed in the last of the light and the river turned a shade of rose. Already the dust and sand was being washed downstream creating a ribbon of murky light between the orange coloured banks. The papyrus shook the dust from their stems in the breeze.

Amisi arrived with her baskets. The cats could depend on that. After the feeding she quickly tidied up the scraps, gathered up the baskets and started out for home before the light failed completely. A dark shadow accompanied her and later, as she slept, the shadow slept also, curled around her feet.

On the river bank to the south, by the dying rays of the setting sun, the male rat watched with a growing sense of urgency as a flood of rats poured downstream above the level of his burrow. His mate pushed past him and watched in consternation the mass exodus. All around them, neighbouring burrows had anxious faces looking at what should have been a flood of water but wasn't. Every so often one of the lone rats from their community slipped into the stream and disappeared. Some ran, some swam, some floated on debris but all were most certainly on the move.

There was no question as to the cause of the migration. It was hunger. More than hunger, it was starvation, and the flood of rats was going north in search of food. Many of them had already travelled a great distance and as they went they collected more and more of their number. The Nile had not, in their lifetime, ever failed to provide. Their population had been well supported by the ample fertile land farmed on the flood plain. The rats had no intention of leaving their benefactor so they headed down the Nile to Lower Egypt in their struggle for survival.

By morning the stream of creatures was slowing but the male rat and his mate had already deserted the burrow. With their offspring, they were heading north along with old rats, young rats, thin rats, pregnant rats, familiar rats and strangers from the south.

The new day in Per Bast dawned with an orange sandy glow. The residents were recovering from the devastating but not unfamiliar sandstorm. They were sweeping the sand and dust from every imaginable crevice and corner. Amisi told Halima 'You stay indoors and let me clear out the courtyard and sweep off the window ledges. I'll clean out the animals' feeding troughs.'

'Thanks my sweet. The pigs and goats don't like sand in their food any more than a human does.'

Not one person in the course of the great sand clean-up failed to pray to the God of the Inundation. 'Hapi, hear our plea and send us a fresh cleansing flood of Ethiopian mountain water.' But where was Hapi this year? The river had the biggest, widest, mud banks seen in a generation and the remaining flow was low and dirty. Catfish were stranding and the papyrus was turning brown. Long-legged birds jostled with cattle and goats for drinking water while the Nile hippos sank lower and lower in the mud. Only the crocodiles seemed unaffected and gathered in large groups to share the available muddy water.

The temple canals ran low and water for ordinances and washing was rationed. Many offerings were made at the altars of the Temple of Bast in the hope of a reprieve from the drought. Life continued for the temple cats. Their fish were a bit muddy but that wasn't a problem. It had taken them all a while to rid their fur of the sandy deposits. They had just settled back into the routine of being adored, pampered and worshipped by the followers of the cult of Bastet when another event was to disrupt their privileged cat lives. This one would be remembered for generations to come.

The rats ran on. They left a strip of barren ground behind them. It was as if a swarm of locusts had passed that way. Their diet now included anything that would fuel their passage north. The floors of granaries were scoured, animal pens were raided, farmers rose to find their emergency supplies had mysteriously vanished overnight but were just too late to see the brown tails receding into the distance. The rat family was holding its own in the crowd of rodents. The young had changed almost overnight from nurselings to sturdy healthy youngsters for whom the journey was an excitement. Their independence was a relief to their mother. It was every rat for himself now.

Rasui was in the temple grounds. He saw something was happening. The High Priest had called a meeting with all temple workers, high and low. Priests and servants were arriving in droves. By mid-morning the courtyards were crowded with people and the cats had retreated to the perimeter wall to watch the proceedings. Always, when there were people, titbits were usually donated to the sacred animals.

'My Brethren', began the High Priest, 'We are gathered here today as we will soon be in a state of emergency. We have decisions to make. As you will realise, if Hapi does not favour us, we will be facing a potential famine even here in the delta. Our granaries are still almost full thanks to our bounteous harvest last year. Our emergency supplies are intact but we have the festival of Bast almost upon us and potentially a year with little or no crops to replace our stores and sustain us until the next harvest.

It is too late to cancel the festival as worshippers will start to arrive anytime now and we could not get word out in time to prevent their journey.' A gasp went up from the listeners as they heard what sounded like sacrilege coming from the lips of the High Priest but he followed it with words of practical sense. 'If we provide food for the expected seven hundred thousand extra mouths we could be jeopardising our own supplies which may or may not be needed depending on the waters. Our choices are this; we could curtail the festival and instead of a week reduce it to one day and one night which would allow the basic pledges, offerings and petitions to be made but minus the feasting and celebrations or we could carry on with our planned programme. As you are aware this is the highlight of the year in Per Bast, the time when we do our Goddess the greatest honour. If we fail to put our trust in her, and fail to honour her, what kind of subjects are we? Would we forfeit the blessings that we have to come? I am your High Priest. I know you look to me to make decisions for us all, nevertheless I am not prepared to make this one. It is yours to make. Will we trust that all will go well for us if we go forward and celebrate the Festival of Bastet?'

There was a hurried murmur which rippled through the crowd and then all the cats stopped whatever they were doing and pricked up their ears as a massive shout rumbled forward from the outer limits of the crowd until the crescendo reached the front ranks before the High Priest. 'Celebrate!' they cried with one voice over and over again.

The decision was made and the populace threw themselves wholeheartedly into the preparations for the inundation, not of water but of people. Stalls were erected, barrels of drink were rolled into place, makeshift shelters were set up to protect from the heat of the sun, tents for sleeping were positioned wherever there was space. Rasui abandoned trying to keep track of Amisi as she seemed to be everywhere at once. The cats made themselves scarce as this frenzy of activity intruded on their normally uninterrupted cat-naps and all their favourite spots seemed to have become dumping grounds or pathways. The air of frivolity was unmistakable.

And the rats ran on.

It was dark. Rasui watched as the sacred fires were lit. The braziers framed the main temple building. They were ignited simultaneously in a shower of sparks which shot upwards and momentarily joined the stars in the clear night sky. The cats had mostly enjoyed the extra attention from those who came to kneel at the feet of the effigy of the huge cat-goddess. She was surrounded by flowers and offerings which filled the vast auditorium of the inner sanctum. This was the only time of the year that the worshippers were permitted to approach the Goddess. Many people came to avail themselves of this privilege. The cats mingled with the crowd and the spectacle was almost dream-like, as if the Goddess was made manifest in the glowing green eyes of her sacred animals. To stroke their warm fur was to make physical contact with Bastet herself while their melodious meows echoed the voice of divinity. The crowds swayed in rhythm with the chants of the Master and some fell into a trance, lulled by the hypnotic effect of the event.

Unexpectedly Khenti appeared at the side of the Master and with him was another fisherman who appeared to be in a state of agitation. The Master handed over the ending of the ceremony to the under-master while the stranger continued to talk rapidly, gesturing wildly. He had a look of desperation in his eyes. The pilgrims had reached the point in their day when they turned into revellers. The crowd was breaking up to continue the cycle of drinking and feasting. It normally lasted far into the night and caused more than a few to have unpleasant symptoms the next morning but that would soon be medicated by more of the same.

Rasui who had been perched high above the courtyard entrance descended and followed Khenti to the priests' quarters where the distressed fisherman was pouring out his tale to the High Priest. 'We came downriver by boat. All of the boatmen had heard rumours of a plague travelling north along the length of the river. We know that these stories can be exaggerated and there is always someone scare-mongering on the river. But this came from men who had just sailed in horror from the town immediately south of Per Bast. But the rumours turned out to be mild compared to the reality. It was then I saw them. It is real. We only just got away by leaping onto my fishing boat with a horde of rats at our heels. We had to beat them off the sides with the oars. They were clinging to the papyrus then others were clinging onto them. I've never seen anything like it in all my life on the river,' he gasped. 'They devoured everything in their path. They had even chewed through the mud-brick walls of the stores and destroyed the grain. All the supplies were consumed at an unbelievable rate and the people had fled with nothing. Now they were moving on, heading straight downriver for the Festival of Bastet. I've never sailed downriver faster than I did today.'

Rasui could sense that something was far wrong. He waited and watched. Suddenly the High Priest was issuing orders to the Master and all the available priests but very few were present as most had been absorbed into the throng which extended far beyond the temple perimeter into every corner of the city. The priests fanned out through the crowd, shouting warnings and trying to convince people of the imminent danger but no one was listening. They were too drunk. Only a few realised what this plague of rats could mean and ran in panic to fetch whatever implements they could lay hands on to use as weapons against the rat horde.

Rasui now knew what was happening. He could smell the danger. Very quickly the other cats also realised that their temple, their city, their very lives were about to be overrun by odious rodents advancing on the town. And they were not about to let that happen.

Khenti had assembled what few locals were in a fit state to act and a small crowd of men, women and children were marching along the canal banks towards the river. They carried farm and household equipment to fight the rats. Rasui saw Amisi and even Halima in the group. Shalam was at the forefront with his father.

Rasui stopped. He looked behind him. They were all there, as he knew they would be. Cats of all shapes and sizes had emerged from their special places in the temple. These cats were animals of great value in the land of Egypt. They were not just pets but also were defenders of man's staple necessities of life from the rodent and the snake. They earned their keep. And they now moved as one behind Rasui, step for step, following him like his shadow.

As the defenders of the city progressed along the canals they were enveloped in darkness however a few carried flaming torches as weapons. As they drew near to the river they heard the strangest sounds.

A faint rustling became a constant hiss punctuated by high-pitched squeaks. The rats were using the canal as a route from the river into the city. They moved like lava along the shallow waterway, up the banks, along the paths, tightly packed, their bodies obscuring the earth and water beneath them. Unstoppable!

The small army of defenders gasped in horror as the swarm flowed effortlessly through their midst. The people swung and chopped to no avail. Children were swept off their feet and it was all they could do to run out of the path of the invasion. In its midst was the big male rat, his mate not far behind, their offspring scattered nearby in the throng.

Ahead the rats could see the illuminated temple and city. They could hear the sounds from the human habitation and best of all they could smell the food, enough for all it seemed. They salivated as they ran on. As they neared the head of the canal they were in a frenzy and food was the only impetus. It was overwhelming, making them wild, careless, driven. They couldn't stop their headlong rush for anything, not even for the sight that greeted the desperate eyes of those at the front of the rat regiment. As far as a rat's eye could see, reeking of feline danger, cats, with hardly a space between them, standing, silently waiting, waiting for them. The front ranks broke but their bodies were either tossed in the air and bounced backwards over the heads of those following or were trampled underfoot. The cats had no need to advance. They didn't need to move at all. The rats streamed into an impenetrable wall of fang and claw. The carnage was horrendous.

As the rodent forerunners were decimated, the centre of the group managed to slow their headlong dash slightly. This gave the rats the opportunity to split sideways and try to get around the feline barrier. But the cat barrier was a giant curve, not a straight line. Rasui made a cunning enemy with tactics like this. He ran from one side to the other, stretching the line of cats to meet whatever demand the rats put on them. When the number of surviving rats became more manageable the cats very slowly, but very thoroughly, began to advance. The rats were losing ground. The rear of their ranks was still running forward unaware that there was no way through.

Rasui observed that, despite the valiant efforts of Bastet's sacred temple cats, the sheer number of the rat horde was not going to be easy to defeat. The battle raged on but the cats needed reinforcements. Some of the weaker cats were beginning to tire. That was when he urged the front ranks forward so that not only were the rodents still running straight into their jaws but were being pushed back towards the river.

With satisfaction Rasui saw a commotion in the distance as the rear column of rats was being attacked from behind. The God Sobek had come to the aid of the God Bastet. Sobek, the crocodile God, had brought several large groups of Nile crocodiles upriver and they were devouring their way through the rats still in the river, then in the canals, and eventually those running through the rushes on the land.

The cats attacked with renewed resolve encouraged by the extra support. The male rat saw that those directly ahead were not faring well and then realised that the most fearsome opponent was advancing from behind. He led his mate towards a tiny gap between the two predatory barriers and back up the river.

Closer and closer the two sets of animals, the felines and the reptiles, chewed their way through the rat swarm but before they met, Rasui signalled to the cats to stop. They did but did not permit one single rat to pass. The crocodiles were allowed to have their way. Rasui had never seen so many crocodiles in one place at the one time ever in his life. It was a terrifying sight.

Several hours after the start of the invasion, it was all over. The city's supplies were saved. The exhausted cats lay supine in any free spot in the temple that they could find. None could face their next meal, satiated with the taste of rat. The crocodiles disappeared from that part of the river as mysteriously as they had come. The revellers enjoyed the last of the festival and returned to their homes around the delta.

Rasui went back to Khenti's house and stretched out at the foot of Amisi's bed. She sat up and he crawled up to her. She placed a hand on his head and a tear fell onto his fur. She had no words to express her gratitude. He understood and simply purred under her caress.

The next morning they were awakened by excited shouts. The God Hapi had joined forces with the Gods Bastet and Sobek. The floods had come in the night. Rasui had heard the waters as they had rushed past Per Bast, cleansing the river of rodent corpses, crocodiles, orange sand and had flooded the fields with the life-giving silt. 'But how?' asked Amisi. 'There were no rains in the south.' Shalam told her there had been talk of a large boulder fall in the far off Blue Nile Gorge which had dammed the flow of water into the main channel. The water level must have built up over the last several months despite the low rainfall, and miraculously Hapi had seen fit to release the waters from their captivity and bless all the creatures of the Nile Valley.

Rasui went to the river early that morning. The male and female rats were just emerging from the reed bed. Rasui saw them. The male rat looked him fearlessly in the eye. Rasui turned away. The rats headed south again, back to where they had come from, and Rasui strolled towards the temple to meet Amisi. He felt content that there would still be a supply of rodents upstream should he need one. The sun rose hot and bright and set the Nile waters afire with the possibility of life, life renewed and abundant once more.

———

From Rasui to Vidarr

Rasui evaporated into the night air as silently as he had materialised. He seemed to melt onto his niche. The Nile scene faded and a wilder, colder, windier picture filled their mind's eye.

The cats were beginning to enjoy these scenarios of far flung times and places but couldn't help wondering with some trepidation what their lives would reveal when their turn came.

A light shone distinctly onto Vidarr's niche illuminating the Norwegian Forest cat which stood and stretched nonchalantly. The tall lynx-like male pricked up his tufted ears, shook his thick striped coat and the sound of his soft Nordic melodic voice was heard by all. Ears pricked up and eyes closed in concentration as Vidarr's story began to unfold.

The Norwegian Forest Cat

1002 AD

He had been lying amongst the scattered rocks above the landing place since before the dim grey light of dawn, silently watching. Summer was over but he was impervious to the Norwegian chill, the herald of an Arctic winter. The wind ruffled his thick outer coat but nothing penetrated the tight fur which covered his long feline body and legs. He was watching the boy. The early morning light was filtering up the Norwegian fjord. The winding pathway of water stretched seawards. It was slack tide and the fighting longship, the drakkar, was laden and ready to go at the turn of the tide. Its carved and painted dragon's head prow bucked in the offshore breeze.

Behind the drakkar was a different type of ship, a knarr, built for merchandise and the transport of goods, men and animals. It was smaller in bulk and lower in the water but almost equal in length to the fighting longship and very much an able seagoing craft. In contrast to the fighting crew of the dragon ship the store's master was shorter, stockier and beardless. His home-spun brown woollen tunic was belted with a crude hemp rope and his rough woollen trousers hung loosely. The shouts of the men carried up to the big cat in the rocks as they carried their supplies aboard the four knarrs.

With lots of shouts and cheers the longboat cast-off with its load of twenty-nine Norse warriors, twelve oarsmen to port and thirteen to starboard, one helmsman plus the navigator, also the oars master and the ship master. The warriors were bearded long-haired ruffians; dangerous enemies but considered valued allies abroad. The loading of the fourth and final knarr paused as every man watched spellbound as the sleek wooden drakkar turned into the wind and leapt forward as her linen sail filled and was secured on deck by the sail master. The navigator shouted instructions and the helmsman pulled his oaken tiller, tightened the thongs supporting the steering oar and headed seawards to the north Atlantic.

Back at the loading dock the ship master on the last knarr was shouting his final instructions to the labourers carrying the ship's stores aboard.' By the hammer of Thor will you get this ship loaded? Do you think we have time for gawking? Never seen a dragon ship set sail before?' Sveinn, excited to be taking his first sea voyage to another colony, risked a small smile. He had noticed the twitch of ears above him in the rocks and whispered 'So my friend, I will not travel alone, even over the seas but I wonder how you will like this journey?'

'Here lad, catch!' Sveinn found a sack of oats thrust into his arms and joined the line of traders and their slaves, the thralls, walking up the planking. They passed the stores to the sailors aboard to be stacked below. The ship had two upper decks, one at the bow and the other at the stern. In between, the hold was open to the elements. The oak mast was rigged securely in the centre of the boat and the supplies and animals were arranged either below the decking or around the mast. The ship was deceptive and the long wide hull could offer much more storage space than expected.

'Asmundr, what do we need all this stuff for if we are only going across to Orkney? The longship can make the crossing in two days and we can't be too much longer than that, not more than three or four days at the most?' Sveinn asked.

'Didn't you hear Torquil before they sailed? He's got other plans after Scotland. He wants to follow his friend Leif and his brother on another voyage after this and I suspect some of this lot will be used for that.'

'Are you going with him?'

'I might. If there's something to gain from it, I will. What about you? You look like you have the spirit of adventure about you.'

Sveinn looked serious and said, 'I'll think about it.'

One by one the ships masters pronounced their boats full. Supplies were lashed down and men loaded.

It was late morning by then and the sun wasn't very high in the wintry sky but the sea was blue and bright and the air was fresh and filled with the lure of faraway places. The big cat saw the boy board the ship and immediately slunk down to the littered landing stage. In the bustle of final commands and pulling on ropes no one noticed the stowaway tuck himself below deck and settle quietly behind the water barrels next to the animal fodder, that is except Sveinn who was watching for him.

As Sveinn's boat headed out in the wake of the three other vessels Vidarr took a lingering glance at the forested slopes of their homeland slipping away and wondered if it had been such a good idea for a Norwegian Forest cat to go to sea.

Sleep came easily to the cat as the ship lifted then rolled then sank back down in the gentle swell. The ship master had assigned the crew to their various tasks and all were in position. Sveinn was at rowing station number four starboard for now. No rowing was necessary as the wind carried them westwards, effortlessly it seemed, giving all the Norsemen time to rest and recover from the loading.

Asmundr leant forward from his position directly behind Sveinn. 'You look done in lad. Take my advice and get a bit of shut eye while you can. This isn't your first voyage, is it?'

Sveinn shook his head, 'No, I went with Haakon, my father, plenty of times but never to Orkney, only up and down the coast at home.'

'Where is your father now? '

Sveinn hesitated and then blurted out, 'We don't know. He might be lost. It's been nine months since we last heard of him.'

'Sorry lad! You have courage anyway. The fact you are here shows that. Is he a Berserker?'

'More of an explorer I would say.' Sveinn couldn't restrain his grin of pride. With that they settled drowsily in the late morning sunlight allowing wind and tide to power their passage. By mid afternoon the four knarrs had drifted apart and were no longer visible to one another. When the northern sun dropped towards the horizon the cat stirred in the hold. He staggered to his feet and stretched his front paws out as far as they would go and then did the same with his back legs. With a yawn and a shake of his large head he set off to explore. First he did a discreet circuit of the hull, checking his new perimeter. The oak beams and the curved hull creaked and groaned as waves pressed against it and the rigging tightened and slackened with the vagaries of wind and tide. Vidarr did not feel threatened at all by this new environment. Balance in this moving tilting world was second nature to a surefooted cat with incredibly large paws. The variety of smells from the sacks and boxes, barrels and trunks were enough to intoxicate a lesser cat but Vidarr sniffed and looked and listened until he was the new ship's master, master of the stores at least.

He was content to have detected the squeaking of the young rats in several nests and to have heard scraping and scuttling among the supplies. He even saw the quick flight of a very large male rat out of the corner of his eye as its tail vanished into the dark below the stern deck. Vidarr would not go hungry.

The sheep were something else. He didn't like sheep. He had never eaten one so had not acquired a taste for mutton. They smelled strange and their droppings smelled even worse. They were noisy and skittish and he decided that he would give them a wide berth. They were penned tightly around the base of the mast and had the privilege of the open sky above them. Vidarr wished they had been left ashore but he wasn't going to let them bother him. He knew about sheep as they had dotted the lower slopes of the farms in Norway but as they never ventured up into his forests he basically despised them, cowards and grass eaters. Vidarr awaited his opportunity to join the boy.

Night fell and the wind dropped considerably but the knarr held its course and ploughed steadily onwards. 'Sveinn, you there boy, get up on watch. You have the second dog watch.' Sveinn draped his cloak around his shoulders and with a 'Yes master,' made his way to the watch position on the deck ahead of the mast. He stood spellbound captivated by the sight of the sea and sky at night with starlight descending upon him. It wasn't long before a movement at his feet and a rush of warmth across his legs let him know of a feline presence. His friend strongly clawed his way up onto a fixed wooden rope locker and Sveinn found himself eye to eye with what he thought had to be the most magnificent and stately of all the animals. 'Thank the gods that you made it Vidarr,' he whispered. 'Good voyage so far old boy.' He roughly rubbed Vidarr's head and in companionable silence together they watched the sparkle of the rising stars on the surface of the sea, reflections of light which originated countless light years away, some from planets long dead.

Night followed day and Vidarr stayed on deck past Sveinn's watch and sat out most of the first and middle watches with another two seaman who seemed not in the least surprised to have the company of a large beast with watchful eyes. As the darkest hour approached Vidarr slipped below and dawn found him prostrate behind the barley, relaxed as if he had always lived there.

By mid-morning the smell of fresh fish permeated the hold and set Vidarr's whiskers twitching. Up he bounded and anyone who did not know that they had a cat aboard now knew as he leapt in full view from rowing station to rowing station, running excitedly from fishing line to fishing line, checking on the catch for that day.

When afternoon arrived he was satiated with countless small fish which had been rejected and thrown to him. He had been heading for his post on the bow sail locker but the sailor on watch had a sneer on his face which quickly turned to a snarl when he saw he would have the cat for company. His name was Fenrir the Wolf and Vidarr felt unquiet when he saw the glint of his gutting knife long after the fish had been tidied away.

The constant heaving of the vessel was no problem to a Norwegian Forest Cat turned Norse explorer. His feet found the rhythm of the pitch and roll and, even when he sprang from spar to spar beneath the decks, his surefooted accuracy carried him safely.

On the evening of the first day he appeared on deck with a limp female rat hanging from his jaws. The cheers of the men startled him at first but as nobody appeared interested in taking his prey from him he carried on until he reached Sveinn. He carefully laid his prize at his feet. This became a frequent ritual. The men seemed pleased at his hunting prowess and they were even betting on the number of his total rat catch before Scotland.

Vidarr sensed that food on board would not be a problem. Sveinn always rubbed his head and gently returned his rat to him. Having been given this permission Vidarr carried it off to crunch away, leaving nothing but the offal which was tidied overboard to the fish, a small symbiotic reciprocation for the daily catch.

The sun was just surfacing on the eastern horizon when Vidarr smelled landfall before any of the men. He opened his mouth slightly and the odour of vegetation and livestock was sifted over his heightened sensory organs. The three-day run to the northern Scottish islands had been uneventful due to calmer conditions. It was morning on the third day when the first Orkney headland came into view.

The rugged promontories gave way to an intensively cultivated landscape and Vidarr's first thought was ... no forests! The journey south to the main settlement was only a few hours ' sail and Vidarr could feel the excitement aboard. Many small islands slipped past. The men seemed to share his desire to disembark and explore.

As the knarr approached the sheltered bay of Kirkwall on the largest Orkney island Sveinn could see what a thriving seafront community it was. The masts of the craft almost dwarfed the village. Ships were rafted up together forming large areas of floating dockside while other ships were dotted all over the bay at anchor. The ship's master shouted frantically at his rowers as he struggled to be heard above the furore in the harbour. After much shouting and manoeuvring with oars and ropes the knarr took its place in the queue to unload at the main jetty, a solid wooden walkway extending far out into the deeper water of the bay and built of the sturdiest Scandinavian pine. Sveinn and Asmundr were at their allotted positions, dipping the oars, pulling hard, then dipping and holding them, then pushing hard against the harbour waves as the knarr edged its way into the newly vacated jetty. The jetty was a seething mass of humanity, all laden with stores and trade items. One or two of the tall bearded longboat raiders strode arrogantly in and out of the scuttling porters, their long hair blown back by the lee breeze.

'I can't wait to get ashore,' Sveinn panted.

The sweating Asmundr replied,' Not long now lad. Your cat is ready too by the looks of him,' and sure enough Sveinn looked up in time to see Vidarr unceremoniously scramble up to the bow, up and over the curved prow and take a flying leap ashore. The last Sveinn saw was the bushy tail vanishing through the legs of the crowd at incredible speed. A few stores were to be unloaded and others were assembled to take their place but before the first sacks and chests could be carried up the planking Fenrir also had observed a streak of tawny fur disappearing into the crowd.

Overwhelmed by sight and sound and smell Vidarr headed for the fringe of the crowd in the hope of finding a safe observation site. Much of the scene was familiar to Vidarr as this was a distinctively Norse community but there were so many other strange things that he needed time to assess the situation.

In his flight he found himself leaving the market place in the main square above the landing stage. The throngs of people here, some strangely dressed and differently spoken, were not known to be friend or foe yet and Vidarr sensed that his safety depended upon his wariness. He passed mud walled buildings with thatched roofs which were scattered around the central black house built of stone with whalebone lintels. Smoke poured from the central chimney hole in the roof. He effortlessly scaled a wooden stockade perimeter and ran freely up a rock strewn hillside amidst countless grazing sheep. The grass was lush and damp and green and in the rocky hollows heather sprouted creating cavernous hideaways perfect for an observing cat. Silently he crept into the dry sheltered heather den and not one sheep even raised its head to wonder. The bustle below was almost too much to take in. Pigs and chickens wandered at will through the tables, stalls, sacks and racks of the market area which even extended down onto the beach and along it for quite a distance.

Vidarr looked out beyond the floating township of boats to the shallows at the far side of the bay. The fields, reaching gently down to the sea, were covered in late barley still to be harvested or in the stubble of already-scythed grain. This was a very different landscape from the steep sided fjords and densely forested mountain slopes that were his home. He twitched his whiskers in pleasure in what he realised was much milder air. Here there was an abundance of land for growing food, for grazing sheep and cattle and easy maritime access to it all. There must be rain too, evidenced by the lovely green of the vegetation. No wonder the Norse ships had been sailing to Orkney for the past 200 years and now, in the year 1002, many colonies had been established. Trade was thriving, cultivation as well as the always available plunder

Vidarr's attention was drawn to the many ducks rafting in the sheltered waters of the inlet with oystercatchers, sandpipers, dunlins and the occasional curlew at the water's edge. Iceland gulls had not yet left for the summer and wheeled noisily overhead. A pair of buzzards floated silently over the dry land searching for prey. The croaks and wails of a late summer black throated diver punctuated the screeches of the flying seabirds.

All of this was thrilling to observe and exciting to absorb but what pulled Vidarr from his shelter was the smell of food from the market square. Also he wanted to check on the whereabouts of his friend Sveinn and find out what kind of broth or roast he was feasting on in this new land.

The landing, disembarking, unloading and the reverse seemed to go on in this place from dawn to dusk. How many ships called here anyway? Vidarr had never seen such a spectacle before. He moved from stall to stall in wonder and curiosity. One place was just a lean-to with an amazing pile of bones displayed on the ground. That was worth investigation. Vidarr crept to the side and sniffed and watched as people separated which antler-rack they would choose to carve into handles for pots and knives and combs and even for ornaments to wear as jewellery. Expensive metalwork was being bartered while craftsmen hammered and carved and women at looms wove and sewed all manner of clothing.

Meanwhile the Store Master was doing what he did best, supervising the unloading. He knew the cargo inside out. Not one item was either unloaded or left aboard in error. His guttural cries instructed the port thralls which timber to take off, which pelts and ropes and livestock. His beady eyes missed nothing. 'Get the sheep off next,' he hollered.

'I thought the sheep were part of the cargo for the next voyage,' challenged one of the crew.

'Sheep, yes, but not those ones. Get them off.'

No one waited around to be told again and, in what was almost an orderly fashion, the little flock was herded into a holding pen at the top of the beach. The relief of the animals to be back on dry land was evident by the feeding frenzy which ensued and short work was made of the freshly cut fodder in the pens.

The master released the crew to their liberty ashore once the work was done and Sveinn followed Asmundr into the village, bemused by the strangeness of it all. They wandered briefly around the stalls looking at all the goods on offer until Asmundr interrupted Sveinn's reverie and said, 'Let's get to that alehouse up there. Everyone is heading that way'. Sveinn allowed himself to be led but could not help noticing a blonde girl with a flock of geese who seemed to be looking back at him. Her head wrap failed to conceal the two long fine plaits of hair swinging as she bent to guide the cackling geese. Her linen apron was pinned to her woollen dyed red dress with two round brooches worked in pewter, one set with amber and the other with jet. She wore goatskin boots laced with leather thongs and the wooden staff she carried was covered in hand carved runes, telling tales of gods and men.

'Astrid, are you dreaming girl? Get those geese moving,' shouted her father. While staring at Astrid, Sveinn almost tripped over as he entered the alehouse door. It was set in a mud walled hut with a turf roof. The barley brew was being consumed in copious amounts. The only thing noisier than Norsemen in battle was Norsemen drunk on brew.

From his vantage point Vidarr had seen many of the men from his ship. He caught a glimpse or two of Sveinn and, satisfied that all was well, retreated to a corner where some meat scraps had been thrown. As he settled down to enjoy his new find, a strange scent assaulted his nose. He leapt up in alarm and went in search of the source of his concern. It didn't take long to find it. He knew that smell all too well, it was fresh warm blood! He saw two women and a man and the job they were doing made his stomach rise into his throat. No, thought Vidarr, no, the savages! These could not be Norwegian people. How could they be doing this! Surely trade of this kind was not acceptable in this country?

What Vidarr was looking at were nine cats in various stages of being processed. None were alive. They murder cats he realised with horror. A man sat at a tree stump using it as a chopping block to cut the animals. Then two women skinned the creatures and their bloody bodies were thrown into a wooden half barrel. The skins were hung on a wooden rack to cure in the air.

As he turned to flee a pair of large rough hands fastened around his middle. Vidarr let out a squeal and as he breathed out he flattened his body and slipped right through the fingers of his assailant. With a fleeting glance backwards Vidarr saw the frustrated face of Fenrir but before the man was able to pursue him the big striped cat was gone and had vanished safely back into his heather cavern, shaking and panting.

How quickly paradise is contaminated by the deeds of man, the murderous deeds of humankind, and so Vidarr discovered that first impressions can be false. Whatever the plan to settle in Scotland had been, Vidarr knew he had to leave and to leave soon. What he didn't know was that his fate was being sealed by actions beyond his control as Sveinn had also made an enlightening discovery in the market in Kirkwall.

Sveinn found a beaker of brew thrust into his hand by Asmundr who then disappeared into the inebriated throng with much backslapping and cheers from fellow sailors from other knars, some of whom had not seen one another in months. After a few sips Sveinn put his drink down on a long sturdy wooden table as he had a thought, 'Some of these sailors may have heard about my father. I should take this opportunity to ask around as I may not be in such a large group again for a while.' For the next couple of hours Sveinn did the rounds of all the men in the inn, many were too drunk to answer his questions coherently but persistently he carried on despite the occasional push and slap to get out of the way as if he were an annoying insect. 'Have you heard of Haakon of Bergen? Did he pass through here? Do you know where he might have gone? Does anyone know what has happened to him?'

He had asked everyone in the inn when the innkeeper beckoned the boy to the storeroom door. He said 'I don't want to get your hopes up lad but there is a local man here in Kirkwall who knows everyone's business that you could ask. His name is Thord and you will find him at his place beyond the far side of the market and up the hill. You'll know it when you see the geese.'

Sveinn thanked him, called to Asmundr that he would be back soon and left as fast as his legs would carry him. Soon he was approaching a sturdy dwelling house with a live turf roof. There were also many smaller outbuildings and lots of pens containing geese. There was a glimmer of firelight from the one small window and as Sveinn stepped under the canopy of the rough hewn log porch, the door opened and Sveinn found himself face to face with Astrid who did not show as much surprise as he did. 'Your father, Thord, is he here? Sveinn stammered.

'I am Thord. Do you want something?' came the same gruff voice Sveinn had here earlier in the marketplace. Thord stepped out, edging his daughter to the side.

'I heard you may have knowledge of the whereabouts of my father'', blurted Sveinn.

'You'd better come in young man', Thord replied less aggressively than before. Sveinn stepped into the dim, smoky atmosphere of the longhouse and saw that the walls and beams were covered in intricate delicate carvings and the central hearth was well-stocked with wood. This was not a pauper's family. Two large cauldrons simmered over the fire which both lit and heated the comfortable home. Astrid followed Sveinn and her father and stood a respectful distance behind them but close enough to listen. Sveinn was offered a stool a little way from the fire. He was aware of others around the hearth but his attention was riveted on Thord. 'Now boy, what is it you wish to know?'

Sveinn told his story of how his father Haakon had left their home in Norway nine months previously for a run to Scotland and back which should have taken less than two weeks but he hadn't been heard from since. The ship he sailed on had arrived safely in Orkney, did its business, then returned on schedule to its Norwegian base but Haakon had disappeared. His family had waited for his return and then sent out enquiries but there had been no word. He told Thord his mother had been reluctant to let him go off but the thought that he might be able to track down his father overcame her fears for her son.

'I may be able to help you and in return you might do something for me one day.' Sveinn nodded his assent and Thord told him what had happened a while back.

'We had a bit of trouble in Kirkwall. Rivalry of some sort. You know what it can get like, family feuding which escalated into a big fight and you know how quickly these things can get out of hand.

Anyway it ended up with a raging battle down at the quayside and it seemed like neither group were winning or showing signs of losing when Olaf, one of the leaders, suddenly shouted 'Retreat!' to his men then swept a load of spectating sailors off the quay and onto his boat, waiting only long enough for the last of his men to leap aboard and they all swiftly rowed out of the bay into the waters of the Atlantic.'

'And my father?'

'Well, he was one of the men swept on board at sword point by Olaf, wasn't he? I've known Haakon for many years. He has been in and out of here many times over the past several years. He is not a fighter, is he? More a thoughtful type. So that was in the early winter of last year and Olaf has never returned, nor any of his crew.'

'Where did they go?'

'I heard but I can't be sure of the truthfulness of it that they were seen in Iceland this past summer. Olaf had always wanted to head up there and I suppose the frightful brawl made the decision for him.'

Sveinn was on his feet and heading for the door when Thord called him back. 'Hold on lad, I want you to do something. Now, are you planning on following your father?'

'If I can I will ship out with the knarr I arrived on.'

'I want you to come back here to Kirkwall after your trip to Iceland and I would like a first-hand report of your impressions of the place. I might like to do business there one day.'

'I see', said Sveinn, hoping that everything would go well and he would be able to make the long and treacherous sea journey.' Of course I will return if you wish.' Sveinn's heart beat faster as he looked into Astrid's eyes and he felt it was more to her than to her father that he was promising to return then he raced off down the hill to find Asmundr.

He needn't have hurried. The inn was still full of drunken sailors but by now they were spread out on benches, slumped against table legs, not only sleeping off their overindulgence but also exhausted from the sea travels, the rowing, the loading, the unloading and the sleepless nights.

Sveinn went back to the knarr. Even the night watchmen were drowsy and no one challenged him. As he slid down into his skin bag to sleep he saw

Vidarr battle over the side from the quay to join him as if all the hounds of the heavens were on his tail. Sveinn didn't know of Vidarr's dramatic discovery in the market place of Kirkwall and Vidarr didn't know of Sveinn's news about his father but both knew they were eagerly awaiting the morning when they would set sail again, one escaping this dreadful place and the other heading with hope in his heart to a remote and frozen island a great distance away.

By sunrise the next morning the quay had come alive again. Vidarr stayed safely below, unwilling to risk an encounter with the cat killers. The sailors returned to the ship in small groups, their heads wet from the mandatory dip in the water barrel to waken up, clean up and sober up. Sveinn sat on his sea-chest which served as rowing bench and which was lashed to the wooden support attached to the sturdy curved oak keel. The keel had been fashioned in one piece by axe strokes along the grain of the wood. A Norse ship was never built from wood which had been sawed.

Asmundr arrived with the others and hailed Sveinn in his unfailing cheerful manner. 'Hey Lad, you didn't come back last night I don't think!'

'No, I discovered news of my father.' Smiling and nodding, Asmundr took his place on his own sea-chest behind Sveinn and they both soaked in the early morning sun. The islands in the Orkney archipelago were rising gently from the darkness of the sea to glisten and shimmer. Storm petrels were leaving their roosts to feed on the abundant fish offshore. The first of the local fishing boats were heading out of the sheltered harbour to sail north and west past the spectacular coastline fringing this, the largest of the Orkney Isles.

'Tighten your straps there Boy', Asmundr advised Sveinn.' They have worked loose. When we head out into the Western Ocean you are going to need that seat to hold fast and not be sliding around. As Sveinn struggled with the lashing Asmundr leant forward and added his strength to the task. 'You see how your seat is attached to the main flooring there and not to the side of the ship?'

'Yes,' said Sveinn, looking more closely at the construction of the interior of the knarr.

'Well, everything is attached to the centre keel there. That is the secret of our boat building and is how we Norsemen can sail across the world! Boats have been built for as long as can be remembered by constructing a wooden frame with the timbers fastened to that frame but our Norse ships are built like you see here. The timbers all come from the solid oak keel and are attached to one another so that our mast, floor, benches, everything you see, goes down to the keel and the hull is free to take care of itself. It has none of the stress of all these other encumbrances. It can bend and shift and twist as it blends itself to the forces that oppose it. Because of this design masts are taller and stronger, our sails are bigger and there isn't anywhere we can't sail to,' he finished proudly. 'I did a bit of boat building in my time', he added with the warm twinkle in his eye. 'Is that beast of yours aboard?'

'He is, but he is not happy about something.' Sveinn replied. Vidarr had retreated to the bottom of the boat and watched as box after box of supplies were brought aboard. Most of the trade items from Norway had been exchanged for some timber and agricultural supplies. Vidarr took himself to the very rear of the hold but climbed consistently on each new layer of cargo sniffing and checking, a feline store-master. Vidarr watched as finally the new sheep were herded on board into their pen around the mast. The first ones had smelled like old mutton but these new ones were young and had lambs of various ages with two tups separated from the ewes and lambs. Vidarr eyed their curling horns with respect and decided not to short cut across that pen in the dark.

The sound of children's voices caught Vidarr's attention and peering from the top of a pile of crates he saw two families being shepherded to the middle of the boat. Some of the sailors were not the ones he remembered but Sveinn was there, as was Asmundr, but to Vidarr's consternation so was Fenrir the Wolf-man. Vidarr gave him a wide berth.

The smell of salt was in the air and the sea breeze felt mild and inviting. The sail was hoisted. With very little need for the oars the knarr was pulled onto a steady course, leaving a white wake hissing on the surface of the sea as her stern disappeared in to the morning light. Mesmerised, the forest cat watched the swirling pattern of the sea-foam and with only a little longing saw the shore grow more distant, then the shape of the islands grew darker and indistinct. He watched as they finally sank beneath the grey-blue of the sea. Vidarr retreated to his favourite corner out of sight of sailor and sheep for a long nap. After initial tightening of ropes and straps and the securing of any loose cargo, the rhythm of the swell and the constancy of the wind lulled both seamen and passengers into a peaceful day's progress west. Later the setting sun shone full on the curved prow of the knarr throwing a living shadow across the deck, up the mast and over the sheep who were quietly settled in their pens, fodder consumed, and rocked into complacency.

It was well into the night when Sveinn was called to replace Asmundr on the Morning Watch. It was not the easiest of tasks as the four hours in the middle of the night to first light could seem to be never ending. However the nights were growing shorter in the northern regions and the wait for dawn was less than in the winter when first light never came at all to the northern seas.

Vidarr perched on his favourite locker and Sveinn leant his face close to his friend's twitching whiskers. The boy whispered to Vidarr, 'I don't know how much you are going to like this but we are not heading home to Norway. It only took us a couple of days to get here but now we are going far far away to another place. If all goes well we could be there in two weeks, or it could be longer. You see I'm going to find my father. Vidarr's gaze never left the eyes of the boy and his ears twitched as if in response to his murmured words. Vidarr did not know the meaning of his friend's words but he felt his closeness and he sensed his excitement at the prospect of this new voyage and where it might take them. If all was well with Sveinn then Vidarr was content to go along wherever it might lead and for now it lead into a starry night with the dip and swell of the ocean, an unknown darkened vastness. Vidarr stared ahead, ready for whatever might come.

Daylight revealed Sveinn back on his sea-chest gutting the morning catch, codfish in abundance from the northern waters of the Atlantic. Despite this, Vidarr was nowhere to be seen. He was good at vanishing like that, like smoke into thin air when it suited him. He may have been causing disquiet to the rats in the cargo, or he may have been curled up asleep on the top of the highest pile of stores in one of the two holds on board. The wind had increased with daylight and the ship was running north to find the route out into the great unmarked northern ocean.

'Asmundr, why are we going north if where we want to go is west?'

'Well you see Lad, the Navigator who came aboard in Scotland, Radulfr, is a highly experienced sailor, a man gifted and informed on all these sea roads.'

'There are sea roads?' interrupted Sveinn.

'Oh yes, there certainly are! He knows exactly where we are going, but sometimes the wind and the waves go against his plans,' laughed the older man.

'And how does he know these sea routes?'

'This man Radulfr has collected information from all the other seamen and voyagers. He can read the stars as if they had runes on them. He can feel the change in the currents beneath the hull. He knows the direction of landfall by mists and winds, by birds and whales. He also has some navigational devices that are kept secret. No one else knows how they work. He alone has the expertise to understand them. We would never undertake a voyage like this without his knowledge and proficiency.

'That's good. I feel better about doing this now. I wonder if my father has learned these skills?'

'You can ask him when we catch him up.'

'Iceland, here we come. So, why are we going north?'

'Do you fancy rowing all the way to Reykjavik?'

'No, not exactly', replied Sveinn.

'Right, it's north first to clear the Orkney Isles and to leave the Shetlands to starboard and then we will catch the wind and the current west.'

These words were no sooner out of Asmundr's mouth when the sail master ordered the square striped sail raised fully and the ship surged forward. The sail was rotated around the mast until it billowed out, filled with the necessary wind at just the correct angle. The ship leant to the one side as she sped through the waves. The oars were secured on board. The day passed into night once more with minimal adjustment of the angle of the sail to the prevailing wind. As the night wore on the swell grew larger and before daylight the helmsman was under orders to change course... westwards.

Vidarr showed up with the offer of a baby rat for Sveinn and as his catch was customarily returned to him he sat, ate and listened to Sveinn's description of whereabouts they were in these great darkening waters. Sveinn was interested in sharing his new found information and told Vidarr: 'We have left the islands behind us. We are sailing west between the Faroe Islands and the little Rock of Rona, the furthest out land before there is nothing between us and the island of Iceland.' Vidarr had finished his meal and although he could not see the Rock of Rona he had heard the far distant cries of the countless seabirds on the cliffs and the stench of their nesting sites had travelled over the waters to his powerful sense of smell. He couldn't label the direction this came from as south but he could have pinpointed its exact location with his nose. Vidarr was not lost at sea, not in the slightest.

The taller waves and the long rolling swell had made the passengers in the two families feel unwell. The Norsemen were seasoned travellers and it took more than this to unsettle them. The sheep were stoic with only occasional bleats when the boat was tossed more violently by the larger waves. Vidarr kept as much distance as he could between himself and Fenrir and actually managed to stay out of his line of vision almost totally. He could not rid himself of the association of the man with the skins of murdered cats.

Day followed night and the journey progressed. Some days they lacked wind and little progress was made. The oars were plied with rhythmic long strokes but ocean rowing was a back breaking task. The sailors took it in turns in two hour shifts until the wind got up again. Some nights the wind blew fiercely and little rest was had as items had to be lashed down then re-lashed as barrels broke free and rigging snapped and had to be replaced. Vidarr dodged the shifting loads with skill but was dismayed to find himself in the sheep pen one night sitting amongst the woolly bodies crowded around the mast. It was either that or be swept overboard as part of the cargo was tossed backwards when the bows crashed into a massive Atlantic wave which came rolling across the deck where Vidarr was walking. When order was restored Vidarr crawled under the fencing of the pen and walked away with his head held high as if he sheltered with sheep on a regular basis and there was nothing demeaning in a forest cat doing such a thing. He found a quieter corner and nearly wore his tongue out cleaning the frightful odour of sheep out of his thick coat.

One night after what seemed like a very long time since leaving Orkney Vidarr sensed something different in the air. It was not a scent he had ever smelled before. He couldn't think what it even resembled – smoke, no, fire, no. Both of these he was familiar with but he knew it had something to do with heat. Burning rocks he thought but that did not seem likely. He had been sensing this change in the atmosphere for some time and somehow under the ship the waves felt different, as if they were surging mightily over mountains on the sea bed. Vidarr was finding all of this unsettling but there was nothing apparently alarming on the surface of the sea itself. The wind blew steadily but gently, the swell was not particularly large, and the air seemed to be mild with the occasional cooler draft. He had been increasingly aware of these changes for several hours when Radulfr gave a shout that they were sailing parallel to the coast of Iceland which was a short distance due north of them and that they would round the south western tip of the island in another couple of hours then berth at Reykjavik.

Shortly after that the moon burst through a gap which appeared in the cloud covered night sky and there was a sight for weary voyagers' eyes. The cliffs of the south of Iceland shimmered in the gleaming moonlight. The waters were alive with dancing ghostly shapes as the crests of the waves reflected the cold white light. The Vesterhorn was faintly discernible on the distant horizon, a steep dark shape protruding into the open sea, outlined by silver moonlight. It would appear and disappear as the ship rose on the crest of the swell and sank again into the troughs of the sea, confused further by the disappearance and reappearance of the moon as the clouds which clung to the land shifted and parted.

By dawn the lower hills of the coastline showed colourless in the distance but it was land and Vidarr was watching eagerly from the bow. Both by moonlight and dawn's pink glowing sunrise a vast whiteness framed the coast, a great gleaming ice sheet reflecting back any celestial light; starlight, moonlight, sunlight. Vidarr's powerful eyes blinked as the unexpected gleam from the land temporarily dazzled him. After he had blinked once or twice he could make out a huge dark cone shape apparently floating in the field of ice and he began to realise that this was a very different landscape from his native Norway.

Leaving the icefield behind the ship continued its progress along Iceland's southern shore away from the forbidding south easterly coast. Vidarr could see neither welcoming harbours there nor any signs of settlement but he could still smell the burning and the air was tinged with an unpleasant and unfamiliar chemical odour. Two more of the mountainous cones were now visible just inland from the cliffs while others were faintly visible behind them. Vidarr was staring intently trying to make sense of all that he could see, smell and feel when the helmsman brought the ship round and headed inland towards the Port of Reykjavik. Vidarr noted several things. First and foremost, no trees. Was Norway the only place with lovely frozen forests? Secondly, and of even greater concern, was the unfamiliar scent which was becoming more than a smell, more of an actual sensation to the big cat. There were some strange clouds in the distance; seeming to come up from the land instead of down from the sky and that was certainly different for Vidarr. Another of the mountain cones was situated not far from Reykjavik, towards the south. It had burning ash pouring from the crater at the top and that was what was causing Vidarr to catch his breath and gave him a burning sensation in his throat.

They had arrived safely after a 700 mile sea voyage in an open boat, a safe arrival that was cause for relief and celebration. The port itself was not as bustling as Kirkwall had been and appeared sparse in comparison. Torquil was recognised by the quay chieftain who shouted a welcome to him and his crew. Several of the sailors saw familiar faces and were also welcomed with shouts and cheers. The expected bustle of unloading had not taken place. Not even the sheep were relieved of their confinement. The two families had been helped with their possessions and had struggled ashore to find their kin and former neighbours now resident in this strange cold island.

Vidarr, who normally leaped ashore, waited until most of the crew and all the passengers were off, Sveinn and Asmundr also, then, instead of leaping ashore, walked gingerly down the planking as he had an uneasy feeling about this place... but he didn't know why. Not yet. But he did as soon as he put his paws on Icelandic soil. He had taken only a few steps when he leapt up onto some barrels on the quayside. Even on top of the barrels he could feel it. Beneath his paws was a deep and dreadful rumbling coming from the core of the earth itself. No one else seemed to be bothered by it and everyone was cheerfully going about their business. Vidarr was encountering volcanic activity for the first time in his life. He had smelled the molten lava out at sea. He had seen the volcanic ash which spewed skywards regularly from the cones of the always active volcanoes. On board, he had felt the ocean's surge against the mountainous mid-Atlantic ridge of which Iceland is the only part above the surface of the waves. Now, through his paws, he could feel the molten rock pour from the centre of the earth, upwards through fissures, to erupt from craters in the centre of the island and fill the sky with ash clouds, obscuring vast expanses of the heavens as the winds caught it and took it away over the seas. I don't like this place he thought and headed back on board.

For the remainder of the day Vidarr watched the unloading of the supplies for Reykjavik from his knarr and other smaller vessels which were used locally as they were not big enough to be ocean going. It was early evening before Vidarr decided to try again and crept down the gangplank. It wasn't really a town as such. Reykjavik, although on a more welcoming coastline, appeared to be a port without a township but still a Norse port with many rugged Norseman. Sveinn saw Vidarr heading along the quay and called to him. 'What's the matter boy?'

You don't like it here, do you? Your tail is dragging and your ears are flat. Don't worry, stick close and you'll be fine.'

'Will I?' worried Vidarr.

The light was starting to fade and now Vidarr could see bright fiery sparks shooting upwards from the ash cloud emanating from the crater which was just visible to a keen cat's eye at the top of the southern volcano. To him the land beneath his feet was alive and wafts of stinking heat blew over the township. Even the people were beginning to give worried glances in that direction but they seemed to be used to this kind of activity here. Vidarr could not know that he was standing on the newest piece of dry land on the planet, that every rock on the surface of the island of Iceland had emerged molten and flaming from the centre of the Earth via the depth of the sea.

Torquil shouted to Sveinn when he caught sight of him approaching along the quay. He had gathered what looked like most of the crew with him but he took Sveinn apart and put his hand on his shoulder, an unusual familiarity from the older warrior and seaman. 'Sveinn, I believe you hoped to find your father on the island, is that true?'

'Yes, I was told he had voyaged here last season with Leif.' Sveinn felt himself tense and desperately hoped he was not about to hear bad news. He looked searchingly into Torquil's eyes but the chieftain was looking kindly at him and even smiled as he asked,

'If I told you your father was even further west than here would you still be willing to voyage with me?'

'Is there a part of Iceland west of here?' Sveinn questioned.

'No my boy, this is as far as Iceland goes. I've just been told that your father sailed from Reykjavik to Greenland. Will you travel there?'

'Greenland,' sputtered Sveinn. 'Yes, yes, I will, of course' and at that he was heartedly slapped on the back and swept up into the crowd of sailors.

'Now', Torquil shouted to his crew, 'Head for the boat before this island blows itself to Valhalla,' at which point the volcano erupted with a mighty roar which blew half the crater into the air. The bright yellow flow of lava started down the steep dark slope in the direction of Reykjavik.

Panic ensued. Sveinn yelled for Vidarr to come with him but he needn't have bothered as with the penultimate rumble before the top blew off the mountain Vidarr was tearing along the quayside and boarded the ship with one of his more spectacular flying leaps.

Chaos erupted at the port. Everyone stampeded for the boats. Torquil's boat was already being rowed out of the sheltered bay as the others were being loaded with all items of value which could be plucked up and carried instantly.

All eyes were glued to the slow progress of the lava flow. Torquil and his crew were jubilant at their lucky escape. Darkness fell and the rowers hypnotically dipped the oars, pulled them back in rhythm, rotated the oar and repeated the action. All hands rowed the ship away from the coastline which was illuminated by a terrible sight. The shouts and screams of terror faded as they put distance between themselves and the island.

They were several miles out when the lava rolled over the town having consumed the southern farms on its way. Even at that distance the hiss from the cloud of stream that rose from the shoreline was audible to the crew. The sky was highlighted by the plume of violently boiled sea water, vaporised in an instant as the lava rolled over the beach and into the north Atlantic. The enormous wave that erupted from the coastline travelled outwards into the sea towards the knarr. The curved stern lifted majestically upwards as the giant wave passed harmlessly beneath them, settling them back onto the blackness of a starless night in a starless sea.

Direction had not been an issue the night before and now with morning Torquil was urging Radulfr to plot a course westwards. 'Can you do it?' Torquil asked.

'Yes of course but give me a chance. I will need to do some calculations then I will give you directions.'

It was all bustle on board the boat. Stores were being checked. With such an unceremonious departure not everything was in order. The store's master was abundantly relieved that he had loaded freshwater on arrival, and old sailors trick based on years of experience and an expectation of the unexpected.

It was a thousand miles from the volcanic island of Iceland to the western coast of the more peaceful ice covered Greenland. Firstly they would seek the East Coast of this new land, a land part of another continent. They were leaving the old world for the new. However the sea voyage would take them across the strait which would not be for the fainthearted. At that time of year the Northern sea ice would have broken up and the many glaciers would be shedding large chunks of ice into the sea, all of which would float south with the current until they reached a southerly latitude warm enough to melt them into harmless snowballs. Next the journey would follow the long coastline south around the tip of Greenland and then westwards to the settlements.

At this point Vidarr was infinitely relieved simply to have left Iceland and he made a mental note never ever to return. He resumed the familiarity of his life on board ship content with a fresh supply of new boarded rats which only tasted faintly of burning rocks. He was found on top of his favourite rope locker much of the time; his head into wind, fur flattened around his face as he earnestly kept watch for Greenland and the icebergs.

Not all of the crew had planned to leave Iceland so were not with the rest of the sailors when they set sail and some who had rushed aboard had not intended to make the voyage to Greenland but here they all were, all choice removed by natural occurrences. The two families had also been left behind but to Vidarr's satisfaction both Sveinn and Asmundr were on board and that was all he cared about except for qualms about the continued presence of Fenrir who never failed to sneer in Vidarr's direction whenever the opportunity arose. That was one crew member who never had Vidarr’s company on the locker. No, he saw Fenrir for what he was, like his namesake, Fenrir the Wolf God.

The sea voyage continued as all sea voyages do. The daily rota of crew on duty, eating, sleeping, all rolled around with relentless regularity. Vidarr had his own routine without need of a master to direct him. Sveinn had many conversations with Vidarr about the wonders of life on the ocean and Vidarr also listened in to the many items of interest Asmundr imparted to the boy.

'Tell me about the sea ice situation,' Sveinn questioned.

'You know in the far north of Norway we have the ice line above which only the great ice-bears can live?'

'Yes, I've heard of that.'

'That ice line extends in both directions over land and sea. Iceland lies just below it and is a fairly small island in comparison with other northern land masses but Greenland lies mostly north of the ice line and is so vast we don't know if it is an island or not.

'So why do we call…'

'I know, I know, why do we call the warmer island Iceland and the larger ice-covered land Greenland?' interrupted Asmundr. 'It was to encourage Norse settlers to keep moving westwards. If they thought Greenland sounded like a good place to farm then they would leave Norway willingly. There's a lot of people now at home and the land we can farm will not support all that many. Anyway, it's an adventure to go to sea, don't you think?'

Sveinn nodded knowingly with his ready smile and reached absently to pet Vidarr's warm head.

One day while the sun shone brilliantly as they steadily moved over a sparkling sea Radulfr called from the bow 'See ahead, the distant white cap of Greenland and looked behind, do you see the highest mountains in the centre of Iceland?'

'My goodness,' said Sveinn, 'I would never have expected to see both lands at once. Isn't that an impossible distance? Shouldn't Greenland still be over the horizon from us?'

Radulfr heard the boy and came down to his place to explain to him. 'It doesn't happen very often. Only in certain conditions of sunlight and cloud we can actually see a reflection of what lies over the horizon. We call it an ice-glimpse. Today is one of those days. Mark it well.'

Sveinn stared at the illusionary Greenland ice-cap and realised he had been looking at it for a while but had put it down to unusual cloud formation ahead. Vidarr stared along with the entire crew in the direction of the land that lay before them, magically revealed above the horizon. He was the first to smell the ice and despite his thick coat he shuddered as a chill went through his body. Shortly after that a cry went up from the Watch, 'Ice ahead!' Vidarr stood with Sveinn as all eyes stared over the prow at the island that seemed to be bearing down on them, gleaming white with blue and turquoise light, enormous, beautiful and deadly.

'All hands to the oars, NOW,' came the order. The sail was lowered because the wind was blowing them straight into the path of the oncoming moving mountain of ice. It was still some distance away but the current was pulling it towards the knarr and the wind was pushing the boat towards the iceberg so the distance was closing noticeably.

For a full hour the sailors strained hard at the oars and it was some time before Torquil saw that they were actually altering their course, but not by much. Never would anyone sail a ship directly at a cliff on a lee shore but here was a magnificent luminescent cliff sailing at them. All could feel the chill in the air now. There was silence aboard except for the grunts and sighs of the powerful rowers, two per oar.

Finally Radulfr announced that by his calculations the berg would pass in front of the ship and safely drift on its way south allowing the ship to leave it to port. His calculation was more of an estimation but he was rarely wrong. All eyes watched its progress in awe. It towered beyond the height of the mast many times over. Its curves were coloured yet it seemed to glisten whitely all over. In parts it looked transparent as if they could see into its heart and in other places it seemed opaque but lit from within.

It drifted silently past followed by all eyes, male and feline. Only the sheep baaed disinterestedly. When it fell away to port and all danger was passed excited chatter broke out.

'How come a huge thing like that doesn't sink in the sea?' asked Sveinn.

'It's because it is made up of fresh water so it floats on the salt sea,' Asmundr replied.

'Fresh water!' Sveinn exclaimed. 'My goodness, what a surprise. Who would ever think that! I expected it to be frozen sea water.'

While all the chatter was going on one man was silent. It was Fenrir. He was watching the cat intently. No one was to know that he was plotting and had hatched a plan of fiendish evil and cruelty which he intended to implement at the first opportunity.

Torquil doubled the watch at night. Due to the ability of floating ice to be wind driven, current driven, becalmed or any other mode of travel upon the surface of the sea, they had to be extremely vigilant in case one came at them not just from in front but from the side or even the stern. Vidarr found that he was able to smell the ice or rather to feel the ice in his nostrils long before the Watch sounded the ice warning.

Radulfr had the ship brought back on course and the sail was hoisted, reset and lashed in place. Sveinn was now a competent crew man on the Knarr. There wasn't much that he couldn't do and he rowed and watched and pulled on ropes and fitted in with the seasoned sailors as if he had been at sea for a lifetime. And Vidarr in his own way was the same.

The afternoon was coming to a close. Soon it would be evening. Vidarr was at the bow watching the sea ahead as his nose felt full of ice. Besides ice-bergs the water here was cold enough for pieces of sea-ice from the frozen winter shoreline not to have fully melted. Small ice-flows leisurely floated past the boat, seemingly not a threat as they were barely more than the consistency of mush and soon would be gone forever beneath the waves, water once more. Vidarr was leaning over watching the passage of a particularly interesting little ice-flow which had a miniature curved ice-berg shape, resembling a sail almost. 'A little ice-boat !' thought Vidarr and at that instant two chill hands seized him around his middle, plucked him from his perch, launched him up into the air and overboard towards the freezing water. Vidarr let out a blood-curdling screech and flailed backwards in the air as if he could fly and stop his descent to his frozen death in the sea.

His scream was heard by several of the sailors and Sveinn, who was on his sea-chest at the side of the boat, saw with horror his cat, his companion, fall through the air. A group of the nearest sailors rushed to the side and peered overboard but were almost trampled by Sveinn who burst through them and charged at lightning speed towards the stern. One of the sailors was already dropping the sail to slow the ship and everyone was shouting confusing instructions to everyone else. Never had such panic been seen on the orderly Norse ship. Next Sveinn was seen launching the harpoon from the stern into the sea with an unprecedented dynamic throw. The men now rushed to the stern to watch. There was Sveinn lashing the harpoon rope to the boat. The harpoon was firmly embedded in a small boat-shaped ice-flow which was now drifting with the ship and there huddled on the ice-flow itself was one terrified Norwegian forest cat.

The men crowded around and many more hands than were necessary pulled that rope until the ice-flow was in contact with the back of the ship. Its top just reached the stern deck. Vidarr scrambled up the ice with claws fully extended and never was more relieved to find himself being rubbed dry and warmed in Sveinn's jacket. A cheer went up from all on board and Sveinn smiled weakly, still in shock himself and somewhat astounded at his quick witted action and amazing rescue.

As the cheer went up from the men no one saw the man trip over the harpoon rope. No one saw the wolf-like head sink into the icy sea as the boat sailed on its way. It was many hours later before Fenrir was missed when his turn on watch was called and the only witness to the incident had been the slanted eyes of a damp-headed cat emerging from his friend's jacket... and he wasn't going to say a thing!

The ice-glimpse of Greenland had faded with the setting sun which had erased the image as it sank colourfully in the western sky. It was days later when a smudge on the horizon caused the excited cry of 'Land ahead'. This time it was real land and the New World slowly darkened on the distant sea.

The knarr had plodded faithfully onwards, evading treacherous waves, volcanoes, ice-bergs and it had crossed an invisible boundary deep below the sea, the meeting of the vast tectonic plates which formed the old and the new world.

Vidarr was watching the approaching coastline of this new world but he still had a long time to wait to get ashore. Colonies of sea-birds were heard from the inhospitable cliffs of the eastern coastline joined by the cacophony of their grown chicks, gannets and gulls, puffins and storm-petrels. Vidarr thought he might like to investigate some nests when he got the chance. The ship headed south and as they neared the southern cape a low keening sound was heard.

Vidarr of course was first to be aware of it and in its initial stages he blamed the sheep but he soon realised this noise could not be made by any sheep and as in his ears it roared to a crescendo he recognised its meaning and fled below to shelter in the snuggest spot he knew of on board the ship.

The long hours of sunlight which they had been enjoying disappeared altogether. The sky was blackened by dense clouds which turned the now turbulent sea a slate-grey broken only by the dark hearts of huge waves crested by grey-white foam. Rowers became bailers, supplies were secured, all hands took turns with leather buckets on ropes emptying the waves back into the sea. Hour after hour the little ship bucked and plunged and nothing seemed as if it would ever be dry again. Violent gusts of wind howled through the rigging which rope by rope was dismantled and dropped onto the decks or over the side as even the hardiest lines gave way. No one rested. It wasn't possible; except for Vidarr who was wedged between the sacks of grain in the rear lower hold sheltered under the aft deck.

Radulfr and Torquil discussed the situation while clinging tightly on the foredeck to whatever was fastened down or permanent. 'We are alright Torquil: the wind has carried us away from the shore so we are in no danger of being wrecked there.'

Torquil shouted his reply, 'When the storm is over will we ever find our way back to the shore?'

Radulfr shouted back, 'We should be able to. The boat is sturdily built and as long as we have the mast… and they both raised their eyes to the unyielding mast, built into the hull of the knarr… and both gave thanks to their gods for its reliability.

At first the wind and the waves had thrown the Knarr one way then another. Wherever they looked the waves were tumultuous, irregular, coming and going in all directions but after a while the storm seemed to abate ever so slightly and settled into a consistent speed and direction. Radulfr reckoned they were being borne away from the Eastern Settlement of Greenland, their planned destination. Now they were heading at an unprecedented rate in a south westerly direction. When he told this to Torquil he looked at Radulfr and said in a quieter tone, 'This may be fortuitous after all.'

Two days and three nights passed with all control over the ship being given over to the mighty oceanic storm. The morning of the third day found a battered Knarr bobbing peacefully (in comparison with the previous several days) in a thick Atlantic fog. As the wind died down and the sea settled one by one the sailors lowered themselves wherever they stood or clung and slept the sleep of the exhausted. When the sun finally burned off the sea mist Vidarr was the only one awake. He was cleaning the remainder of the sea water from his fur, perched happily on his bow locker. He was the one who first saw the distant coastline, the first one to realise this was not Scotland, Iceland, or even Greenland. This was a new land and he couldn't wait to put his paws ashore and explore.

It was the afternoon watch before the ship started to come to life again. Hot gruel was prepared and everyone hungrily emptied their bowls. Fresh fodder was passed into the sheep who seemed to be able to withstand the battering of the waves, insulated and padded with their massive woollen fleece. The spirits of the men rose as the afternoon passed into the Dog Watch. The fleeting afternoon sun had warmed the ship and started the drying out process on board.

Vidarr had left the observation of the new land to the navigator and came down to sit with Sveinn. Vidarr found him sitting dejectedly, his head in his hands, immune to the air of cheerfulness around him. Vidarr pushed his head against his friend and getting no response forcefully injected his warm head between Sveinn's face and hands. Sveinn looked up and sorrowfully told Vidarr the reason for this depression. 'Oh Vidarr, what am I to do now? I've come all this way with you from our homeland, our lovely Norse mountain homeland with your beloved forests and our family all in the hope of finding my father. I was sure I would find him in Greenland and now we have no hope of berthing in the Western Settlement. We have been blown so far off course that we are heading for some great unknown vast land. Even Radulfr has never ventured this far before. And Torquil seems quite happy about it too. I suspect this was his planned destination all along although he couldn't have anticipated a storm like that. I'll never see my father again. I may never even see home again.'

Asmundr overheard the boy pouring out his heart to the cat who sat with his head on one side listening intently to Sveinn, sensing his grief. Asmundr put his hand on Sveinn's shoulder and Vidarr stretched out a paw onto Sveinn's leg and the three of them sat like that for a long time.

That night Sveinn had the middle four hour watch and was on the foredeck, well wrapped up, as the ship forged ahead into the darkness. The sail was set, all the lines had been pulled taut and the ship seemed to be racing ahead with purpose and determination. Vidarr was sitting by the prow, eyes fixed on the sea surging beneath the hull.

The clouds which had gathered earlier in the evening had broken and increasingly the sea was lit by starlight and then the full moon rose and seemed to sail across the sky with the boat.

The storm had dissipated the worst of the sea ice, broken it apart and reduced the icebergs to liquid. Only once in a while a lone giant was sighted travelling at right angles to the knarr, floating north to south in ghostly moonlight. None came near the ship but Sveinn and Vidarr had no intention of relaxing their watch.

Sveinn had been looking up at the sky, mesmerised by the light from the myriad of stars, layer upon layer of them extending from the planets which shared our revolution of the sun to the tiniest faintest of lights still travelling from the furthest reaches of the universe over countless light years of time away.

Suddenly Vidarr stiffened and stood leaning over the rail, his ears pricked forwards. He uttered chirrups every few seconds. Sveinn came over and stood beside him looking over the hull. He thought his eyes were still seeing the stars only now they were in the sea. 'What?' he muttered to Vidarr. The two of them stood in astonishment as the entire sea was lit from within, wave after wave of sparkles shot under the boat only to be replaced by a further army of shooting iridescent lights. Gradually Sveinn realised what they were witnessing and laughed, the first time since the great storm. 'Look Vidarr, fish, hundreds of them, no thousands, maybe even millions of them, all lit with phosphorescence. See, every time they move they shine and illuminate the sea.' The two of them remained in that spot watching until the end of the watch and when they were relieved around 4 a.m. the last of the fish were still passing under the boat and across its bows. Vidarr retired to Sveinn's sleeping bag with him, tired but excited. He had just witnessed his first new world cod run when countless fish headed south towards the Grand Banks off of Labrador. Sveinn had been cheered by this miraculous sight and was thrilled that Vidarr had shared in the excitement with him. They slept soundly, the boy in his bag of skins, his cat in his arms, warm and comforting and close.

Radulfr and Torquil were frequently found on the foredeck, their heads bent together in serious conversation. Vidarr took to sitting at their feet as if listening in to their conversation.

Radulfr explained to Torquil that although he had never sailed to the new world himself he did know something about it as they were not the first to travel this far across the ocean. Other fishermen from the Old World had been intercepting the cod for centuries. The natives from the north of Green land had also travelled across the strait and explored some of the extensive Eastern coastline. Bits and pieces of information had trickled through the navigator's grapevine giving Radulfr a sparse and basic knowledge of what they should do now. 'Follow the coast south, leaving a safe distance from the coast itself. We will have to watch out for some skerries which will lie in our path but other than that we can have a clear run to where you will hopefully join up with Leif and the settlers. The storm has blown us so far south we are well below the land of bare rock and glaciers and now we are approaching the land of trees. Somewhere to the south lies a vast river estuary big enough to shelter islands and beyond that is the fertile Vinland where the wild grapes grow.'

'Right' said Torquil and scanned the horizon for the famous trees he had been promised. 'Fine' thought Vidarr and joined him in his watch.

As the knarr voyaged southwards the air turned milder. The cries of seabirds were a constant reminder they were not far from land. Vidarr could smell pine. His nose tingled, his whiskers twitched, his claws extended themselves involuntarily and he was unable to sit in one place for long. The land slid past, agonisingly slow for all on board. Days passed and nights. Finally around the middle of the forenoon watch Radulfr announced their destination was coming into view. What appeared to be a huge peninsula running north from a vast tract of low-lying land (later proved to be an enormous island) stretched towards them. In the entire journey south no sign of human settlement had appeared. The trees grew everywhere. It was indeed a land of forests. Vidarr could not help but observe that while the trees covered hillsides, valleys, hung over streams, clung to cliff faces, they most strikingly grew to the high tide line on the rocky shores. But now straight ahead without doubt was a settlement marked initially by the smoke twirling on the sea breeze from their home fires.

As the knarr approached a cry went up from all of the people on the shore and out of about six or eight Norse houses came a stream of people all waving and shouting excitedly. The sea was shallow but the knarr slid perfectly up to what seemed like a tiny shipyard complete with smithy shop and timber yard. The settlement was situated on a curving marine terrace with a fresh water brook running across it and into the sea. 'My goodness' said Sveinn, 'where did all these people come from? There must be about a hundred of them!'

Suddenly unsure Vidarr did not do one of his flying leaps ashore but waited until Sveinn and Asmundr crossed from the ship to the makeshift quay then pursued them down the planking. Land at last. Terra firma. Joy. No Fenrir. Friendly faces. No sign of cat skinning and there before Vidarr was the initial row of trees which stretched from this coast to a far distant unknown coast in an unbroken, thick, tangled, wonderful forest waiting to be explored. Vidarr took a deep breath and Sveinn saw with a smile a striped tail rushing into the undergrowth.

It would be impossible to describe the confusion which followed the arrival of Torquil's knarr to Leif's little Norse settlement at the tip of the island that in later years would be called Newfoundland, a worthy name befitting its location.

Hours later when all the crew and livestock and probably a few, a very few, surviving rodents, were all safely accommodated ashore Vidarr found an exhausted Sveinn in one of the turf houses and joined him inside. The storm, then the realisation that Sveinn could be missing being reunited with his father had taken a heavy toll on the boy and he just wanted to sleep and sleep and sleep some more.

There was an excited squeal from the woman at the hearth fire when she saw Vidarr and before he knew it a bowl of warm stew was placed in front of him. He did not hesitate to lap it up and while he did so his new friend, Freya, told him he was the exact image of her beloved pet cat she had in Norway as a child.

It was several days later when all were rested and used to firm footing instead of a heaving swaying deck beneath them that Torquil called a meeting. 'I want you all to know that as free men you can make your own decisions now we are here. You have several choices. Due south of here

Markland ends at the large estuary. The south shore of this river system has a milder climate and is more sheltered from the sea. We have reliable information that the wild grape indeed does grow there, also wheat and other grains self-seed and grow wild.'

A murmuring broke out as the crew commented in these amazing facts.

Torquil continued, 'The settlement here will make anyone welcome who wishes to stay. The sheep have opted to remain.'

Laughter broke out at Torquil's joke. He seemed to be in exceptionally fine spirits.

'You will realise soon enough that we are not the only people in the area. This is not an uninhabited land like Iceland. There has been very little contact with these natives. They call themselves 'Skraelings' and they seem to be a primitive tribe. Some trading has taken place but they can't be trusted yet.'

Further murmuring broke out as the men digested this surprising piece of information.

'As you can see this land is rich in a commodity which is lacking in both the Greenland settlements and in Iceland.' The shout of 'timber' went up from some of the men. 'Yes, very valuable timber. These other settlements are more desperate for a supply of wood than any other commodity and I plan to provide them with it' he announced with a smile. A cheer went up from the men. 'The situation is that you can stay here, you can travel south in further exploration or you can return with me with a load of timber, first stop Greenland.'

Sveinn looked up in interest at this suggestion and as he did so Torquil noticed him and added 'Oh yes Sveinn, by the way, your father Haakon is here and will be back in the settlement in a couple of days after a trip to the south.'

Before Sveinn could even take this in Torquil had gone on to discuss the fact that it was now half way through the summer and there was only time for one single journey back if they went all the way to Norway.

Sveinn almost fell from his stool when Asmundr gave him an almighty slap on the back and a dazed young man was surrounded by a group of his sailor friends congratulating him on his luck.

Vidarr missed this piece of news as he was deep in the forest lured by the scent of a cooking pot and he was watching a young girl chopping vegetables and herbs and adding them with venison to the large cooking pot in the middle of the Skraeling camp. He kept his head down until a band of men arrived in the camp looking for supper. Vidarr slipped away through the undergrowth, unseen but intrigued.

When he arrived back at the settlement he found Sveinn in a great state of excitement. He couldn't sit still; he paced the length of the house then turned and repeated this action over and over. Vidarr watched him but saw that all was well so happily sat down to a bowl of stew but it didn't smell as appetising as the Skraeling girl's supper.

The next day Vidarr set off into the forest again. Sveinn was preoccupied, anxiously scouring the horizon to the south for the return of the group sent out to explore the legendary Vinland. This new world forest was full of wonders to an inquisitive cat from the old world. The smells were totally different, especially the animal ones. He encountered some strange new creatures but kept his distance until he knew more about them. He tracked the stream for quite some distance and was astounded when he came to a deep pond formed unnaturally by a carefully compiled log jam and watched from the safety of one of the only nearby trees left standing as a family of beaver swam to and fro in the pond while their young played in the shallows diving and chasing and slapping their flat tails on the surface of the water. Other rodents were visible along the river bank and Vidarr made a mental note to sample a muskrat which seemed to be prolific and an easy catch, except for the swimming bit.

Vidarr headed off to where he had seen the Skraeling camp but when he got there it was deserted. He sniffed around the cold ashes of the camp fire and was bombarded with new and interesting odours: roasted meat, animal skins, human tracks, all made his head spin. Silently in the undergrowth a slim dark hand parted the foliage and a pair of black eyes fringed by straight jet black hair observed Vidarr's explorations with interest.

Vidarr sensed a movement behind him and without pausing to turn his head he flew off in the opposite direction and did not stop until he was certain he was not being pursued. He stopped, panting next to a fallen log, alert and ready to run again when from behind the log a huge shape covered in massive spikes lumbered over the log towards him. Never had Vidarr seen such a grotesque creature and in a flash he was up the nearest pine tree and did not pause to look down until he was perched on an alarmingly high branch. The huge male porcupine showed his disinterest in the cat by trudging off into the forest without as much as a backwards glance. That was a close encounter, thought Vidarr and he was very glad not to have tested out just how deadly those spines were.

From his perch above he watched squirrels run from tree branch to different tree. These he recognised. He smelled but did not see the offending skunk and was glad that the scent seemed to be airborne from quite some distance away. That was close enough. Its deep muskiness was overpowering.

A family of racoons marched slowly but purposefully across the clearing below him, the youngsters tumbling and rolling their way behind their parents.

Vidarr had never seen so much wildlife all in one place anywhere else. This place captured his interest. He started to feel part of this new and strange land.

Curiosity overcame him and on his way back to the settlement he passed close by the Skraeling camp once more. The girl was at the cooking pot again. She was younger than Sveinn, tall and very slim and very dark skinned. Vidarr watched her. She seemed to sense she was not alone and very slowly she lifted one of the strips of venison she had been about to add to the pot and threw it in Vidarr's direction. She almost scored a direct hit. He leaped upwards but the smell was so tempting he leapt down upon it, grabbed it firmly and ran off into the forest with his gift. The tinkling sound of her laughter followed him through the maze of trees.

That evening Sveinn was even more fretful. Vidarr stayed close to him as he felt his friend needed his warm presence next to his legs to comfort the anxiety that was emanating from his every pore. Vidarr also had a moment of concern when he heard the cry of another cat in the dark of the forest, not a small cat, no, but a menacingly large one, a cougar. Vidarr made a mental note to stay well away from a predator who outweighed him by far like that. He had once encountered a wild lynx in his homeland but it had not been interested enough in him to cause him a problem. The prolonged scream of the new world panther was something altogether more threatening.

Sveinn had been given his father's place in one of the communal houses. Some of his possessions were there and Sveinn recognised them from his house. A hood his mother had sewn. A blanket his sister had made. He had not realised until then how much he missed his family and all he wanted now was to see his father again and to reunite his family.

Vidarr was thinking differently. He wanted to go further and further in his explorations. He was learning so much about this place, rich in plants and wildlife, birds and insects. His curiosity about the native people drew him back daily to observe this different way of life.

The following day Vidarr left on his next trip into the great forest. The Skraeling girl was watching for him. She lifted a piece of meat again but instead of throwing it to Vidarr she simply held it out and spoke gently to him in her guttural language. He didn't know the language but he knew a friend when he heard her way of talking to him and saw the friendly tilt of her head and the smile in her dark eyes. He approached cautiously and took the meat from her hand but stayed beside her crouching form to eat. She gently ruffled the fur on his head and let him finish his meal in peace.

It was a week before the exploration party returned. Vidarr was sitting at the tree line watching the settlers gather on the shore to help bring the small boat into the shallows. Sveinn was pacing the water line like a man demented. Eight men waded ashore laden with sacks of things of interest they had gathered on their travels in the big estuary. The fifth man ashore walked in a familiar way and even with his head down, his back bent to carry a large sack, Sveinn knew it was Haakon, at long last.

Haakon raised his head in amazement when he heard an oh-so-familiar voice shout 'Father' and he could hardly believe his eyes at the sight of his eldest son running through the shallows towards him.

Vidarr couldn't wait to join in the happy reunion and rushed from his vantage point to join the crowd on the beach.

That night the three of them sat together at the fireside. Sveinn and Haakon had so many adventures to relate but every so often Haakon looked at Vidarr and stroked his fur and told him 'I cannot believe you have come all the way from Norway with my son.'

Torquil said that they would only have another ten days in Newfoundland to prepare to leave for home and all hands worked to gather lumber from the tide line and load the knarr. More and more Sveinn noticed Vidarr's absence. Vidarr was away overnight some nights and Sveinn knew that things were changing. 'You like it here boy, don't you? I don't think you want to be a Norse ship's cat anymore, do you?' Vidarr gave a short purr in response. Sveinn didn't voice any more but both of them knew what the other was thinking and what the outcome of the next few days would be.

Asmundr came to Sveinn and Haakon and said, 'I have decided to throw in my lot with these settlers here in the new world. I am getting on in years so I can't keep sailing forever. Anyway I like it here. I feel younger again. Sveinn was too choked up to say anything but Haakon thanked the old man for all the care he had given Sveinn on the journey. 'You might land here again and don't forget to stop off and see that girl in Scotland you have waiting for you,' Asmundr said with a smile to Sveinn who nodded manfully. Neither mentioned Vidarr. That was a whole other subject.

The day came when Torquil and his men boarded the knarr and Haakon stood at the side of the ship with his arm around his son. Vidarr stood at the edge of the tree line. The knarr was pushed and pulled out of the shallows and the sail was raised. Sveinn did not take his eyes off Vidarr. The ship quickly left the shore behind and Vidarr became a tiny speck in the distance, disappearing out of Sveinn's life. Haakon tightened his grip on his son and Sveinn felt a surge of unexpected happiness as if everything was working out as it should.

Vidarr watched until the ship disappeared over the horizon then with a bound he vanished into the forest, the first Norwegian Skaukatt in the New World.

From Vidarr to Gatto

The New World scene faded slowly in the minds of the cats perched on the rock face. The ancient forest into which Vidarr had disappeared was replaced with the forest beyond the clearing in front of the cats, barely visible in the subdued light.

The voice was heard collectively once more. 'You have been chosen tonight for the memories of your earth life held captive in your mind and also for your recollection of how it felt to experience these events, not simply for what happened.'

Vidarr sat upright awaiting his successor and the tale he had to tell. 'Attention please Wutki, your turn will come,' said the voice as Wutki leant across towards Vidarr and asked him what he had done next in the forest.

Gatto blinked as the light started to illuminate his niche and the voice introduced him, 'Gatto will you please come forward,' He slipped easily from the ledge to ground level. They all could see this was an agile cat who was comfortable on rocky ledges. He was not difficult to see in the subdued light and not just because of his colouring or his agility but because confidence seemed to emanate from his every posture and movement. 'The Roman cat will now share his life experiences with you.' All eyes were trained upon him as this white and grey cat stood comfortably before them all. His story began and yet another change of surroundings and climate in a different time appeared.

The Roman Cat

Carrara, Tuscany
Early 1500's

The sky was an unblemished turquoise above the rocky peaks which sloped down to the sea, sparkling and dazzling in the sunlight. A sharp pair of green eyes peered in wonder from the lip of the crevice high up in the mountains. There, the lush dark green vegetation was punctuated by an equally dazzling brightness. Slits of white rock, as pure as snow, transformed the terrain into a shimmering illusion.

He was perfectly camouflaged. His fur was identical to the white of the stone of the mountain. The blue grey stripes on his head, legs and tail exactly matched the streaks in the exposed area of the rocks.

The spring sun was rapidly warming the morning air. Behind the unseen cat, the mountains seemed to unfold in layers, each one higher and more jagged than the one in front. They stretched endlessly into the azure infinity, generously revealing their glistening scars. Buried within the seams of marble, and soon to be brutally extracted from their slumbering ancient beds, lay the greatest works of art the world would ever know.

The cat pricked his ears forward and lent over the edge. He looked down. The final destination of Carrara's marble, the best in Italy, probably the finest in the world, was not his concern. However he was fascinated by the movement below. He crouched low to observe. From this height the quarry workers resembled mice on a granary floor. Already there was a rising haze of marble dust. The olive-clad foothills and the vines of the lower slopes had a grey patina which at first hung over them then descended to rest on the foliage. Finally it was swept away by the breezes or the less frequent showers provided by the Tyrrhenian Sea. These offered some respite from the searing summer heat and the powdered products from the mining.

The cat knew the comfort of the touch of marble on his body. While the sun rose high in the Tuscan sky and even the birds remained still in the trees, the little cat had been comfortable in his first marble home, a sanctuary of coolness where his mother had always come to give birth. Now his four siblings had scattered to different places of their choice and his mother had returned to her spot beside the Carrione River. He had stayed on in the quarry.

Silently he raised himself up, stretched, and after a rapid lick at his paws he fearlessly descended the broken surface of the mountain. He wended his way from slope to slope jumping from half excavated chunks of marble to scree slippery with small broken pieces. He was in a familiar landscape, sure-footed and most of all, curious.

The quarry reverberated with the necessary daily sounds which somehow failed to echo up through the mountain passes but were absorbed by the dusty marble haze. As birdsong is to a forest cat so is the sound of hammers, picks and chisels to a Carrarese cat. The shouting of the labourers, the crack of the whips over the backs of the toiling oxen and even the occasional gunpowder charge all failed to prevent the cat's enthusiastic descent into the world of man.

One man stood out to the small cat. This man moved at a different pace. He walked with a different gait. The cat's gaze was continually drawn back to this tall thin figure. The man would spend many hours just staring at the lumps of marble freshly cut from the mountainside, touching it, lowering his face to the surface until he must have been breathing directly onto it. Seeing this, the cat recognised something in this man alone. Like him, the man knew the coolness of marble, the comfort of its touch, the beauty hidden in its limestone depth, the secrets it held there.

The rush downhill was not unprecipitated. The cat knew exactly what he was doing. To be more accurate, he knew exactly what time it was. Before he arrived on the quarry floor, the gong had sounded. The men were filtering down to the shacks at the base. It was the morning break. The cat knew that the men's packs held a delectable feast of hams and sardines, cheeses and smoked meats. He lived in hope of a scrap or two being thrown in his direction and usually he was not disappointed.

His descent led him past a massive block of quarried marble, almost too heavy to be man-handled onto a regular ox-cart. This was one for a strong cart with reinforced flooring and double wheels plus a lot of ropes. The tall stringy man was standing motionless by the side of it, one hand placed on its side, his palm gently touching the surface. It was as if he could feel the calcite rich cells left behind by the marine creatures whose desiccated bodies formed the limestone in another long-forgotten age.

The cat skidded to a halt at his side and looked inquisitively up into his gaunt bearded face. He was younger at close range than he appeared at a distance with his lank body and preoccupied demeanour. As their eyes met the man inclined his head in recognition of the cat's interest and murmured one word only in greeting, 'Gatto'. He went back to his contemplation of the marble and the cat walked on, more slowly now, replaying the name he had just been given, over and over in his head, 'Gatto'.

From dawn to dusk, day in and day out, Gatto observed the apparently endless toil of the quarrymen as he leapt from the surrounding scrub and remaining forests into the dazzling noisy world of the precious marble. He couldn't stay away. His adventuresome nature was opening doors in his young life that would to lead to unimagined places. Always, he knew where the strange young man was and he watched his doings with an undiminishing fascination.

It was late afternoon and the days were stretching out as spring slid into early summer with all the growth and warmth of the Tuscan season. The men sweated more. Gatto watched as fresh-water barrels were moved into position more frequently. They were brought from the streams to the quarries. He headed for the watering area to lap up the cold mountain water dripping below the barrels when he didn't want to climb back out of the quarry to the streams. Men were gathering at the water for a few moments' respite and for an exchange of remarks, jokes and insults. 'Giovanni, behind you.'

Giovanni looked round in the direction of his friend Paolo's gaze and recognising the dust-covered scarecrow-like figure waiting behind him said, 'Excuse me Master Buonarroti, please go before me.' He just shook his head and waved Giovanni on who quickly drank from the wooden ladle and moved away. At Michelangelo's heels was Gatto, drinking alongside his new found friend. Gatto had been stalking the artist for weeks now.

'Master, I see you have your little marble cat with you', Paolo joked good naturedly and a few of the queuing labourers laughed out loud. Michelangelo paused and looked down at Gatto as if noticing him for the first time. Gatto sat down as close to his large feet as he dared and contentedly washed the water splashes off his fur. Michelangelo said nothing but turned and walked away. Another burst of laughter went up when Gatto, suddenly noticing his departure, leapt in the air and scurried after him.

Michelangelo went back to the job in hand which involved cutting a large irregular chunk of marble. Michelangelo spoke quietly to the cat. 'Do you see this block of marble Gatto? Now it is rough and misshapen but inside it is an idea. One day it will adorn the tomb of the Holy Father in Rome and the entire world will adore at its feet.' As his little shadow looked up into his eyes, Michelangelo stretched forward and gripped one end of the swinging saw which was suspended by ropes on a wooden framework straddling the block. He methodically began to push and pull the narrow blade through the solid limestone. His helper on the other end sawed in rhythm. As the marble dust began to float to the ground, Gatto leapt nimbly away and ascended to his lair for the evening, leaving the men to their industry.

It was a few days later when that sense of complacency, which comes to man and beast when all is going well, was shattered. Gatto was perched just above the level of the block-mining activity, his spot of preference. The less marble dust that he had to shake from his fur the better. Gatto observed.

Domenic, the head marble mason, had spent considerable time marking out the faults in the seams of marble which were still embedded in a vein in the mountainside. He knew that these faults were the weak spots. Next, Domenic, with the help of his assistant, used a hammer and small chisel to cut a groove into the marble. Gatto thought they were making little more impact in getting that marble out than if he were down on that ledge scraping at the stonework with his claws. This was part of the fascination of the work of man to a cat's mind. How could you find two more diverse creatures than a human and a feline? But Gatto was to learn that opposites can be drawn to one another and, for mutual benefit, entwine their lives forming a relationship that can endure for life.

Gatto jumped a little when Domenic roughly hammered in some wedges of olive wood carved from the ancient Tuscan olive trees. Next buckets of water were hauled up on ropes and using rags, the wedges were soaked repeatedly until the wood started to absorb the water. This went on until the men took a break. Gatto crept a little closer to see exactly how the liquid was disappearing. Domenic saw his approach and sounded a warning, 'Watch out little cat! This marble is going to move soon,' and at that there was a crack like thunder and a large section of the marble seam separated itself from its bed. Gatto fled.

It didn't take long before Gatto was descending from his perch once more. He had spotted his friend below. He was busy shouting instructions to a large group of workers who were gathering to help bring the chunk of marble safely to ground level.

A team had mounted to the ledge beside the seam and were engaged in roping the lump of stone. Great levers of wood were positioned under it. It took the weight of many men to raise the rock even a little but just sufficient to coax the net of ropes under and around it. Gatto hopped from spot to spot anxious not to miss a thing. This was quarry work which had been taking place here all of Gatto's one season of life, and much more, but he had never paid such close attention to the work before. It had something to do with his new attachment to the artist. It was almost as if he could see through another's eyes and something new was becoming of interest and of importance to him. What Gatto hadn't realised was that he was growing up.

Next to arrive on the rope pulleys were piles of logs with all the appendages carefully removed. They were laid out in a line forming a pathway which led to a previously prepared chute carved from the natural stone of the mountain.

The levers were back in position. The men threw their weight into nudging the gigantic chunk onto the roller road. The ropes were ingeniously looped around anything solid and stationary to form pulleys to help ease the stone to the head of the slipway.

This was too much for Gatto. He bounded to the head of the chute to look down the gradient which had been designed to be as gentle as possible while still harnessing the pull of gravity. Gatto could see the master on the ropes below. Suddenly Gatto recoiled in horror as the smell of rancid animal fat polluted with lye assaulted his nostrils. What was that caustic stink? The chute had been greased with a layer of soap to facilitate the descent of the stone.

It was being man-handled again. Gatto saw it move with much manual exertion onto a wooden skid, a sledge of planking, then multitudinous nets were fastened around the entire contraption. The ropes were anchored to posts strategically placed beside the chute and Domenic lent over to give the signal, 'Coming down'.

To Gatto's amazement the massive block hovered at the edge fleetingly and then seemed to melt away over the drop. He ran to his ledge expecting to see the block shattered at the base, but no, it was travelling in a controlled, and apparently effortless, manner ground-wards.

It touched down with barely a crunch. Then a lot of shouting ensued. Gatto headed for the base at top speed but not by way of the foul smelling chute. He arrived in time to see a large wooden sling being towed to the bottom of the chute where the block lay. The sling was attached to the marble, complete with skid still attached, and the next task was to crane it onto a waiting bullock cart. This involved swinging the marble from its current position through 180 degrees and elevating it onto the broad wheeled cart. The ox-herders firmly held the heads of the six oxen waiting to take the load to the work area to be trimmed into a rectangular shape.

The block was in the air but suddenly Domenic was yelling something from above. He was waving his arms and pointing but no one could make out what he was saying or what the problem was. He could see something the workers below couldn't! With a resounding twang one of the main support ropes gave way allowing the heavy stone to swing down to one side and all the adjoining ropes snapped like thread, one by one.

As the piece of rock weighing several tons came crashing down all the men holding the ropes leapt aside in all directions. Two men were left in the direct path of the falling rock. One was the young master artist. The rock clipped the neck of the other worker and his fall knocked Michelangelo backwards off his feet but out of the path of the runaway marble. As everyone dusted themselves off and ran to help the two men up, only one of them got up from the ground. Gatto frantically rubbed himself against Michelangelo's ankles and kept almost tripping him up as the artist walked away alone.

At last the final day dawned. Gatto descended to the base to mingle with the workers, the carts and dozens of oxen. He had witnessed this commotion several times before in the previous eight months as Michelangelo directed the loading of tons of marble onto carts for shipment to Rome. Every cart in Carrara had been commissioned. Gatto saw block after block of the precious marble being slung on their beech wood skids on to the carts. Several times he had retreated to slightly higher ground in fear of being kicked by one of the many excited oxen which were being strapped noisily into position. Gatto noticed that the most dangerous animals had red dye painted on the tips of their long horns. This warned the workers that this one was a feisty beast but Gatto did not require to see the dye, he could smell their belligerence.

The sun rose higher and higher in the sky and it was well after noon before the last of the carts was moving out of the quarry. The master artist mounted onto the bench beside the cart driver and, as the quarrymen raised a cheer of farewell to

Michelangelo, Gatto realised that his friend was actually leaving along with his load of marble. This hadn't happened before. Michelangelo stood up and raised an arm in farewell and nodded a silent thank you to the workers. He scanned the nearby rocks. Gatto stood, his ears pricked up as far as they would go. Their eyes met. With a gentle smile Michelangelo gave an almost imperceptible nod. It was enough. Gatto reacted instantly. He virtually flew from the hillside and took a flying leap onto the top of the now rolling cart. Skidding to a halt he dropped down onto the cart bed just behind the figure of his friend and the two of them departed the white marble mountains for the greatest city in Christendom.

The convoy of laden ox carts bumped and rumbled their way down the track. It was not fit to be called a road. It twisted and turned between the hills, slid on patches covered with loose rubble, stuck in dips with muddy bottoms but always the faithful oxen kept the carts moving slowly towards the sea. It was a journey they had made many times before and nothing knocked them off their plodding stride. Gatto was crouched in a corner watching the huge lump of marble which rocked and swayed but never parted from its wooden sledge or shifted within the security ropes. Gatto was glad of that.

It was almost dusk when a new set of sensations reached down to Gatto in his little corner; sounds, smells, movement in the air, the cry of sea-birds. Gatto climbed cautiously to the side of the cart and looked at the sight before him in wonder. It was the distant sea which from high in the mountains he had seen glistening many miles away on the far horizon. Now it was right in front of him. He was overwhelmed by the enormity of it, stretching beyond the port, merging with the sky itself. And the movement! Gatto was not used to the water around his solid mountain home shifting before his eyes, rolling in towards the land and being sucked out again with a hiss of terrifying ferocity. The incoming waves roared while the outgoing waves pulled at the shingle of the shoreline like a world full of angry cats. Gatto decided to remain in the cart for now until he understood more of what was going on around him. The salty sea breeze blew his fur in all directions. The noise of the gulls was frightful, a piercing, shrieking, screech. One of them glided overhead inspecting the unusual arrival in the cart. The bird observed that this tiny furry creature, the colour of marble, would pose no threat to his kind and drifted away on the next updraft. Gatto saw his vicious yellow eye, his sturdy beak and his sheer brute size, judging it to possibly out-weigh himself. He knew he had met his match.

The port was alive. Gatto surveyed the rows of wooden barges lying abreast of one another at the quayside. This was a busy commercial dock and the loaders were no strangers to massive blocks of marble swinging on slings from the carts to the dockside and from there into the holds of the little ships. It looked as if the boats would sink under the load of heavy rock but they only settled more firmly at their watery berths.

As each barge was filled it was drawn out from the quay by ropes pulled by dock workers and the next empty barge was pulled into position. Suddenly Gatto was startled by the jolting of his cart as it pulled up beside a boat. The noise was frightful. Oxen were bellowing. Men were shouting, the descent of the marble into the hold caused crashing and banging. Men were hammering hold covers into place with huge heavy mallets. The skippers were shouting instructions to their crew. Gatto could not even bring himself to utter a growl but gaped in wonder at the apparent chaos before him.

As Michelangelo walked up the gangplank onto the boat Gatto leapt expertly onto the rope beside him and boarded the vessel as sure-footed as any river rat. In no time at all the boat was towed, pushed and pulled, away from the quay and the long triangular sail was raised. At the bow a white and grey cat stood with its four paws planted firmly on the deck, its fur blown flat across its head, ears back and face into the wind. He rolled with the swell as it passed beneath the boat, lifting the bow high above the waves then dropping it smoothly back into the troughs in the sea. Gatto was undauntedly sailing to an unknown Rome with his artist friend.

He stayed there in the forecastle until the sun had disappeared below the horizon like a fiery ship with blazing sails of vermillion Even then he waited in the dark, savouring the salt smell of the night air.

The vessel ploughed its way south following the darkened bulk of the Tuscan coast now outlined by a myriad of celestial lights.

The moon emerged from the distant waves. It hung low in the sky, created a shimmering path which led straight to the boat and picked out the white head and the glittering eyes of the cat as he kept watch. The ship sailed on through the night.

Satiated with the heaving movement of the black night sea and to avoid the increasing sea spray Gatto retreated across the deck. A silver glow shone up through the spaces on the decking over the hold; marble reflecting moonlight. Gatto cautiously padded across the top of the hold feeling comforted by the proximity of his native marble not far beneath his feet. The lateen sail worked well in these conditions. Gatto felt the boat surge beneath his feet as the area of low pressure in front of the sail effectively pulled the boat along, a perfect airfoil. He watched the helmsman with his steering oar keep the boat on a steady course which wasn't difficult as the heavy cargo lessened the wind drift to which boats with this type of shallow draft were prone. Gatto looked for a corner to sleep in. Where the sides of the boat rose from the bilge line, clinker style, strakes overlapping strakes, Gatto found his bed for the night in a pile of his familiar marble dust and chips and before he knew it he felt the warmth of the morning sun on the tips of his ears.

The onshore breeze had strengthened overnight. Gatto tried to dodge the fine spray which broke over the wide deck as each new wave crashed into the bow. He watched the flow of sea water as it drained harmlessly away down through the hold where members of the crew pumped it back into the sea.

Gatto had never seen land from this perspective before and he was torn between watching the Tuscan hills slip by and going in search of breakfast. The smell was too much for him and he raced down a laddered stairwell straight into the galley. It was tiny but there was his friend sitting with some sailors around a small table. A cheer went up when Gatto appeared in the doorway and a sailor said, 'Cat, we thought you had drowned.'

But Michelangelo answered with a laugh, 'Not likely. This animal can ascend vertical mountains and descend marble quarries blindfold so you needn't worry about him,' and at that a shower of scraps came flying through the air towards him. Gatto devoured it all with a growl and settled in the warmth and shelter of the galley for another nap as close to Michelangelo as he could get.

The day wore on and it was late afternoon when Gatto heard a shout go up from the watch. The mouth of the Tiber had appeared in the distance but was still some way off. The Master and some of the crew were discussing the worsening weather in serious tones. Gatto felt that the heaving had increased and now the front of the boat was banging down onto the surface of the sea with each passing wave. It wasn't a pleasant sensation for a well fed cat and Gatto started to feel nauseated but stalwartly held onto his stomach contents. It would have been a terrible waste otherwise.

Unbeknownst to the artist, or to the cat, two hundred and fifty miles to the north the heavy winter deluge had arrived early. The sea lay approximately fifty miles to the west from where there was an endless supply of moist air, which, when it hit the raised land, condensed into rainfall. Once the ground was saturated, the valleys began to run with countless streams which gathered momentum with their descent. The river, flowing south through the beech forests of Emilia Romagna on its way to the Tyrrhenian Sea, was swelling with excess water. It ran off the Apennine Mountains to which the river ran parallel. When eventually the Tevere was joined by the Aniene River it expanded immediately into a torrent hurtling towards Umbria and the city of Rome.

When Michelangelo left the galley and headed back up onto the deck Gatto roused himself and followed. He knew instinctively that he needed fresh air. On emerging out onto the lower deck they were struck by wind and spray which heralded a full blown storm. The two of them worked their way towards the centre of the boat where the hatches covered the hold. Michelangelo peered down into the darkness below and muttered that his best piece of marble would be pounded to dust by the time they got to Rome if this dreadful banging of the waves didn't stop. There had been a sharp crack every time the hull crashed down into the troughs of the waves but now there was an ominous rumbling from the hold as the marble shuddered, following the movement of the boat, a rumble that was echoed aloft as thunder joined in the storm chorus.

The crew were also on deck, lashing goods down. Michelangelo reached out and restrained one of the sailors, Giovanni, by the arm. 'Is this going to be alright? My marble is starting to shift below.'

Giovanni gave a short laugh and said, 'Master Buonarroti, we have been plying this route for close on two thousand years. Our fathers and grandfathers before us sailed this coast, so leave it to us and,' he added as an afterthought, 'don't be concerned about your chunk of rock down there, we'll look after it for you.' Michelangelo gave a glimmer of a smile which failed to reach his eyes. Only concern showed there.

Despite avoiding showers of salt spray Gatto felt better in the fresh air. Somehow the experience, although challenging, was exhilarating. The driest and safest spot seemed to be behind the central mast. The two of them hunkered down, averting their heads as one, each time a wave splashed over them. When the rain poured down they were both so wet already it didn't matter. Gatto gave up snarling at the water being thrown over him.

The sun had not set yet but the darkness was increasing as the storm clouds obscured the sky. A call from above alerted the sailors. The mouth of the Tevere had been sighted in a flash of lightening. The sea changed colour and consistency. It was now a mottled yellow due to vast quantities of silt washed out from the land. The sky turned green. It was as if an artist had gone colour blind and painted a surreal landscape.

It had become a battleground. A tiny triangle of sail was all the crew could allow themselves. Three men were on the steering oar. Gatto had his claws fully extended and firmly embedded in the lines running from the mast. He wanted to run for shelter but he was deterred by the wind and water traversing the deck. Michelangelo roped himself next to Gatto and they sheltered together, helpless in the face of the storm.

A cry, that now they were turning towards the river, was briefly heard before being carried aloft by the gale. Beneath the waves an invisible danger was menacing the already distressed vessel. A slowly subsiding tectonic plate had created steep shelving off the coastline. This resulted in a strong sea current which flowed closely in to the shore, strong enough to wash away the silt from the mouth of the Tevere. No delta was permitted to form there as every tiny particle was picked up and borne northward with a fierce determination.

The ship had to enter this current and cross up into the mouth of the river avoiding being hit broadside by such a force of nature and spun helplessly onto the land. The shallow draft of the vessel was no help in a situation like this but at least it had the ballast of Michelangelo's marble.

The crew were familiar with the foibles of the estuary of the Tevere and joined the current to the south of the mouth of the river. The ship was gripped in a tidal race. They were swept alarmingly close to the shore line and at what seemed the last possible moment they swung the boat round sharply. Amazingly they exited the current in the Tyrrhenian Sea like a cork from a bottle and shot up into the country's third longest river.

The wind dropped immediately under the shelter of the land but the black and green storm clouds still rolled aggressively overhead barely above the height of the mast. The Tevere was not a deep river, in places as shallow as seven feet and never deeper than twenty feet. Gatto saw with horror that the yellow flow from upriver raced and foamed like a waterfall. The waves were even more gigantic than at sea. Now the crew had to navigate away from the teeming shallows.

Gatto succumbed and vomited until he could retch no more. It seemed as if the boat was moving upriver pulled by an invisible rope which sometimes pulled strongly, sometimes weakly, sometimes as if it forgot to pull at all. In this manner they battled their way towards Rome. Ostia Antica, the original harbour for Rome before it became land bound, had passed by unnoticed close to the mouth of the river. Sixteen miles of navigation lay ahead.

Sick and weary Gatto lay stretched, almost flat, his faithful dagger-like claws holding him fast to the rope with a strength his muscles no longer had. The out-flowing river battled against the wind and the incoming tide. The rain was still swirling in aerial torrents when the boat gave a heave which felt as if it had taken wings. The crew were all essentially God-fearing Catholic Christians and cries for help from Mary the Mother of God echoed around the boat In later years more than one sailor swore he saw the muscled body of the God Tiberinus rise from the river, water flowing from his hair and beard, the merciful guardian spirit of the Tevere. At that precise moment the vessel slammed down onto a shoal and broke her back. The bow and stern were simultaneously raised out of the water and the mast descended into the deep in pursuit of one of Carrara's finest blocks of marble along with one artist and one cat.

Drowning is a strange sensation. Once Gatto's head sank below the brown and boiling surface all the raging storm sounds were silenced. Not even a hiss came from the waters. The marble cleared a pathway downwards. Gatto followed hindquarters first, his head still straining upwards towards the light but too shocked to even move his front paws. The marble came to rest in an explosion of mud and Gatto landed inelegantly on top of it.

Sailors who have survived near drowning experiences describe the sinking twice followed by a resurfacing but alas the third sinking is the final one. Your life is said to flash before your eyes in those last moments of awareness. Gatto had no such experience. Obviously it must be different for cats.

Instinct closed Gatto's nostrils and lungs against the river water and now he pushed with all his feline might against the hard rock below him and paddled his strong forelimbs ferociously. He coursed through the fathoms, fleeing death, seeking life. His face shot above the surface of the water, fur moulded to his skin. The noise of the river crashing and the boat breaking up was deafening. The next thing he knew a hand with long strong fingers grabbed him by the scruff of the neck. He opened his eyes to find himself lodged against a fallen tree trunk which once grew at the edge of the river but now extended over the water with its roots still holding onto the land. He was in the arms of his friend being held securely.

Gatto hung like a skinned rabbit as Michelangelo worked his way ashore and held Gatto close to share what warmth they had between them. That night the crew were given shelter in a warm barn with hot food, bread and wine from the nearest farm. Gatto lapped his stew thinking that food had never tasted so good, as life did also, but forever at the back of his mind there would be a wariness, a fear of dark floating shadows swirling over a muddy murky river bed and no matter how long he lived it would always silently lurk there, as if waiting.

'Cheer up Master Buonarroti. The other barges made it. You still have plenty of marble to work with', said a crew member but Michelangelo was morose and in mourning for his specially quarried block. In time however he was able to haul it ashore when the river was not running in spate so all was not lost.

The next evening Gatto rolled into the Holy City on the back of a cart looking as clean and fresh as if he had never known a muddy river. His astonishment grew as the city of Romulus and Remus, of Romans and Christians, of gladiators and temples unfolded in a moving panorama before his eyes. It was obvious to him that the food smells and the garbage stink meant that this would also be a city of many of his own kind. Then he saw them. They seemed to emerge from everywhere. It was a city of cats. This was going to be a whole new experience for a Tuscan cat from a marble quarry. He wondered if he would be welcome or not. For a moment he felt a pang of longing for Carrara.

Nothing escaped Gatto's curious inspection: the pealing of the church bells, so many churches, so many buildings, labyrinthine streets all begging to be explored, cooking odours, oh the food in Rome. What ecstasy! And the people and even more people!

So this is the fabled Holy City wondered Gatto but at that moment the cart rounded a corner and in front of him was the sacred church, the famed Old Basilica of San Pietro. In a state of transformation it sat solidly overlooking what was the best possible sight to both Michelangelo and Gatto; a massive pile of cut marble, huge blocks, small blocks, irregularly shaped ones, pyramids of broken pieces, all creating a miniature city straight from Carrara. Michelangelo's stock pile had safely arrived and awaited the touch of his hand to be transformed into the Holy Father's magnificent tomb. He could see it in detail in his head, the levels, the statuary, the grandeur as never before seen. Yes, in this creation Pope Julius would be remembered forever.

To Gatto, the raw marble was simply home from home. Here he would explore and hide as no other

Roman cat knew how. He would establish dens and defend them with all the ferociousness of a feral tom from Tuscan hills. He would find mates, see his offspring born, hide from the rains of winter, then stretch out in the Roman sun, warmed and content but for now he was off to a tiny studio behind the Church of Santa Caterina where Michelangelo had his home. It was the first and the last night that Gatto spent indoors and at first light he was outside, lured by scents and sounds that had hung in the Roman air for centuries.

Gatto adapted to his Roman life with all the tenacity and determination of a proud Carrara cat. Food in abundance was to be found everywhere. Life in the city of Rome meant a well-stocked larder owned by well-fed people whose wastefulness rather than their largesse supported hordes of workers, clergy, builders, artists, poor people and cats. Dogs were also to be found but not in the same proliferation as the cats.

Gatto grew to love his San Pietro marble home. As the rock pile diminished it was replenished and the ever changing scene reminded him of quarry life. A little before dusk every day, Gatto would slip inside the remains of the old Basilica and race wildly under the carved wooden pews, up the aisles and round the altars in a frenzy of not quite religious fervour but as a cooling off in the shade of the building out of the summer heat. As winter replaced summer, and the temperature dropped outside, the warm glow of the candles served as a warming attraction. From there Gatto would make his way to the studio where his friend would make him and fellow artists welcome. Gatto knew half of Rome and they knew him.

Shortly after his arrival in the city Michelangelo had suffered a disappointment which caused him some terrible distress. Gatto knew there was something wrong but he was unable to understand the politics of the Holy Church and its dealings with the painters, sculptors and architects within its patronage.

One day Gatto heard raised voices from the studio and scampered up from the roadway to the apartment door. It was ajar. He knew Michelangelo's voice but not the other one. The argument sounded bitter. Gatto crept in and looked in amazement from behind the artist's legs at the figure in the large dark cloak. His hair was silvery grey, his eyes were piercing and his authoritative voice was as sharp as a rapier. Beneath the cloak Gatto could just make out the folds of a pure white robe overlaid with elaborately gold-stitched garments and on his head, a small white skull cap.

Gatto had arrived at the end of the discussion and at that point the visitor strode imperiously towards the door. Gatto jumped aside to be well out of his reach. The man turned and spoke to Michelangelo in the coldest calmest manner, 'I am Julius the Second, the Holy Father, and you Michelangelo Buonarroti are my humble servant. We command you one thing now and one thing only: the Sistine Chapel vaulting,' and suddenly spotting the cat on the floor the Pope stared him straight in the eye and held his gaze as he disappeared through the doorway.

Michelangelo stood as though paralysed until he dropped to his knees, covered his face with his hands and moaned like the wind in a storm, crying out, 'No, no, no!' Gatto pushed his head against his strong sinewy fingers inserting his nose here and a whisker there and together they stayed in that position for a very long time. Finally Michelangelo whispered to his only confidant, 'I am a sculptor, I am not a painter, not in fresco! I have told him this. I came to build his tomb. Not this chapel ceiling, no never!'

Trapped by the Papal politics of the time, by the wealth of the Vatican, by the conspiring of the artists and architects who were not his friends and not least by the immeasurable talent he had displayed as a sculptor, Michelangelo began a task of unimaginable creativity and agonising labour for himself and his assistants with Gatto as witness.

It was April 1508. Spring was well established in the city and Gatto felt energised, as did Michelangelo. Gone with the gloom of winter were the disappointment and the fearful lack of self-confidence he had experienced earlier. Cardinal Alidosi had overseen the signing of the contract for the work. The agreed payment of 3,000 ducats upon completion was a generous amount but was still less than he would have been paid for sculpting the Pope's tomb. However, as he really had no choice,

Michelangelo felt committed to the arduous task. Gatto was left in no doubt about his friend's enthusiasm as he constantly had to leap aside to avoid being trampled as Michelangelo energetically set about the organisation of his men and materials. There were assistants to be carefully selected, trustworthy and capable workers but also willing and compliant ones. This was not going to be easy for anyone involved. Before anything could be accomplished the scaffolding had to be built to transport the artist and his workers the sixty-seven feet up to the vault. Rope and wood had to be purchased and of course he was responsible for all his own materials and tools. Gatto witnessed a transformation in the face of his friend. No more sad lines and drooping eyelids, instead a face animated by challenge and eyes that burned with an unworldly fervour.

It was early morning and Gatto caught sight of Michelangelo striding purposefully past his Carrara marble pile in the Piazza San Pietro. In an instant Gatto was at his heels. Wherever Michelangelo was going so was he. They were heading for the Sistine Chapel in the Vatican complex. Strangely this building was one of the least likely looking churches in all of Rome. Standing adjacent to the Old Basilica of San Pietro in the Vatican complex it looked more like some kind of fortress or barracks, never a church. It had been designed by a military architect of course. Completed in 1484 it had taken 14 years to build by Pope Julius the Second's uncle, also a pope, Sixtus IV. Its redeeming architectural feature was that it has been constructed in the exact proportions of Solomon's Temple in Jerusalem. It was indeed more than a chapel. It was a place of privacy, retreat and safety for the Pope and the few who were permitted inside. Gatto looked at the walls: 10 feet thick at the base, no windows until the upper level, no portals, pillars, domes, no exterior decoration. He did not think much of this box-like structure when his sharp eyes noticed the external walkway at the top of the building, a temptation for a quarry cat. That revised his opinion.

To enter the building you had to go via the Vatican hallway. Michelangelo slowed his pace as approached the east doorway almost tripping over Gatto. If any of the clergy noticed the tomcat enter the sacred chapel they said and did nothing as they all had received strict instructions that there was to be no impediment to the artist's work.

Two pairs of eyes were raised heavenwards, and surely that was heaven up there, the bluest of blue skies dusted with golden stars that shone down on them. Already Michelangelo was deliberating, calculating, his eyes narrowing as he saw the task stretching apparently endlessly onwards. The vault spanned twelve thousand square feet! Gatto twitched his whiskers and padded irreverently over the 15th Century mosaics on the floor. He looked up at the high windows where the morning light filtered in between the statues of former popes and marvelled at how the vaulted sky dropped in peaks beside each window as if it was truly all encompassing as nature intended the sky to be.

'Well, that starry sky will have to go,' Michelangelo said aloud and only Gatto was there to hear him. The first decision had been made. The artist barely gave a second glance to the eight murals which decorated the lower windowless walls, large panels representing the life of Moses on one side and the life of Christ on the other. They may have been painted by great artists such as Botticelli and Ghirlandaio, Michelangelo's early tutor, but they were not on his agenda. Now it was all up to one man, himself. Gatto sensed the tension which felt like a coiled serpent ready to strike.

Gatto looked up at the high windows where the morning light filtered in between the statues of former popes. He marvelled at how the vaulted sky dropped in peaks between each window as if it was truly all encompassing as nature intended the sky to be. He had the suspicion he would be a regular visitor here as whatever his friend had planned surely Gatto would find a place for himself in its midst.

Spring evenings in Rome were amongst the most pleasant of any weathers to be found in the Mediterranean. Everywhere there was a gentle light which belied the dusty oppressive heat to follow. Gatto had made a discovery. He felt sure it must have been designed to enable Roman cats to traverse the narrow winding lanes between the Vatican and the fortified tomb of the Roman Emperor, Hadrian, on the banks of the Tevere, without setting a paw at ground level. Unknown to Gatto this aerial walkway was the personal escape route of the pope. If the Vatican was to come under threat then the Holy Father could flee unmolested to the safety of this fortress called the Castel Sant' Angelo.

One evening as the sun was close to setting Gatto scrambled up his own personal route from ground level to the parapet of this walkway. Needless to say stray chunks of Carrara marble were involved in this access route. Gatto was scampering along the edge of the wall peering down occasionally at the street life below, surveying the cats in particular. There was one aggressive tomcat that he liked to keep an eye on as he now had several small but deep scars received from this beast's swipe of claw, also the potential fathering of progeny with a particular female had come into dispute and had broken out into a heated cat fight.

Unexpectedly a dark shadow passed behind Gatto and a stern voice spoke in his ear almost causing him to overbalance. Gatto jumped down onto the walkway path to regain his composure. He found himself face to face with the Holy Father himself who also was strolling in the mild evening air. 'Cat, we know you. You are that obstinate artist's little shadow. Don't think we don't know where you have been. We know it all.' Gatto was cringing a little by now and was preparing himself for flight or perhaps fight. He felt his claws appear and contract. 'We know you have been in our Chapel,' and at that he lent forward closer to Gatto's face and hissed, 'If we see you or that artist doing anything you shouldn't in there we will…' but Gatto did not stay to hear the papal threat as he was up the walkway, over the side and into his marble tunnels with a flash of a grey streaked tail.

Gatto now knew the route from the studio to the chapel and quite happily made the short trip frequently to see what was going on. If he was bored he would stroll over to where there always seemed to be frantic activity and no shortage of fuss. He could watch from the side or race about in the middle of it causing a few shouts and curses if he misjudged his steps.

He inadvertently was witness to the dispute over the nature of the all-important scaffolding which would enable the plasterers and artists to access the vaulting. Massive piles of rope and stacks of wood had appeared. Gatto had checked all of these supplies by nose very thoroughly.

One day Gatto sauntered into one of those heated disputes. The standard means of accessing the ceiling would have meant the construction of a scaffold standing on the floor and reaching in levels to the required height. However Pope Julius had presented Michelangelo with yet another challenge. Knowing this work could run into years, or rather fearing that it could, he insisted that space at ground level be always available for the scheduled ceremonies held in the chapel. Gatto watched the humans argue from behind some sacks of lime and sand. Michelangelo was face to face with Bramante, the Vatican architect, and they were both very red in the face. 'What!' Michelangelo said, 'You want to bore holes all over the vaulting and hang scaffolding on ropes from the very area I will be painting. No, think of the finished work. A scar here and a scar there, a whole ceiling pitted with scaffolding scars. No! It will not do!'

Bramante started to protest. Gatto did not like the enmity from this man and crept to Michelangelo's side. He was pointing up into the north west corner of the vault and Gatto's eyes follow his pointing finger. 'Look how badly that white jagged crack in the corner looks against the sky. You want that effect all over the finished fresco?' Michelangelo was almost shouting by now. Then he looked down straight at Gatto and immediately lowered his voice and said very quietly but very powerfully, 'I have another plan.' Gatto left at that point as he was satisfied that his friend knew what would be the final outcome.

On the following visit Gatto encountered a stranger in the chapel. When he caught sight of the cat moving cautiously into his domain, the elderly man continued his work without disturbing the cat's inquisitive inspection of his supplies and tools. Finally Gatto approached the man and looked into his wrinkled face. The man's eyes twinkled and he spoke to the cat, 'Good. A new assistant has come to help me get this old plasterwork down. What do you think if you and I bring down this sky?' With a gentle smile that reassured Gatto he said, 'You can call me Piero and I will simply call you Cat.' At that Michelangelo arrived and threaded his way through the hundreds of sacks of the raw materials for the fresco. His arms held rolls of paper, his plans for the design for the scaffold.

'Good morning to you my friend,' Michelangelo said, 'Look at this and tell me what you think', and he unrolled the scrolls. Gatto considered a new game of chasing the paper as it unfurled but something stopped him as he had the feeling that might not be a good idea. Gatto watched Piero Roselli who had come from Florence with the artist to do this work. Gatto knew he was going to like this new friend when he saw the brotherly affection between the two men as they poured over the drawings made by a master, an instinctive engineer, a genius of creativity.

Over the next few weeks Gatto watched in fascination as an elegant curved bridge soared from one side of the chapel floor to the other spanning the entire 44 feet. Many times, as Piero locked the archways in position, a whiskered face would appear on the step ahead of him apparently supervising the process, a little feline totally unafraid of heights, sure-footed, courageous and maybe more than a little foolhardy.

Gradually these stepped arches covered sixty-five feet, half the chapel's length and enabled the labourers to reach the first half of the vaulting. Gatto fled in horror the day the starry sky was assaulted by picks and hammers. He wondered if the end of the world had come as the sky fell in dusty chunks around him.

Spring burst into Roman summer in a cloud of plaster dust. For three months Gatto's visits to the chapel were fleeting as the activity there was quite unsuitable for the presence of a cat. Once the scaffolding had been constructed according to Michelangelo's ingenious design, Gatto ceased his aerial acrobatics which had delighted the workers. Square foot by square foot the sky fell. Only when the work commenced to replace the ceiling with a layer of perfectly smooth plaster, the base for the actual fresco, did Gatto resume his visits to Piero whose work seemed to never stop.

It was the end of July and after the three months of frantic activity the Sistine Chapel was ready for the real work to begin. Gatto was sitting beside Piero who was packed and ready to return to his Florentine home. Piero stroked Gatto's head and throat. Gatto may have been a friendly curious cat but he was now also an independent feral Roman cat so rarely did he bestow such an honour on his human companions. He couldn't help but listen to the kindly voice of this old man. 'I have finished this work Cat. Now I return to my home. I am ready to go. I am old. I am not a well man but I would not have foregone this task for anything. I do not know if I will ever see the finished work but this I know, your friend Michelangelo has a determination and drive burning within him and the end result will be nothing short of perfection. You stay here and witness the marvel he will create. Like the book of Genesis, which describes the creation of the world, our friend will do likewise, but in paint not in words. The world will acknowledge his version of God who made the earth, the air, the sky, the sea and the message of Genesis will come alive to you and all who see it'. With a final pat to Gatto's head Piero was gone, paid to do the vital work, having expended the last of his energy but happy to have been a part of it all and content to have made a friend who listened.

Gatto observed with wonder the four-month progress of the sketches for the new illustrated ceiling. He saw Michelangelo working feverishly using different methods and techniques all of which were a mystery to Gatto but which commanded his respect. When he felt the terrible urge to pounce on a scroll rolling onto the floor, and to shred it, he would rush from the studio to the streets to the watery places where he knew the rats surfaced to forage and he would do his pouncing and shredding there. Michelangelo was unaware of this behaviour which enabled him to have both Gatto's company and his designs unmolested.

The preparations were complete by the beginning of October. The sweltering heat of summer had subsided. The temperature in the chapel was cool but suitable to labour in. The ceiling was perfectly smooth with Piero's *arriccio* base. The scaffolding was back at the first half of the chapel, the pigments had been purchased, all necessary tools and materials were on hand. The assistants were anxious but keen and Michelangelo was impatient to start.

Gatto would never forget the day he was confronted with an agile cat's wildest dream. All of the choking dust and broken plaster had been meticulously removed. The mosaic floor was pristine and due to the arched scaffold, free for the Pope and his cardinals to perform their ordinances. In fact, a mass was taking place at that moment and the haze of incense rose up towards heaven.

Gatto's nose followed the updraft of scent and there, high in the air, was another world. Gatto headed for the forty-foot ladder and competently and silently ascended to the first level of this new world in the sky. This took Gatto to the tops of the windows where he stepped confidently onto the planking forming the first of the wooden bridges spanning the width of the chapel. Then excitedly he climbed another twenty feet on a ladder with protective railings this time. Nothing pleased him more than being sixty feet off the ground. He wasn't at all concerned about his sense of balance and the presence of a safety net of canvas slung on ropes below the scaffold was of no interest to him. To the artists the canvas was literally a life-saver. They had been known to fall to their deaths from a scaffold whilst painting. The Holy Father and his entourage were also grateful not to have falling artists and paint splashes on their robes as they went about their business. Gatto was privy to another reason for appreciation of the canvas barrier, muttered to him out of earshot of the others by Michelangelo, 'It stops prying eyes watching my every brush stroke, judging, criticising, I don't want it to be viewed until I have finished and not until I say so.'

Gatto scampered around his new elevated playground and on that first occasion managed to descend to ground level effortlessly. He was also unadorned, in this instance, with non-feline colours in his fur. And so the labour continued. Gatto watched his friend, with his team of experts, toil, grow weary, barely rest, and then toil again.

Gatto was oblivious to the privilege afforded him as he observed the world's greatest artist perform his miracle on the Sistine Chapel ceiling. Michelangelo's secrecy was becoming obsessive. No one was allowed to observe the work or view even the completed panels. This however was a source of impatience and curiosity to the Holy Father and gave him no rest. The Pope had been expressly forbidden to mount the scaffold to look above the canvas screen. Who else in all of Rome and Christendom would dare to command the Pontiff? Not to be beaten the 'Warrior Pope' devised a strategy to get his way.

Julius chose an evening when the work was completed for the day and all the workers had gone home. Michelangelo had remained behind and Gatto stayed behind to enjoy his company. Gatto always felt a sense of peace and security while the artist worked but something was different. Michelangelo nodded appreciatively at him. He was not working. He lay down flat on the floor of the platform concealing his presence totally. He dipped his hand to signal Gatto to be still. Gatto stretched out close to him thinking this was a fine way to spend the evening resting undisturbed in solitude in the peace of the chapel but Michelangelo knew something Gatto did not know. The artist had informers within the Papal entourage. Plotting and conspiracy was a way of life in Renaissance Rome and to survive you had to play a strategic game with the Papacy.

A sound from below caused Gatto to raise his head and look over the side. He peered in amazement at a man dressed as a labourer carefully climbing the scaffold. Gatto was not fooled for an instant. He could detect with all of his cat senses the identity of the visitor and the odour of deceit assaulted his nostrils. Gatto looked up in alarm at Michelangelo, wondering what he would do, fearing that this situation could not end well.

From his vantage point at the level of the ceiling Michelangelo had also spotted the ascending intruder. Without hesitation he began hurling the planks of wood from the top of the platform. Gatto was rooted to the spot then, as he feared for his own safety, he leapt back to crouch behind the paint pots. The first plank went wide but the crash as it hit the floor was shattering. The next plank skimmed past the man who was now flattened against the ladder in terror and disbelief. Gatto's curiosity overcame his alarm and he crawled on his belly to look down. Michelangelo's temper was ablaze, that was obvious, but if he was trying to knock Julius to the ground surely his aim could be better? Julius did not hesitate and slithered back down the ladder at almost the speed of the flying wood and disappeared below. Not a word had been spoken by either man, or cat, and the only damage was the streaks of green and orange paint from the paint pots now transferred to Gatto's flanks.

Michelangelo and Gatto walked in comfortable companionship home to the studio for their evening stew and uncharacteristically Michelangelo smiled all the way.

As the Holy Father regularly processed the length of the chapel with his clergy, attended by choirs of angelic children, he never failed to look aloft. Michelangelo seemed to sense the exact moment Julius would pass directly below the scaffold. He would pause his work and look down. Gatto would simultaneously peer over the edge of the topmost platform and stare in fearful awe at God's representative on earth, a man he recognised as powerful, dominating, someone to be feared by man and beast alike.

Without missing a step Julius would hiss up into the ceiling, 'Too slow! When will you be finished?' to which Michelangelo would unfailingly reply,

'When I can.' His papal anger would fly like an arrow upwards and engulf both Gatto and the artist. Michelangelo ignored these jibes and criticisms so Gatto did likewise.

The Pope's aggression was not always as passive as this. One day as Gatto approached the chapel he could hear raised voices which made him slip furtively along the wall and position himself underneath the scaffold where he could observe undetected. Pope Julius was there alone with Michelangelo, his face red and contorted with rage. 'What is this Drunkenness of Noah that takes you this length of time to complete? You have been painting it for over a month!' In his defence Michelangelo answered,

'It is a larger image and of course takes longer than the smaller areas to cover.'

'We want this work completed. Do you hear? Finished. What are we expected to tolerate with you artists? We have Bramante's building, Raphael's painting and you with this fresco. Do we have to come in here and force you to get on with it? We feel most days like having you thrown off this scaffolding.' The pope continued to rant.

Michelangelo attempted to reply. Never one to apologise for his art Michelangelo started to talk about the difficulties causing the halting progress when Julius interrupted, his face purple with fury. 'We don't care about that. When will you be done? When?' he shrieked.

'When I can.' the artist replied in a cold and steely tone.

'When I can. When I can. Is that all you can say?' and at that Julius raised his staff and set about Michelangelo's head and shoulders. He tried to defend himself by shielding his body with his arms but he feared damage to his fingers and hands so most of the blows rained down on him undeflected. Gatto dropped to his stomach and flattened himself to the floor but panic overcame him and he fled from the chapel unseen by the Pope but Michelangelo saw the flash of fur and was glad that Julius would be unable to turn his stick on the cat.

Gatto was in full flight; his lithe body energised by the flow of adrenaline into his nervous system, his heart and lungs pumping uncontrollably. Expanded blood vessels charged his muscles with an excess supply of oxygen and his feet barely touched the ground. With pupils already dilated he covered the short distance from the Sistine Chapel through the courtyard to the construction site of Julius the Second's new church, his shadow merely a blur on the bronze fountain, and on through the façade of the remains of the Constantinian Basilica of San Pietro.

No worshippers now sat at prayer or meditation in the ruins of the chapel. No one saw the moving shape streak up what remained of the left hand aisle of the long nave of what had been the transept of the church and vanish behind the altar which still stood on a raised step. Bramante in 1506 had been charged to build a new San Pietro, one worthy of being the greatest church in the world. The task would take until 1626, one hundred and twenty years later but for now it was still in its initial stages. Gatto had become familiar with not only the piles of Carrara marble being used to construct the new building but with the remnant of the Old Basilica still being removed by Bramante, aptly named 'il Ruinate' by the people. At the rear corner of this altar step, unbeknownst to the clergy or architect or stone mason, was a split with a small subsidence beneath it. This had been somewhat enlarged over hundreds of years of passage by countless generations of cats and rats.

Down and down, down through cracks and tracks, channels and tunnels frequented solely by his four-footed animal kind, he ran. Earthquake and flood had both preserved and concealed this secret way into the catacombs of ancient Rome. Neither the Holy Father nor his humblest servant would have been able to follow Gatto down into this undiscovered way.

Gatto twisted and turned past countless tombs guarded by the rat population since the days of antiquity. It was a place of the dead. Dead pontiffs, clergy, royalty but Gatto was headed for sanctuary, a place of safety, the tomb of the crucified St Peter himself. Two niches in a red wall behind a sheltering shrine were where the long-dead disciple lay, his bones awaiting excavation in a later day. Beneath was a third niche below the ground level of the ancient necropolis and this was a place of refuge for all who entered. Gatto squeezed down into the hollow and relaxed as he felt the adrenalin drain from his system to be replaced with peace and merciful sleep. The blows from the staff of the Papacy could not reach him here.

Gatto witnessed many conflicts and confrontations between clergy and artist. He had sensed from the start that Julius was a soldier first and Holy Father second. Gatto, with all of Rome, watched him ride out in full armour on more than one occasion, a warrior pope at the head of his Roman legions, more reminiscent of his name sake Julius Caesar whom he obviously emulated. The State of Venice was raged against; foreign invaders were cajoled then repulsed while the Italian states were being sucked within his domain whether by force, treaty or friendship.

Michelangelo was uninvolved with the machinations of Julius and as none of this reached down to the level of the Roman cat Gatto continued his semi-feral street life relatively uninterrupted. It was now the year 1510 and Gatto witnessed his friend reach the half way point in the vault. Half the ceiling was completely covered in his art work and he could paint no further until the scaffolding was moved when another storm blew up. Pope Julius commanded Michelangelo to unveil his work so far. The scaffolding and the canvas cover were to be removed and guests were to be invited to the viewing. Gatto could only listen as the artist fumed and raged but then he admitted quietly to Gatto alone that he would after all be interested in the reaction of the public to his work.

Michelangelo's voice followed Gatto one night as he was gliding effortlessly down the ladders. 'And what do you think of my work, cat?' but the only answer he got was a cat's tail disappearing out of sight while the prophet Ezekiel and the newly created Eve looked down sightlessly on the Roman world. Had Gatto been able to comment and to express his feline opinion and become an art critic he may have commented that God the Father seemed to be a benevolent old gentleman but the paradisiacal Garden of Eden looked a lot less enticing than the marble mountainsides at Carrara Also the surrounding *ignudi* seemed more real and compelling than Father Adam and Mother Eve but that would only have been a cat's opinion. Gatto also could have commented on the portrait which flanked the freshly painted Creation of Eve. The prophet Ezekiel emerges from the vault with power and strength, his feet and hands alive, his body stretching compellingly across his illusionary alcove. Gatto believed he could be a real human being. And where were the cats of Eden? Hiding from God behind the pile of rocks?

There was scorching heat in Rome that summer. Gatto longed for the cooling mountain breezes. The coolest spots were in the shade by the river but the stench from the pollution of man made it a fetid undesirable place. Plague and malaria were rife. Despite the conditions Julius was in warrior mode and the unveiling was pushed aside in favour of the preparations for the Pope's next military campaign. Michelangelo was in despair.

Gatto sat in what little shade he could find in the piazza. A new band of soldiers had arrived courtesy of the Pope. This was a smart army, dressed in black berets, a uniform of crimson and green stripes, swords at their sides and speaking in a foreign tongue. Despite the intense heat they exercised relentlessly. Gatto felt a shiver of fear but also of respect as he watched the way they drilled. One afternoon they appeared carrying pikes eighteen feet in length and suddenly, on command, the battalion broke into tight units and charged across the square in disciplined formation, pikes lowered, straight at Gatto. He turned and fled faster than his legs had ever carried him before. He had encountered the invincible Swiss Guards, the most feared infantrymen in Europe and who were to remain a feature in the Vatican from then on.

In August, Julius was ready to go to war. He set off northwards to take Bologna, leaving Michelangelo vexed and in need of payment. Once more Gatto heard his complaints. 'What am I to do? No unveiling and no money! It has been a year since he has paid me anything. Oh why does he torment me so? By October Gatto was just thankful for the ending of the terrible summer heat and was unconcerned about the dull drizzling rain.

It was after Christmas before Michelangelo showed up once more in Rome having received a further 500 ducats from his employer and impatient to continue his work. Gatto was spending more time in the studio with him. Nothing had been done in the chapel for four months and still nothing could be done as Julius was delayed in Bologna by serious illness. 'Gatto, already it is the year 1511 and still I wait. While the Holy Father is away the Sistine Chapel is not in use I could be in there painting undisturbed by all the Vatican's goings-on but he has to get back here for the unveiling before we can begin on the other half of the ceiling. This is too bad.

A tragedy. I need to work,' and so he moaned and groaned in his anguish. Gatto stayed with him at home while he continued working on his next set of drawings.

Gatto was crouched on the studio table the day that a nude figure of a man resting on the ground with an arm outstretched appeared on a smallish sheet of paper in red chalk. Gatto was later to witness an enlargement of that same figure take pride of place in the scene of the birth of Adam. Gatto was to wonder how a shape so small could become the identical shape but larger than life in another location in another medium. He would not be alone with this question and no one then, or later, would be able to give an adequate explanation. It remains a mystery still to cats and humans alike.

The next year wore on. In June Gatto was unaware of the arrival of Julius. Apparently he entered the city via the Gate of the People but, as no fanfare greeted him after his ten month absence as a soldier of God to rid his holy land of the much hated French, he managed to reach Piazza San Pietro unsung. Gatto did see his arrival at the Vatican and stared at the almost unrecognisable bearded face, a first for any Pontiff in Rome.

Still Michelangelo waited. Finally Julius announced the date for the unveiling, the auspicious Assumption of Mary. Gatto entered the chapel the next day after the date had been announced to find the air was thick with choking dust and falling timber. The scaffold was coming down and bringing with it the plaster and dust of three years worth of fresco work. Gatto left. Unlike Gatto, Julius rushed in to the dust and tumult of the dismantling, unable to wait to see the transformation of the vault from a blue starry sky to the sacred Book of Genesis come alive. He was not disappointed nor did he feel he had wasted his money.

Gatto now had mastered quite a variety of different routes to and from the chapel, many of them involving rooftops and acrobatics high in the air. He used one of these high roads on the morning of the Feast of the Assumption of Mary which fell in mid-August. There were so many people packed into the chapel. Gatto travelled unseen from one end of the chapel to the other amidst the feet of the onlookers. The whole of Rome wanted to see Michelangelo's masterpiece. Julius had put on a show for the world to marvel at. He entered in his chair, richly robed, attended by his cardinals and Swiss Guards but when Gatto saw this he withdrew from the front and slunk off into a corner of safety. All eyes were raised and all who passed through the Sistine Chapel that August morning were witness to a new style of painting, the original work of an unsurpassed master. Gatto sensed their reverence. He was not to realise of course that from this day onwards the art of fresco had been changed forever.

The final challenge awaited Michelangelo. Eagerly he arranged for the scaffold to be erected under the western half of the vault. It was a busy time but Gatto enjoyed that. The hustle and bustle reminded him of the best days in the quarry.

But a further obstacle raised its ugly head. Gatto could tell that something was severely wrong with Julius. His weakness and infirmity had given Gatto the confidence for a couple of forays into the Papal apartments until some churchman aimed a kick at him and ordered him out. Gatto heard the word malaria mentioned in hushed tones around the Vatican. Gatto had seen this illness before in the people of Rome. Those who frequented the swamp land of Ostia often fell prey to it and it could result in death. Julius had been pheasant shooting there and no doubt made a good meal for a malaria-bearing mosquito. Julius was once more a victim of his rebellious and careless flouting of the holy rules of his office as Supreme Pontiff.

With the imminent death of the Pope, Rome became a frenzied city with the Vatican leading the madness. The idea of a change of rule made some people panic, some avaricious, some ambitious but everywhere Gatto was obliged to get out from under the feet of the preoccupied. He retreated to the studio but it was filled with such great anxiety over the future of the second half of the vault that Gatto eventually went back to his marble den in the square, glad to be away from the human chaos.

Pope Julius the Second was administered the last rites but in true warrior-pope fashion surprisingly made an almost instant recovery. 'Thank you Heaven for that', Michelangelo was heard to utter and to Gatto he said, 'Do you know it has been fourteen months since I painted? Now, I will finish.' Gatto could feel the energy emanating from his friend and together they set out on a nine month journey to completion.

His brush moved at speed. The colours flowed from it like a river in spate. Gatto took up his regular visits to the new platform and watched even larger figures appear, figures which seemed alive. Michelangelo worked like a man possessed of divine yet demonic passion. Julius must not die before the completion of this sacred commission.

Time passed steadily. Long hard days passed into weeks which rolled into months. The book of Genesis appeared, scene by scene, as the fresco emerged as if from some other world. Michelangelo's health suffered as he stood on the platform, day in, day out, neck craned back at an unnatural angle, eyes raised to the limit of his sight, arms stretched and strained to reach the plaster surface while fingers cramped around the brush. He worked in pain and discomfort but still he worked. Seemingly endless figures emerged and intertwined with the story of the creation of the world, sibyls and prophets prophesised from above, cherubs and nudes displayed the perfection of both divine and human form. Ultimately the face of God himself transplanted itself into the chapel through the miracle of Michelangelo's mastery of his paint brush. The finger of God reached out to give life to his ultimate creation, the miracle of man. And still he painted.

While Michelangelo feverishly worked, pushing his assistants to their human limits, Julius was still plotting his political schemes and military campaigns. Using his papal power he assaulted any who crossed his path regardless of whether they were sovereigns in their own right, foreigners or from the Italian States. His warmongering knew no rest.

Winter persisted. January of 1512 came and went. Still the troubles continued. The French army under Louis the Second threatened to advance on Rome. Gatto detected the undercurrent of fear which swept Rome and held it in its clutches. Michelangelo had kept himself apart from the political turmoil and uninvolved in the speculation but once more Gatto was his confident and he was told that if these four years of work was ravaged by the French then it would be the end of everything! Gatto listened thoughtfully but disbelievingly. The French, for reasons of their own, failed to attack and despite ongoing antagonism and threat Gatto's life remained undisturbed.

As Gatto observed Michelangelo paint a mass of human bodies writhing with poisonous snakes he hoped that this would be an end to this gargantuan never-to-be-completed task. The snakes made Gatto squirm. He couldn't make out where there was any more space that Michelangelo could possibly paint on. It seemed to take an interminable time to finish this snake scene and after six weeks Gatto wondered if his friend seriously ever intended to stop work on his aerial creation.

It was the end of October, a full nine months after the start of the western half of the vault and four years after the commencement that Michelangelo's family in Florence received a letter saying simply 'I have finished the chapel I have been painting.'

Eleven weeks later Guiliano della Rovere, the unecclesiastical pope, lay dead. He died in a syphilitic fever following a draft of powdered gold administered in ignorance and superstition by his physicians.

Michelangelo prepared to make the trip to Tuscany once more. The materials used to paint the Sistine Chapel had been packed away forever. His assignment as a painter was thankfully over. He could hardly wait to make his return to being a sculptor as he had adamantly declared he was to Julius many years before. 'Well cat, you alone have been my faithful companion throughout this long and arduous time. It would be of no use paying you in ducats but there is something I can do for you which I feel sure is your heart's desire. Come…' and the two of them headed out together. The crowds thronged the Piazza San Pietro. There was a buzz of excitement. Eyes lifted regularly to the chimney above the chapel. Gatto and his friend waited at the edge of the onlookers. Inside the Sistine Chapel, below Michelangelo's work of art, the College of

Cardinals was meeting. Dressed in all their finery; their red capes and gowns, their white lace tunics, their close-fitting tricorn hats, adorned with their gold chains and crosses, they were voting for the successor to Julius the Second. The Swiss Guard stood dutifully outside the locked doors protecting the sacred rite of passage taking place within the chapel.

It was not long before a ripple ran through the waiting crowd. It grew to a roar of approval. Gatto saw the white smoke pouring up from the Vatican chimney forming a little white cloud as if painted in the sky. A Medici pope was on the throne of St Peter.

Some time later Michelangelo and Gatto came within sight of the white mountains of Carrara. On entry into the quarry Gatto's little feline heart leapt at the familiar sights sounds and smells. Michelangelo was there to prepare fresh marble for the tomb of his late benefactor and nemesis. Gatto started at a run for the slopes of home but then stopped and looked back at his friend. Michelangelo's rugged, creased face broke into an uncharacteristic smile and with a wave of his hand he released Gatto back into the wild.

One memory of the Sistine Chapel ceiling stayed with Gatto for all the rest of his life. None of the other features in all of that glorious work of art had made an impression like this one. It would come to him in sleep or awake. He was forever haunted and somehow puzzled by the space Michelangelo had left between the hand of God and the seeking finger of man.

From Gatto to Wutki

As Gatto disappeared up into the quarried mountains of Carrara his audible purr of satisfaction brought all the cats back to their cloistered space in time. Gatto slipped gently back to his ledge. He contentedly licked his chest and legs. Wutki was leaning over the rocks perilously close to landing on top of him but she managed a fleeting lick of appreciation on one of his ears which he gracefully accepted. 'We lived at the same time, didn't we?' she said pensively. 'But we never met', she added sadly.

Otherwise no one moved or murmured. Gatto's story had been a long and remarkable tale, his time in Rome an unexpected interlude in the life of a quarry cat. A pause in the proceedings seemed to be in order and all was quiet for a little while.

'All right Wutki.' The voice once more. 'Please come forward now.' Wutki slithered down the rock face and crouched in front of the gathering. 'Do not be apprehensive. All cats and their past lives have validity. Down through the ages of man you have all shown valour for which you deserve respect.'

As her account commenced she realised that she was before her peers. She straightened up, raised her head and bravely took her place. Hers was to be very much the tale of a female unlike the males who had preceded her.

Wutki's Solution

Early 1600's

It was somewhere around the early sixteen hundreds. The mountains and forests of Maine were as yet undeveloped by the pioneer settlers. They came from Europe to carve out a life for themselves and their families from the thickly forested but fertile lands of the New World. It was the beginning of a new age and changes were creeping slowly over the face of the American Continent. The area would eventually become known as the Moose River Valley. The mighty Kennebec River would offer man a route into the heart of the region. After the white man's arrival it would never be the same again.

But for now there was silence in the woods. The blackness of the moonless night enveloped the aspen, the ash and the beech. On the hillside, in discomfort, the restless cat rolled in her heat. Suddenly the wind caught the clouds in a violent embrace. As the moonlight flooded the mixed forests of oak, pine and maple, her call shattered the stillness of the silvery night, travelling upwards to one who was listening.

Wutki's cry was unmistakable. It penetrated the darkness of the den beneath the pile of rocks strewn haphazardly across the hillside. Aguara stretched his full length and shook his heavy jowls and the thick skin of his neck. He was large and lynx-like, wild, rugged and shaggy. He had lived on this mountain for all of his ten years of short, hot summers and long, cold winters. He unsheathed and sheathed again his magnificent claws, long, sharp and lethal. He licked his broad feet paying cursory attention to the extra toes and claws on each front foot, the legacy of his kind that nature had seen fit to bestow on him. He was well prepared for this feral existence.

One yawn and he was outside turning towards the sound of her calling. It was rising in a crescendo then falling, as if pleading, but never diminishing. It seemed late in the season to be summoning her mate but in response to her need he bounded willingly from rock to ledge, his own desire fuelling his rapid descent from the coniferous upper slopes towards the deciduous woods below. Once or twice he stopped to raise his striped tawny nose allowing her scent to energise his maleness. His fur seemed to ripple with an impatience born of an uncontrollable need to be the one chosen to continue their species.

Wutki was suffering as never before. Her desperation to have one more litter of kittens before the arrival of the cold and snowy Acadian winter was contrary to her condition. She was tiring more easily. Things bothered her. Her agility was not quite what it had been. Not that she limped or anything like that and she could still clear the stream in a single bound, even in spate, but something was happening. Now there was the gnawing agony of longing for the attention of the mate who had fathered her young on too many occasions to count.

She knew he was approaching the small safe clearing in the woods, backed by the protective sheer wall of stone which had served her well as den and nursery to her summer broods. It wasn't that she could hear or smell him yet but she could sense his speedy approach through the brush, the magic of his presence. Her wildness of spirit overcame her need for a safe haven. She ran screeching, massive tail streaming, into the night to find him, Aguara, to feel the pressure of his long heavy body on hers, to be enveloped in the warmth of his long layered fur, to flex her hindquarters in opposition to him and then feel the muscular power of his entry reaching her convulsing depths.

He leapt the last fallen log and burst from the bracken. He was there. Her hysteria was deafening as she pitched herself at his feet and crouched. In one fluid movement her brush of a tail was swept to one side and she was powerless to resist the grasp of his mouth as his teeth sank blissfully into the muskiness and warmth of her oh-so-familiar and welcoming neck.

Wutki's relief was short lived and with a blood-curdling screech she rounded on Aguara as he rapidly withdrew. He deftly swung away from her raking claws and retreated to his lair, licking himself with quiet satisfaction, knowing, that in a few hours, the whole process would repeat again and again until she was satisfied that the outcome would be life, new and continuing.

Her entire body throbbed with the violence of the act and she also retreated to her safe place. In a bed of leaves she too licked her wounds, knowing that before long she would once more raise her strongly defined head with its high cheekbones and square muzzle and call for the male, source of her offspring's genetic strength, to carry on with the irresistible urge to mate, over and over.

It wasn't long before Aguara's presence was not only unnecessary but seemingly unwanted by the now pregnant cat. She was not unfamiliar with the workings of her body at this time. The unwelcome rigours of rampant hormones driving her into a breeding frenzy were not missed. Wutki settled into her twenty-four hour round of hunting, feeding, resting but she constantly had an awareness of the life within. She slept more than usual. She took extra care in all her comings and goings as it wasn't only herself she was responsible for but also her swelling progeny.

There was something happening in the forest or rather at the edge where many trees had been cleared and activity of an unknown kind reached the ears of the ever-vigilant female cat. She raised her head and listened intently. It was a rhythmic sound as if a giant tree was being attacked. Something wasn't right.

Her heart pounded as she crept forward although the sounds were coming from a long way off. She followed the small stream, fairly gentle in the late summer, unlike the raging torrent it became in the spring when it carried the run-off from the winter snow. She descended into the valley still following the stream bed but halted in her tracks as a new and strange odour hit her sensitive nose. She was approaching the area where the trees thinned out and patches of shrubbery were filling the gaps. In alarm all her hackles raised as she recognised one of the smells. It was burning, wood on fire. At that moment a small herd of white-tailed deer burst from the thicket and raced almost over her in their anxiety to flee the smell of smoke, the terror of all forest creatures.

Wutki, in her intelligence, unlike the deer, did not give in to panic. Despite the definite scent of burning wood, where were the choking fumes driving all creatures great and small in front of it? Where was the terrifying wall of fire consuming all of nature in its path? No, this was something altogether different. She felt a prompting to go just a little bit further but to protect herself from the threat of fire and of the unknown she crouched low and headed into the bog-land on the near side of the stream. Normally the last thing she would wish to do would be to drag her sensitive belly over anything as wet as cranberries and black chokeberries, especially in her present condition, but she held herself as clear of the water as keeping her head and back hidden would permit. She inched her way forward. Little did she know the impact that this act of feline curiosity would have on cats of her kind for all time to come.

Further down the valley she spotted movement and to her excitement and surprise she saw a creature the likes of which startled but intrigued her.

She thought at first she had spotted a bear as he was standing on his hind legs, but he was apparently unafraid of the burning stumps of the trees. His scent, the acidic whiff of human sweat, was a whole new experience for her. The felled trunks lay in piles at the edge of the water-meadow. Wutki knew there was no way this was bear behaviour and backed off into the cotton grass in consternation. Suddenly the burning stump closest to her side of the meadow exploded with a resounding crack and the air was filled with a shower of sparks. Without pause, she was up and running, no thought for caution or concealment, her tail a rapidly vanishing striped streak.

The man turned. Out of the corner of his eye he had spotted movement in the shrubbery. Ishmael smiled to himself and wondered if it was a raccoon he had startled with his efforts to make a clearing big enough to build a homestead for his young family. He returned to work.

Extra vigilance had to be maintained at the future cat nursery if survival was to be ensured. The waiting period, the time of fulfilment but also of anxiety, was upon her. For Wutki, this time, it seemed different somehow. When she awoke from sleep she sniffed cautiously at the air to discern if there was any hint of danger. She knew that she and Aguara were not the only felines in the vicinity of the spreading rolling hills of the Katahdin. She carefully padded the perimeter of her hidden den then waited tensely in the wild raisin shrubbery or in the low sweet blueberries, making full use of her cat's olfactory senses, almost tasting the scents of those who roamed the forest floor. This was part of her normal hunting pattern as many a small bird, feeding on the wild fruits of the forest, fell prey to her clawed and fanged skills. There was today, an ache deep within her which gave the whole process of reproduction a sense of urgency and made her role as protector of her unborn young seem imperative as never before.

Tracing the route of the descending stream of frigid mountain water, cold even in summer, she went down to the water meadows where the hillside ceased to slope so steeply downwards. She ignored the temptation to leap upon the salamanders which scuttled out of her path, tails wagging invitingly as this was only sport and she had more important matters to occupy her. Likewise the wood frogs held no interest as they floated in the shallow pools formed by the undulating terrain. She heard a movement in the undergrowth directly ahead and dropped to a crouch, hidden and silent. She waited and as no further threat appeared she continued to advance through the shrubbery of goldenrod towards the St John's wort. Without further warning, with a croak that vibrated around in her sensitive ears, a large bullfrog erupted from his resting place as she came within a paw's distance of him. She recoiled and swerved blindly to the right, doubly startled that a lowly creature such as a bullfrog would get the better of her. Her instinct to claw and rip was upon her almost before she could refocus on the offending creature so she pounced in a high arc, up and over the foliage, in the direction the doomed bullfrog had taken.

It was almost the last thing she ever did. In that instant the sky was blacked out. Her ears were deafened by the rush of a mighty beast as it hurtled over her and her nostrils filled with the fetid stink of wet fur. Its legs were long like tree branches. Upon its head was the biggest rack of horn imaginable. Wutki had no time to consider all of this as she had done exactly what she would have travelled out of her way to avoid. She had disturbed a bull moose, not just interrupted him but startled him sufficiently to cause a mid-air collision. As a deadly rear hoof flew towards her skull she knew her survival depended on an almost impossible in-flight turn. There was no time to think. Using all her muscular ability instinctively she swivelled her body, succeeding in avoiding the life-crushing foot by a hair's breadth.

She slunk away, decidedly shaken by the unexpected fear that had overcome her. She climbed back up to her lair and licked her thick coat of fur more as a comfort to her shocked system than for any cleaning purpose. She felt distraught. She ought to be taking better care of herself at a time like this. Was she losing her abilities? Was this the aging process in action? Was she getting to be too old to still be mothering? What were these aches and discomforts she hadn't felt before; difficulties with her hips, shooting pains in her chest. She decided there was no time for brooding about such things and put it out of her mind. More important matters lay ahead. Wutki, in her experience as a mother, knew that it would be some time before anything would happen, time for the summer to draw to a close and the fall to reach its multi-coloured tendrils into the forested hills.

Dusk was settling over the hillside and the shadows were lengthening. In the dark of the big rocks Aguara lay in a crouched position, head resting on giant paws. He knew not to impinge on her territory, that his job was done once more, but he still liked to know that all was well with his mate and that his genes would be passed safely down to his progeny. That way the big cats would always be found in the Eastern forest. From prior experience he knew that Wutki could take care of herself but he too had heard the strange sounds coming from the far side of the rolling hills and sensed that something new was happening. Vigilance was the rule until it was established exactly what was causing the sounds and smells. Then if necessary he would act to preserve the wild lifestyle of the big coon cats. He was unaware that the instincts of the female of the species was going to affect a plan more effective and far reaching than anything he could have done to achieve the continuation of the species.

Wutki was restless again. The ache in her hips and the bulge around her normally lean middle meant she couldn't sit, she couldn't lie on one side or the other and she didn't feel comfortable lying flat with her head on her paws as she always liked to do.

That way she was ready to lift her watchful eyes and ears to any approaching sounds. Her swelling sides were alive with the minute movements of kittens equally spaced down either side of her uterus. Her constant hunger gnawed at her innards and her appetite was insatiable. She knew her time was approaching as only that day, as she pursued a clumsy and noisy grouse through the forest, she misjudged the space between a fallen log and a blueberry bush. The momentary recoil as she collided with the unexpected obstacles enabled the creature to make an unprecedented escape. Summer had been kind to the breeding population of rabbits, rats and harvest mice and Wutki had indulged the feeding frenzy demanded by her growing young. Countless tender baby rodents, easily caught and quickly despatched, filled her emptiness and nourished the developing brood.

She awoke one night and sniffed the changes in the air but found them not unpleasant, especially as they heralded the day she had been waiting for. The forest nights were starting to lengthen and a faint cooling crept over the mountains on the wind. She slept fitfully and restlessly wandered at night seeking relief from her physical symptoms. She struggled to clean herself but found it hard to reach all the places that formerly had been no effort at all to lick and groom. A sweet milky secretion flowed from her reddened nipples. Although she loved her den and had felt secure there in the past she had a pressing sense of urgency to relocate to an unknown and previously unused birthing place. It was as if she could foresee the significance of this litter and understood the necessity for caution at all costs.

She sniffed and nudged her way through the undergrowth and found herself descending towards the lower plain but remained above the marshland. A rocky ledge fell away into a slope of rough rubble and scree and she peered suspiciously into the darkened space formed by a pile up of stones and rocks. It was an unlikely hiding place due to the mobility of the surrounding material but it was unoccupied and exactly what she had been searching for.

It had been nine full weeks since the night on the hillside with Aguara. His absence had been necessary to allow Wutki to make the decisions that would give her and her young the best chance for life. Death came too easily to the unwary or the careless in the mountains of Maine. That first night in the new den was a wakeful one for Wutki as she moved the leaf and plant debris from one corner to another, assessing wind direction and chill factor. After much turning and rearranging she finally stretched her laden body and gratefully lay down on the soft matting of the leaf mould and closed her eyes. Her ever-mindful ears heard a small familiar snuffle from the rocks on the topmost ledge of the slope and she knew that he had come to be near, and to protect, Aguara the powerful, her mate.

The sun arose and its earliest rays failed to penetrate the hidden den. A little later Wutki wakened herself with the sound of her own purring. She licked tremulously at her tawny striped fur and felt a rising thirst in her throat. One quick stretch, which ended in a twinge of discomfort, and she was off and bounding down the slope, revelling in the warmth of the sun. There was no sign of the big male cat any longer. The stream ran even colder, another sign of the departing mildness, and Wutki lapped seemingly interminably, relishing every cooling drop. She shook her head, distributing droplets of crystal clear water in all directions and was off again in pursuit of breakfast. This time that grouse was not so lucky and she tore at his gamey flesh with a vigour befitting a mother of kittens-to-be.

Fortified for the task ahead Wutki climbed carefully back to the chosen birthing place. What was that dripping from her rump as she climbed? Every so often she turned and very gently but thoroughly erased all trace of the colourless liquid, less her loss lead a predator to her door. As she slid inside the narrow entrance to the den she turned her face one last time to the outside world to clean the rock from the now bloody markings on the slate. It wouldn't be long now. Aguara crept sure-footedly to the closest spot to the den without sending the scree sliding and crashing to the base of the rocks. His ears were straining to every sound from the den. As he settled down for the wait he heard Wutki's breath coming more rapidly as she started to breathe through her mouth. It was the onset of labour.

Her babies lay within their sacs in the horns of her uterus. Protectively their placentas encircled their small damp bodies. Wutki's abdominal fur stiffened as her uterus contracted time and again; her forced breathing the only outward indication of her labour pains. At first this happened only once every hour but as time passed their rate and intensity increased until Wutki could hardly draw breath in between. Two contractions a minute was the norm. Seemingly sensitive to his mate's distress Aguara inserted his brown tabby head through the entrance and before Wutki could protest this intrusion into the privacy of birthing he licked her face and withdrew. The sight of that familiar proud white ruff disappearing into the darkness gave her the strength she needed for the last stage of labour and she started to bear down with a determination experienced only by the female of the species.

The uterine contractions had been gradually moving the first foetus towards her cervix. Her licking of her genital area had increased and she had been dilating steadily during this time. The first of her offspring was now well established in the birth canal. Two more pushes and the distended balloon of the inner amniotic sac was visible in the opening. Apparently without further effort the first kitten slipped onto the matting, encased in its semi-transparent sac, and was heralded into the world by lusty licking from its mother. She hardly noticed the arrival of the placenta and once the tiny creature's breathing was regular and strong she promptly bit through the cord and devoured the placenta in a few gulps.

It seemed the next kitten appeared from nowhere. One moment it wasn't there and the next it was born. While it was being released from its sack and licked into life, the first kitten was squirming strongly towards its mother's belly and the milk-giving teat. The kittens were wet and looked hairless. After tidying away the second placenta Wutki settled back for a short respite. Thirty minutes passed before her panting became rapid and anxious once more. So far the double horns of her uterus had one kitten each and again it was the turn of the first side to release its little one in to the world. This one was large and strong, a male. He was up and moving before Wutki had a chance to deal with him. His membrane had broken open at delivery and nothing was going to hold him back from the business of living. He burrowed into his mother's fur, pushing fiercely between his two sisters to locate an upper teat, an advantageous position that he would tenaciously cling to during his infancy.

Another rest period allowed Wutki to gather her resources for the final push. This one was not as straightforward as the others had been. Not that the pains were greater or the pushing stronger but somehow it seemed to have stuck. Wutki struggled to move her haunches in an attempt to dislodge the kitten but it didn't work and eventually she lay back exhausted from her efforts.

She tried to look and see what the matter was but all she could see was the tail of her un-born protruding from her own body, a true breech birth. When she realised her pushing attempts were futile she gently disentangled herself from her rooting babes and with one last ounce of strength she launched herself into the air. It was not the highest she had ever jumped, but it did the trick and number four made a flying entry into the den followed closely by a tiny twin, both sharing the one placenta.

She knew immediately that there were no more to come and she settled down in the bedding with her sucklings. As she fell asleep she marvelled at the arrival of the fifth kitten, so unexpected especially as it came riding on the placenta of his bigger brother! Before she slept, all was clean within the den. No sights or smells would give away the presence of the little family. As she slipped from consciousness, she was aware of a bigger form introducing himself to each new arrival with a welcoming lick. Their fur was drying and they no longer resembled hairless, newborn rodents. She didn't see the double lick given to the little twin with the extra high–pitched squeaking voice who was asserting his right to a share of his mother's milk. One adult cat slept in relief. The other climbed to the highest point in his territory to greet the rising sun with triumph. The night passed gently into day. A satisfactory outcome was his opinion and a sense of fulfilment lent power to his morning call.

Wutki crawled from the den, blinking in the sunlight later that morning. The brood squealed as her warmth passed out of the den but they were comforted by the contact with one another and slept again in a heap of little breathing entities. She crept just to the base of the slope and drank long and deep from a puddle of rainwater and dew. The next mouse to pass within sight and smell tasted all the more delicious as she was no longer pregnant and Wutki relished having her body to herself once more. A squeak of hunger from the den sent her bounding back up the slope and in an instant she was stretched languorously in the midst of a pushing, sucking mass of kittens.

Wutki no longer felt the pressing anxiety that had plagued her during her pregnancy and since her confinement she had relaxed. The next three weeks passed uneventfully for the mother and young. At five days or so, the kittens' shrivelled umbilical cords had fallen off. Before the third week they were crawling and had commenced exploration of the den but not outside. They tottered unsteadily around, knocking one another over with ease. The last little boy-twin remained small but determined. His eyes were the first to open on the ninth day. The familiar scent of his mother and litter mates and the shelter of the den all gave him a sense of security. His mother was the fount of all possible warmth and comfort that any kitten could ask for. The two girls were out-weighed by the two bigger boys but all grew fat and fluffy at their own rate and thrived on their diet of mother's milk. Wutki took the matter of kitten-raising seriously and not one speck of dirt infested their fur nor was there one spot of anything offensive anywhere in the den. They were fed and licked and cleaned to a state of perfection. If only her back legs were not so stiff and uncooperative!

Aguara was never far from the den. No predator had the chance to even approach their home in the scree as Aguara saw them off promptly. The big cat was at his fiercest while the kittens were vulnerable.

Wutki worried that something might not be quite right. She felt abnormally tired. However, in those first few weeks as she was required to lie still a lot in order to let the kittens feed, it really was not an issue. The supply of moles and shrews, which supplemented the mice, was still plentiful and easily caught. She never had to venture far from the den to find her nourishment.

It was the start of the fourth week and she went out particularly early one morning. She had a special task in hand. An especially tasty little bird was her first prey but instead of rapidly crunching it up she carefully carried it up to the den. There, she split it open with tooth and claw and pushed it towards her babies. Milk teeth had formed and ears had pricked up. They were ready for food, real food. They sniffed with interest but all turned to nurse from their mother in preference. She batted them away with a soft paw and not until each kitten had at least dipped his nose and tongue into the innards of the bird did she permit them to suckle. This process was repeated at every mealtime and within a week all the kittens were enthusiastically devouring the dead offerings with a fair amount of jostling and rivalry.

Wutki was content to let her children play now at the mouth of the den while she soaked up the last of the warm sun. It somehow comforted her body. She now realised her bones were getting old. Mostly the kittens chased tails, their own or another's. There was much swatting, neck-biting, tumbling and general wrestling. Then, when Wutki started providing fast moving food in the form of live rodents, the kittens were in their element. Little-twin raced courageously after mice but was beaten to the kill by his older brothers. Wutki lent her paw to him and the girls but only at first. Very quickly their instinct combined with their mother's training supplemented their milky diet. Their mother was keen to see them become fully weaned. She was experiencing an uncomfortable dryness in her teats that warned her that there could be an early loss of milk. Whatever happened, these little cats must not starve.

A gradual descent of the scree was now taking place with each outing from the den. The little ones were too light to cause any kind of rocky avalanche and were able to race safely over the broken material. Wutki tried in vain to keep up with them but they were everywhere at once. She spent a lot of time calling the litter to keep them close by.

This difficulty she had been experiencing with her rear hip joints was getting worse and worse. She felt that her mobility was being curtailed. She knew that no animal must reveal any weakness in the wilderness or they would be singled out by predators and killed as a matter of course. The weak were easy prey but it also served to preserve the bloodlines of only the strongest. She hid her problem as only a cat can. She suffered in silence. Soon they would go into the forest for a real lesson in life.

The day dawned cool and fresh. Wutki sniffed the air and set out down the slope with renewed enthusiasm, followed by a tumbling mass of disputing young. She was glad to see that their long-haired coats were coming in well. Their stripes were appearing and different shades of brown helped to camouflage them outdoors. She led them to the edge of the forest with its pine-needled carpet and sheltering canopy. Suddenly the little cats became very cautious and walked by her side, each one jostling the others in their attempt to maintain contact with their mother. Wutki noted this with pleasure, which later turned into relief.

Old pinecones were strewn over the floor. Strongest-brother batted one out of his way and when it rolled, as if possessed by a life of its own, they were all off in pursuit of the new toys. Wutki stood and watched. Amazing how quickly they grow and learn, she thought. Suddenly her keen hearing brought her an alarming sound from behind a thicket of briars not too far away. It was a grunting and snorting and scratching. The wind shifted slightly and Wutki's hackles lifted in horror. The musky smell of bear filled her nostrils and dread filled her heart. He broke through the foliage with a roar and with one quick cry she alerted the kittens and ran. They all flew back the way they had come, little cats following their mother's streaming tail. When they reached the safety of the slope leading to the den it was the kittens that arrived first. They cowered in the back of the den almost under the rocks themselves. But where was their mother? They were too scared to look.

Wutki wasn't far behind them. When she had reached the slope she looked back. The bear had lost interest in a hysterical group of cats. He was more interested in fishing. This had saved Wutki's life because for the first time she had been unable to bound up onto the scree and into the den. She painfully dragged her hindquarters slowly uphill and as she fell into her home she was convulsed with a crushing agony in her chest.

She lay breathless and weak on her side on the floor. The kittens were seemingly unaware of their mother's distress and crowded round to nurse. She was unable to move. She now knew that she was ill and whatever fear she felt for herself was nothing to the terror she felt for the fate of her children.

The next day at sunrise the youngsters wakened their mother with their cries and pushing. The kittens were in fine fettle and ready for a new day of fearless adventure. Wutki tentatively placed her four feet on the ground and stretched carefully. Nothing adverse happened. The attack of the day before had passed but she knew within herself that something had to be done. It now looked as if her strength would not hold out long enough for the kittens to be independent of her. Her rear limbs were not in as much pain but they were reluctant to cooperate and dragged behind. 'This will never do,' she mused as the kittens tumbled down the slope with nothing but play on their minds. 'If only they could fend for themselves and be out of danger'. But that wasn't going to happen overnight and the necessary number of weeks to reach that stage was looking doubtful.

She led them away from the den. The education of the kittens seemed as if it would be their only hope. Rodents would no longer be playthings. Birds had to be caught, not leapt after futilely. Wutki realised that she would probably never see the den again as she would have to take the kittens out into the world and when she could no longer care for them they would have to take their chances with nature. The situation did not look good. The kittens chased and fought unawares.

Each day the little group of cats moved slowly down closer to the valley where the strange sounds and the smoky smells drifted towards them in the autumn breeze. The kittens grew used to these new experiences and were unafraid.

Each night a different spot became a new shelter; a fallen tree, an overhanging rock, a deserted burrow.

Each hunt became a learning experience and Wutki bravely bore her pain as she demonstrated the stalking, the ambush, the leaps and pounces necessary to make a kill. The kittens rushed after her, clumsily at first, but gradually they copied her silent step, the act of freezing with one paw in the air in mid-step. When Wutki killed the prey the kittens would rush upon it and behave as if they were the victorious hunters, ripping viciously at the flesh, fur and feather when actually their milk teeth were not very effectual. Wutki watched their efforts with satisfaction but wondered if independence would come to her kittens before it was too late? Would small-kitten be able to keep up with his litter-mates in the race for survival?

Each day, by late afternoon, Wutki felt an overriding weakness, an exhaustion of the kind never experienced before. She knew that the pressure of caring for and protecting her offspring was all that was keeping her going. Only her determination fuelled her routine of feeding and moving her family closer to the valley, the valley that was being changed by human hands. The sounds of woodland and scrub being converted to fields and farms, the scent of burning tree stumps, the sound of human language and young human's laughter all surged uphill to the cat and her kittens. She tried to remain calm in the face of the strangeness of their proximity to the new humankind as she had a plan, a risky plan, but what else could be done in the face of her growing inability to care for her litter?

The weather was turning. The leaves were losing their green mantle. Reds and yellows predominated. Ishmael saw with growing satisfaction that his efforts were now beginning to bear fruit. He had arrived with John Cabot and his party of English settlers and had set out to carve a place for his wife and children in the New World. He had been clearing brush, felling trees, and burning stumps since he and his family had arrived in the valley. The land was now his. He had staked his claim, registered his name, built a rudimentary cabin and was well on the way to being a farmer as he had been in the old country. His wife came up behind him as he rested at the edge of his newly cleared field and sat beside him. The gentle murmur of their voices floated on the wind up to where Wutki and the kittens were hidden crouched in the long grass. Wutki signalled to them to stay and crept to the edge of the covering grass to watch. She saw the strong young woman with her tall straight body, long brown hair, her skin unusually tanned from the New England summer. She and Ishmael were surveying the scene with obvious pleasure and although Wutki could neither hear nor understand the words, the meaning still reached her. She could almost feel the love of this valley emanating from the couple; their delight in their farm, the appreciation of the fruit trees and bushes, the wooded slopes, the rocky summits. The happy voices of their girls wafted from the cabin and the joy of their parents in having provided them with this space to grow was almost tangible to the sensitive, intelligent cat. The woman stood, shaking the dirt from her long skirt and apron, left Ishmael his bread and soup, and as she walked away she saw him lift a handful the soil and let it crumble through his fingers with satisfaction. Unseen and unheard the five little kittens silently inhaled the varied scents of man.

For several days this process was repeated with Wutki gradually drawing her young closer and closer until the kittens were watching the children play from the edge of the forest nearest to the farm. The human children reminded Wutki of a litter of kittens as they ran and tumbled, chasing their toys and squealing with glee.

The temperature continued to drop as the season progressed. Wutki's pains were increasing. She felt a constant crushing in her chest and there were moments when she thought her back legs would never move again. She knew the time had come.

For one last long night the six of them curled up together in a hollow not far from the cabin. Wutki was awake from the first greying in the morning sky. She looked at the five little bodies pressed against her stomach and saw the firmness in their flesh, the shine on their coats, the straight long whiskers and the twitching striped tails and knew that her job had been done well; even small-cat had survived.

At dawn Wutki stretched her aching body. The little cats woke up and stretched also. Their mother gave them all a cursory wash which they reluctantly submitted to as they were now grooming themselves. She set out across the field and they nervously followed. They had never been allowed out of the cover of the foliage before. The sun had risen over the top of the hill and light streamed down illuminating the strange little procession wending its way up the valley. Smoke had started to curl lazily from the cabin chimney while inside another little family was starting its day. A pot of oatmeal was simmering over the small fire. Ishmael ate quickly and pulled on his boots and jacket. The girls got up from the table to kiss him goodbye.

Wutki's kittens had become familiar with the sight of the cabin and its inhabitants but they had never been this close to it with its many interesting odours. Wutki called them to stay close to her and led them up to the door of the cabin. Timidly but trustingly they followed her. One by one she licked their little faces and ears and then gave the signal to freeze. All of them understood this as their lives had depended on their obedience to their mother many times before.

Wutki slowly backed away. She repeated the command to stay several times over. Bewildered the kittens obeyed and watched her approach the bushes bordering the side of the cabin. Almost immediately the door opened. Ishmael stood there, his arms full of his little daughters, laughing and kissing his bearded face. The eldest saw them first. With a cry she struggled from her father's arms to bend down in wonder at the sight of five pairs of bright eyes with five immobile tails, still obeying their mother, all looking up at her in mutual wonder. The second girl threw herself onto the floor and now five pairs of eyes were fixed on hers which were only inches from their quivering little faces. Ishmael called his wife who appeared with the baby in her arms who cooed and smiled at the sight of the cats. Ishmael and his wife looked at one another and looked at the joy in their daughters' eyes and nodded silently at one another.

Ishmael looked up and caught a glimpse of Wutki heading for the bushes. It's that coon cat he thought. She's left them here. What on earth? Wutki turned at the bushes for one last look in time to see a bowl of food being placed before her little ones. All five little heads were lapping up the warm milky porridge but small-cat turned in time to see his mother vanish into the shrubbery and somehow he knew that he would never see her again.

Wutki had found the solution to her problem. Her last litter thrived and bred a long line of sturdy New England cats. Down through the generations they befriended the settlers, rid their farms and homes of rodents, but none were ever more beloved than Wutki's first domesticated litter in the wilds of Maine.

From Wutki to the Scottish Wildcat

Wutki seemed taller as she returned to her place. She would never have thought that her solution to her family's dilemma would ever be counted as important as the lives the others had led. Somehow she seemed to be sturdier and not quite so tiny. The realisation that her actions had an impact on the future of the land she lived in had given her self-confidence and she was now proud to be included in this company of cats.

Without need for voice of command a large striped shape materialised from the top of the rock face and took her place at the front. Her descent had been so furtive and rapid that not one other cat detected her between her initial appearance above and her arrival below. Quite a few cat eyes blinked in wonder at the serious face before them, a stern countenance, earnest and mature, maybe even slightly threatening but certainly commanding. No introduction was provided but as the years rolled back once more in the minds of the cats all their attention was riveted on this very different animal.

None of them could have anticipated the roller-coaster ride through the creation of this cat's homeland which was about to be played out at speed in their mind's eye. A moving kaleidoscope brought claws from their sheaths and muscles tensed. It appeared as if the whole rock face might tilt and throw the cats from their niches. The effect of this visual cataclysm was sufficiently powerful to make even the bravest cats cower.

The Scottish Wildcat

1812

As she moved at the edge of the clearing, a mere shadow, every cell in her body vibrated with awareness, alert to all around her, above and below her. The voice of the bedrock spoke to her. Her instincts were inherited from her female ancestors, passed down through her genetic code in an unbroken line. She was large and striped in shades of fawn and brown with markings of black in streaks and rings. She was wildcat, one of those who had always been there throughout the generations of time. She was progeny of many survivors, cats who had witnessed tumultuous changes in the land, natural changes and those wrought by the hand of man.

She scaled a small cairn protruding from the slope above the clearing. The great tectonic plates far beneath her had travelled across the surface of the planet over aeons of time. She sensed the agelessness of the rock under her paws. Scotland was drifting slowly away from the Americas at an almost imperceptible rate. This was a rugged wild terrain, not for the weak or the fainthearted.

The ancient ones, her predecessors from the beginning of time, had witnessed the rise of the land she stood upon. Over a vast period of time, massive walls of ice cracked with sounds louder than thunder and fell into tormented seas . Great sheets of savage ice slid down mountainsides and smashed to pieces in valleys below. From these valleys torrents of melt water, laced with frozen slabs, powered down hillsides, carving slashes of brown into the white and blue of the retreating ice. A land was slowly emerging from its frozen cloak, rising in hues of granite and limestone, soil and sand. It was the end of the last great ice-age.

This land, which in later days would be known as Caledonia, undulated, climbed and fell, the steepness and the ruggedness dictated by the rock beneath. Fresh water gathered in dips and hollows forming inland lochs. The sea encroached on the broken coastline forming salt water sea lochs. Cliffs soared and as suddenly dropped into the sea.

Algae and liverworts started to cover the rocks. A succession of life ensued as mosses, grasses and herbaceous plants found enough soil to thrive. Then one day as the warming sun beat down on the planet's surface, one seed, one tiny seed, buried deep within its new found soil lodged in a sheltered gully, sprouted. Upwards it raised its head to the light and rain. A pine tree emerged, grew, seeded, dropped its pine-cone progeny and the trees crept relentlessly across the face of the land, mile by mile, year by year. Every possible site, every slope and ledge, all coastal plains and river banks, every nook and cranny was colonised. A biodiversity of life, of vegetation, first the fish then the insects, birds and mammals, burrowers and foragers, ruminants and predators.

In keeping with the passage of time the old made way for the new. Fleeting glimpses of enormous oxen and herds of wild horses seeking out the valleys of rough grass were seen. The woods were shared by the brown bear and the lynx but they faded with the daylight. Those best suited for survival at that time were the ones who hunted and howled and the silent stealthy one who merged with the forest as an illusion in the dusk, one who seemed as ancient as the rocks beneath her paws, she was a Scottish wildcat.

Her ears pricked up and she turned her strong striped head westwards into the woods. Through the birches and pines came a blood curdling howl followed shortly by a cacophony of canine voices filling the forest. Stealthily she dropped to the ground and clawed her way up to the middle of an old oak tree. She stretched comfortably along a wide branch, perfectly camouflaged in the foliage. She could hear their scampering feet draw closer in pursuit of pounding hooves. All her senses were on alert. She knew exactly from which direction the animals would appear, also how many there were and what they were hunting.

The ragged breath of the prey grew louder and two female red deer burst from the thicket in wide-eyed terror followed by another which was struggling to keep up. With her damaged hip bone, she did not stand a chance.

Almost upon her was the alpha male, the black leader of the wolf pack. His mate was not with him but in his wake came his two adult daughters, an older related male, plus a stranger to the pack, a young golden male who stood out from the others.

None of the wolves exhibited any signs of being the slightest bit out of breath. The skittering, panicked gait of the deer was not echoed in their pursuers who loped along effortlessly, their breath coming in regular controlled inhalations and barely audible exhalations.

The cat lay motionless but for the swivel of her ears and a twitch of her long whiskers. The deer were totally unaware of the presence of yet another ferocious predator above their heads and ran right under the branch where she lay, closely followed by the determined wolf pack. The time had come and the alpha drew alongside the ill-fated deer. He sank his teeth into her damaged leg. That was all it took to cause her to stumble and she went down with her spindly legs flailing wildly but ineffectively. It was over.

The kill was close enough to make the wildcat drool when the smell of the fresh blood rose into the trees but it was safer to remain still and silent. She had tasted the blood of deer before, not a full-grown doe like this one but opportunistically she had taken a small fawn on several occasions.

The wolves gorged on the tenderest parts of their kill. Their muzzles were stained red and their nostrils were filled with the satisfying stench of death when they loped back to their den around the other side of the mountain. They lived on the steepest face of the mountain above the ancient forest. The alpha female and her pups would eat well tonight on regurgitated venison.

The wildcat was not fooled. She would have been at fault if she was to think that her presence had gone unnoticed by the pack. They knew exactly what tree she was in and how far up the trunk she was. It was simply of no interest to the wolves who trotted away, this time avoiding passing directly beneath her. However despite her camouflage, as the young golden wolf came level with her oak tree, he lifted his head, bared his teeth in a semblance of a snarl and, for the briefest of moments, looked the cat directly in the eyes. She returned his stare impassively without a blink. He did not break his stride but followed the others into the gathering mist which swirled around the woodland.

Another pair of eyes had been watching the entire scene. From the crest of the hill which separated the Great Glen from the Glen of the Rowan, hidden behind the granite outcrop, low in the fronds of the bracken, another youngster observed. She had caught a fleeting glimpse of the wildcat as she emerged from the cover of the woods if only for a second or two. She could not see the cat in the oak tree but she suspected she was concealed not far away. She also recognised the wolf pack and had watched them from afar.

What she didn't realise was that both the canines and the feline had detected her presence from the start but had simply chosen to ignore it. After all what interest or danger could come from being stalked by a half-grown human child?

Ailsa Cameron pushed herself up from the bracken, the smell of the fronds on her hands, in her long brown hair and on her rough clothing. She headed back over the ridge towards the settlement before darkness fell. She caught one last glimpse of the pack as they emerged from the wooded area and mounted the jagged summit of the mountain, heading for their den on the far side. They travelled in single file and at that distance looked about the size of mice which made Ailsa grin.

They travelled effortlessly, their bellies full, enjoying the warmth of the late highland spring. Not even a rabbit, which misguidedly ran across their path, deflected them from the journey home. They followed the same route as they had come but omitted the hysterical zigzag taken by the fleeing deer. Their den was many miles away, isolated just above the tree line, and was difficult to access. No one bothered them up there. Occasionally a golden eagle floated overhead as if inspecting the pack for potential weakness but any dive for a closer look provoked a barrier of growling, snapping animals. No eagle would risk feather and life against such fierceness.

To any observer the wolf den was invisible. The entrance lay behind, and almost below, some large boulders broken from the rock face and the tunnel wound round into the base of the cliff itself. No matter from what angle the den was approached only solid rock was visible. The female heard the pack's return. She emerged from the den to greet her mate and the playful, joyful reunion belied the few hours' absence. She was much lighter in colour than the others. All were of the grey wolf species but this pack included the creamy coated alpha female and the young golden male who was a yearling loner who had been permitted to join the pack.

Her mate fed her first, and generously. He could go and hunt for more food if he had need but she was tied to the den for now. Also he suspected that most of what she ate would later nourish the soon to be demanding offspring as yet unborn.

Elsewhere a mother cat was seeking a similar safe environment in which to raise her young.

Ailsa had ascended the hill behind her and cut down through the pass, a fairly easy trek. She continued over much lower hills until below her she spotted the winding roadway leading into the glen, her glen, her home. She was racing darkness as she skipped along the pebble-strewn track heading for her tiny stone house. In early evening the settlement was always busy at the end of the working day with the time for the evening meal. She had hardly crossed the small stone hump-backed bridge spanning the stream running through the glen when she could hear her mother's voice, 'Ailsa! Ailsa, there you are. Where have you been this time? Do you know how long you have been gone?' Ailsa shook her head and linked her arm through her mother's. Her baby brother Ian was held in the other arm as they headed past the cluster of cottages.

Welcoming smoke billowed from the hole in the thatched roof of their sheiling. Once inside the house Morag Cameron turned her daughter round, cupped her face in her hands, and said very sternly 'You haven't been hanging around these wild creatures again, have you? You know what I have told you, over and over. Why oh why do you persist?' Ailsa's father arrived at that moment and ducked his tall lean figure through the frame of the doorway.

'Why do you bother to question her like that? You know she is not going to tell you anything?'

'I know Rob,' Morag answered still looking intently into Ailsa's face, 'but I feel I have to try.' At that she released her daughter who danced off with her eyes shining and a small smile on her lips. Her Dad gave her a playful smack on the legs as she ran silently past. That was the problem. The silence. Ailsa had stopped speaking in the fifth year of her life. She was mute.

The cat inhabited the unique ecosystem of the Caledonian pine forests which thrived in smaller and smaller clumps in the Highlands. She had been raised within sound and scent of man, his cattle, his battles. No two creatures could have been more different on the planet earth than these two, cat and man.

She and her kind had survived for countless aeons without making changes to the landscape in which they lived, bred and died; unlike humans who seemed bent on destruction and appeared to be compelled to slash and burn, consume or destroy all around them.

She had avoided their cattle all her life. They were no threat and of no interest to her and her kind. They were dirty, smelly, noisy, clumsy and came with unkempt, shaggy coats and very large horns. They lived in the control of men who exploited them for their hides, their meat and their milk.

From afar, safely concealed in the hillside rocks, she watched the cattle droves. In certain seasons, with regularity, the tracks and glens echoed to the pitiful sound of lowing cattle. The cat waited patiently knowing that peace would soon return once all those beasts had reached the cattle-markets to the south.

She had seen how the endless demands of man and of deer had whittled away at the habitat which she and many wild creatures particular to that environment had depended upon.

She felt movement now in her swelling belly. The old male wildcat with his territorial marking and possessive stamping of the feet had fathered her young. He was the best choice, strong and forceful. He had answered her calling earlier in the spring leaving her satisfied that his strengths would be passed to their offspring. He had moved on now to the north in search of further territory suited to the life of a solitary male wildcat. His legacy, her developing young, was soon to be born. It was time to find a den.

She lay motionless on the moss at the edge of the tree line. It was soft and spongy. It gave gently beneath her distended abdomen but at the same time provided a cradle of comfort and support. Her swollen teats were tender but were cooled by the absorbent tiny plants. She was not there to relax however and her sharp eyes were recording every aspect of the scene around and below her. She had already scanned the skies for birds of prey. It was a bright day and barely a cloud masked the warming rays of the spring sunlight.

Behind her the trees had thinned out considerably as the fertile forest floor gave way to more and more granite outcrops. Ancient lichens overran these rocky slabs in slow motion, their algae producing food for their fungus from the sunshine, water and air. The heavy female cat inhaled. No danger could be detected. Her nostrils filled with the distinctively sweet yet peppery odour of the liverworts growing over the ragged edge of the drop to the river below her. Her ears recorded the thunderous roar of the waterfall upstream. It was channelled through a narrow crevice to drop thirty feet into the brown river beneath. It created a dangerous eddy of whirlpools and opposing currents as well as increasing the rate of flow at that part of the river. The river had eaten away at the limestone bank causing it to become a rugged cliff face topped by sentinel firs.

Any creature running through this part of the forest would come to an abrupt halt when they reached this impediment and would have to turn around and go back the way they had come. Not even the wolves could negotiate this sudden drop into the river. The approach from below was guarded by the swirling white water. Half way down, an overhanging slab concealed a deep hollow in the eroded stone. Further down, an area of raised beach had been left stranded by the river as it ate its way through the landscape.

The question was, could she find a suitable pathway both up and down and could her kittens safely play on this rock face? She stood up, stretched gingerly so as not to compress her already overcrowded body, and headed over the edge. She followed the line of shrubs which clung in the gullies and by wending her way from gully to gully she gradually descended to the isolated rocky beach. Surprisingly there was much more vegetation here than she had expected. The upright stems of a variety of ferns pushed their delicate fronds directly towards the light. In other spots tough bracken, the largest of the ferns, towered over its rocky base.

With claws extended the expectant mother sure-footedly ascended what looked like an impassable route from the former beach until she had scaled the last of the slope leading into the hollow rock. As she had hoped, it was bone dry. The noise of the waterfall was barely audible and fronds of dead bracken lined the floor. It sloped gently upwards and went back a considerable distance into the rock face until it reached the solid granite deep below the forest floor.

She went back to the entrance and surveyed all the possible routes to and from her new found den. Once satisfied that nothing other than a mountain goat could navigate the rugged topography she disappeared back inside to scrape the foliage into a comfortable pile in a semi-darkened corner and then lay down to await her time.

It was late morning when the little lad came running down the track into the glen, his collie barking at his heels. His breath was ragged and his voice was hoarse but he was yelling a warning as loud as he could manage. 'They're coming, they're coming. Dad! Dad! Help! They are nearly here.' Calum continued to scream like this all the way over the bridge and round the side of the settlement to his family's sheiling. His father straightened up at the sound of his young son's voice in time to see the cloud of dust rising over the hill, the indication that riders were approaching. Dougie scooped the boy up and rushing into the cottage swept his baby daughter out of her cradle. Calling his wife, he headed for the small stone animal shelter behind the perimeter wall of the village. As they threw themselves down below the height of the stone dyke his wife Shona landed almost on top of them as she fled her vegetable garden beside the cottage. The riders were already descending the track and were almost at the bridge while shouts and screams from other villagers echoed through the glen. The Clan Cameron was under attack.

By now, the alarm was well broadcast and people, dogs and chickens were scattering in all directions, crossing one another's paths in their panic. Generally there was a movement towards the higher ground and the tree cover. Seven riders clattered at speed across the bridge. All were rough mercenaries, their faces worn and uncaring, a merciless looking bunch. Some had firearms and others swords. The villagers were without weapons, forbidden them since the Jacobite uprising in 1745, other than farming and logging tools and implements. Shots were randomly fired accompanied by much threatening waving of swords in the air all of which sent shock waves of terror throughout the settlement. Morag had her baby son strapped to her hip as she ran for cover, terrified to feel a slash from a sword or fear of a lead musket ball from a flintlock in her back. She threw herself down behind the stone wall where her cousin Shona was concealed and together the two women clung to one another, their babies covered by their two bodies while Dougie cradled his son Calum in his arms.

To add horror to the attack burning brands were lit and the seven men galloped through the settlement between the cottages sending showers of oily sparks in all directions. Whooping and yelling, they galloped back over the bridge and as a parting shot sent a burning brand into the hayrick of the last cottage they passed. It was over almost as soon as it had started.

All the cotters, men, women and children who were close enough, emerged running from their hiding places and frantically scooped water in leather buckets from the stream. They were passed from hand to hand, dousing the flames in one coordinated communal effort. The soaking prevented the fire spreading to the cottage itself or back into the village. Only the hay was destroyed, the black acrid smoke polluting the entire glen.

Rob had heard the cries. He had been above the glen out of sight of the settlement. Heart pounding he ran, his rough boots crashing through the heather and bracken, his breath rasping and then it hit him, the dreaded smell of oily smoking torches and the smoke rising into the sky before him. Careless of his own safety or of the danger he might be running into he rounded the hillside and the village appeared before him. The riders had already ridden away. A pall of grey plumes, like phantoms, drifted over the settlement. The one small fire was under control. His knees felt weak beneath him. He stumbled the remaining distance with one thought in his mind, Morag and the children. 'Please dear God don't let them be harmed, not hurt, not wounded. Please, please dear God not killed.'

Dougie, his neighbour and kinsman, saw him crashing along the track from the cattle pens, wide-eyed with terror, his whole countenance contorted with concern. Dougie, sopping bucket in hand, intercepted him but before he could reassure Rob that the women and children were safe Rob had sucked in his ragged breath and swallowed hard with a forced measure of control and courage. 'Dougie are they safe?'

'Rob-man, they're safe.'

'Thanks be to God for that!'

'That was only a warning,' Dougie added.

They went together to Dougie's sheiling where a shaken Morag and Shona were waiting with the children. Not given to outward demonstrations of affection Rob only laid a hand on his wife's shoulder and asked in a gruff voice, 'You are alright Lass?' Shona heated some broth and they sat round with their wooden bowls. It was more than obvious to them all that one family member was missing. Morag actually gave a little laugh and said, 'I am always concerned at Ailsa's wandering but this time I am so thankful she is off on her wild escapades this afternoon.'

'Aye,' said Rob, 'She will show up later, none the wiser for today's chaos,' but both parents still had concerned expressions.

Morag wanted to talk to her cousin about her little daughter. She needed to pour out her pent up worries. The men wanted to discuss the situation that through no fault of their own they found themselves in. They settled down and shared their fears and began to make their plans.

Morag repeated, 'It's a mercy Ailsa didn't see the attack today.'

'I know Morag,' Shona said. It was that slaughter on the moor of our granddad and your dad that took away her lovely happy little voice. We did not need a repeat of that trauma.'

'It's been two years come autumn since it happened. I wonder endlessly if she will ever recover from that,' Morag replied.

'I have heard stories about that,' Dougie added. 'Never give up hope. That lass of yours is something special.' Morag nodded, a little grateful smile on her lips.

Rob said, 'We have to make serious plans now. Today's incident tells us our glen is next in line to be cleared.'

'How can they do that to us?' Shona demanded.

'We are only cottars who rent, not land owners,' her husband replied. 'Our homes will burn, our cattle will be destroyed and our rigs turned into grass. This settlement will be razed like all the others.'

'But why would our own countrymen turn on us like this? What have we done to them to be persecuted like this? Haven't we been faithful tenants and always paid our dues?' Shona persisted. 'And what about our Clan Chief? Can he not help us as we have always helped him?'

'It comes from the Parliament in London,' Dougie answered. 'He is powerless now that we have been rendered useless without weapons. The whole clan organisation has been undermined. We are helpless to fight this. I heard it is happening all over the highlands.'

Morag said, 'Well what about the king? Does he think we are all barbarians or wild Jacobites here? Don't they know we just want to live in peace? We have given up so much already.'

Shona burst into tears. 'I feel as if I have lost part of myself. There is a hole inside of me where something I loved and treasured once was. Who would have thought that the sound of the bagpipes or the sight of the tartan or our men in their kilts would have meant so much? They were the symbols of what made us. I mean, those things were handed down from our fathers before us and somehow made us who we are. What right has anyone to take this from us? It may not seem important to outsiders but to be free to speak our language and live as we choose is our heart and soul. The very meaning of life here is being eroded. What will become of our blood line?'

Rob sighed and said, 'I doubt that anyone other than ourselves and all the others who work the land and run the cattle will have a thought in their heads except for the profit they will make on those damn sheep. It's the sheep. It is all about the sheep. We are driven from our glens so that the landlords can bring in that new breed of sheep, Cheviots they call them. They are big white-faced brutes from the south that eat everything. I tell you this, if those beasts run rampant across the whole country, one day Scotland will be a barren moor.'

'Well, that is exactly what is happening,' said Dougie. 'All the smaller bits and pieces of land are being joined up to make vast sheep runs. So what options have we got now that our clan no longer needs us to fight for it, now that we are being driven out? The King does not care. That George is a foreigner anyway and has his sights on better loot than our rigs and cattle. Cameron of Lochiel lost it all after Bonnie Prince Charlie's rebellion. Remember, all the Clan Cameron lands were forfeit to the Government. What can we do? We have no rights left.'

At that point Ailsa arrived as predicted. Morag hugged her and then said 'Off to bed all of you. Ailsa eat this soup first. You can sleep here with your cousins tonight.' That produced a huge smile on the little girl's face. The two families settled the children into bed and the four adults huddled round the stove making their plans long into the night.

The wildcat was content with her solitary existence. She had no desire to live in packs like wolves or villages and farms like men. An annual mating and then the raising of her young was all the company she required. No, she was the silent one, the watcher, the independent and untameable. She had never been and never would be a plant eater. Her teeth and claws were not designed for such a passive existence. However the small rodents she thrived on and would feed to her young were being annihilated by the loss of their habitat thanks to the unstoppable flocks of sheep. Yes things were changing in these high lands. Men and wildlife were being forced to move on against their will. It was becoming, 'Give-in and relocate to survive'.

Now however at the far side of the forest, out of sight, sound and scent of Rowan Glen she knew her time had come. The rhythmic tensing in her belly had taken on a life on its own. This wasn't her first time so she knew no fear. Safely ensconced in her darkened cave, with the protection of the inaccessible cliff and the fast flowing river, she had exactly what she needed, peace and isolation. The elements were kept at bay as were unwelcome intruders. She had chosen wisely and now gave herself over to the task in hand. No murmur escaped her throat and the only indication of her labouring was an increase in her breathing from time to time. As she panted rapidly her mind seemed to soar. She felt more like a bird than a mammal. She let her body deal totally with the task in hand. She did not seem to be present in the cave at all. In her mind she scaled mountain tops and felt the howling gale flatten her ears to her skull. She saw the bolt of lightening explode from the sky and crack open the tallest pine tree, sending its lengthy trunk smouldering to the ground. She ran from the downpour, her striped tail streaming behind her, and burrowed in the mossy floor of the deepest part of the Great Forest. She sat on the edge of the cliff and watched the uniqueness of each snow flake as it fell silently past her whiskered face to fill up the dips and hollows unseen in the valley far below.

To the accompaniment of this imagined drama of the natural world her little ones slipped easily into life and all they knew was the dark, the quiet, the warmth, one another's softness, the tingling roughness of their mother's tongue and the sweetness of her seemingly unlimited milk.

Another mother was feeling the first tension in her belly. It was coming regularly. The blonde alpha female stretched in the safety of her den. She could smell the birthing waters coming from her body and knew now that her time had come. The black alpha male sat outside the den, awake, alert, listening. The rest of the pack rested a respectful distance and lounged about joining in the vigil. As each new pup was licked into life by its mother and voiced its first little squeak in place of its future howl the pack members wagged their tails and milled about happily. The pack was growing. Soon its hunting capacity would increase as the new members grew up into more grey wolves to become the apex predators they were destined to be.

Several weeks passed. Ailsa had discovered that by following the banks of the river it was a short cut through the hills. She had found a spot where she could sit sheltered from the wind and rain. It was downriver from the waterfall and faced a rocky cliff on the opposite shore. She sat and played with the wildflowers, made daisy chains, had pretend kitchens with leafy plates and seeded food all the time talking to herself in her head. She was watched constantly by the mother cat, a source of curiosity. One day the cat emerged and sat in total stillness watching the child play. Ailsa was not unaware of the cat's eyes on her but as neither felt threatened by the other both simply carried on. She had been taught that you can never tame a wildcat or its kittens but Ailsa was just happy to have her silent undemanding company. The cat never stayed long but would glide up the rock face and meld into the woodland above. Ailsa smiled to see her knowing that few of the adults she knew had ever even seen a glimpse of a wildcat.

The settlement was astir with fears, ideas and plans for their survival. It was evident that they could not remain together as a community any longer as they had no way to fight the landlords with their ruthless uncaring factors and their sheep. They had no weapons, even their native Gaelic language was forbidden. A clan was a family, a large merged family, but no more could the clans depend on their chiefs, the landlords, the Parliament in England or the King of Great Britain. They would have to split up into single family units and all make what they could of a life in another location. Morag and Shona wanted to remain together and the men pledged to do their best to make that happen. The two cousins were all that were left of their original families. Too many deaths and too much parting.

The first indication of the threat was detected by the birds of the forest. As the air pressure plummeted the birds first of all became silent. An eerie stillness pervaded the woodland. The foliage drooped and the branches seemed to hang down as if reaching for the forest floor. It was there that the next sign of impending change became evident. Tiny scratchings and scrabblings accompanied by almost inaudible snufflings and snifflings commenced. Immediately the silent birds sounded their alarm and were visible flying in agitated circles above the canopy of the trees. A distinct rustling was evident now as small creatures and insects rearranged themselves in what they deemed to be more secure surroundings.

Meanwhile Ailsa was heading steadily towards the forest. In her little sack she carried some oat bread and sheep-cheese curds. She was never bothered by the varied weather. Her acceptance of whatever the Western Scottish climate chose to throw at her was like her inability to speak, an inconvenience but never a hindrance.

Ailsa tongue may have been stilled but her active mind and imagination more than made up for it. As she climbed up and away from the village she thought of her own family, a bit like the wolf pack, although she felt more like a solitary wildcat herself. She raised her little freckled face as she crossed the hills and gullies and in the wind and the rain she attempted to howl like a wolf, calling to her mother and father, telling her baby brother that she too is part of his family. Sometimes she thought she could make like a tiny sound like a kitten but although close she never quite managed it. Her heart raced with an inexpressible excitement as she thought of what she considered to be her wildlife. Her passion included the wind and the rain, the hills and the gullies, the rivers and bogs. All creatures, whether with fur and claw, fang or feather, moved her little heart to near ecstasy. Of all the sights and sounds of the wilds her greatest joy was the fleeting glimpse of a tawny tail slinking through the rough grass at the edge of the woodland.

Changes were seen in the sky. At first only small white clouds appeared on the horizon but as the breeze strengthened more and more of the blue was obscured. Soon the entire sky was painted in grey which darkened until it was almost black in places. The bright light faded and was replaced by an unsettling yellowish hue.

The she-wolf whimpered quietly, instinctively aware of this first change in the atmosphere. The others wolves were loping around in circles outside the den. Some of the animals appeared to be chasing their own tails while emitting short, sharp yips.

The deer had vanished as only deer can do, blending effortlessly into the shrubbery of the forest.

In the den in the hollow rock the mother wildcat was alert, head raised, whiskers fully extended, sensing the drop in the air pressure. Her kittens suckled and she allowed them to continue while she waited and watched to see what the storm would bring.

The light had diminished to a shadowless glimmer when the first crack of thunder shook the top of the highest hills. The wolf den registered the vibration first. The adult wolves all sought shelter and lay in various groups in the lee of the rocks. The Alpha-male stretched across the entrance to the den where the female lay with their pups. The next crack rent the atmosphere and reverberated all the way down through the rocky banks of the river.

The squall flattened the bracken to ground level. Ailsa ducked into the shadow of some overhanging rocks as the heavens opened and the downpour began. She considered making a dash for the woodland but remembered her father's warning of the danger of lightening striking trees which could fall on you. Ailsa pressed herself as far back into the hillside as she could allowing the wind and rain to blow over the top of the rocks. Unperturbed she started to eat her lunch while watching the sheets of violent rain sweeping as if in formation across the hills towards the river.

As time passed ground which had been dry became saturated, marshes turned into shallow lakes, gullies became ditches and horror of horrors, the high mountain loch spilled over. A torrent of water followed the path of the ancient glacier and swept down through the valleys sweeping all before it. Ailsa's eyes grew wide as she watched a raging stream materialise before her and start to steadily climb the hill towards her.

She was not alone as the wolf pack was experiencing exactly the same phenomenon. Never before had the den come under threat from the elements. The valleys had not filled up with flood water and never with speed like this. The older wolves had outrun flash floods before but no flood had ever consumed the hill tops. This one looked about to do exactly that.

The mother appeared at the mouth of the den, a tiny blind helpless pup in her jaws. She dropped it at her mate's feet, spun round and went back down into the den. She repeated this action four times, presenting a precious pup each time to an adult member of the pack. With the final pup in her mouth they all set off together, up and away from the rising water, the pups hanging limply from their rescuers' mouths. She looked back in time to see the murky water hiss and gurgle down into her dry clean home.

She scampered onwards following the pack which, led by her mate, carefully picked its way across the upper hillside towards safety.

The wildcat shepherded her babies into the back of the den, grateful for its upward slope away from the river. She positioned herself at the mouth of the cave ignoring the squeaks and squeals of the kittens. She peered down into the rising waters judging the point when she would flee upwards with her litter. The thunder of the waterfall now that the river was augmented many times over was deafening. Great chunks of soil and turf from the banks of the river along with saplings, dead wood and even rocks were hurtling over the drop and being swept downriver in a foaming mass. The cat did not panic but silently calculated the danger; better to flee or to remain. Her wise eyes and intelligent reckoning took in all aspects of the situation. The lives of her young depended on her decision. She still had time to get them all up onto the top of the cliff face but it would be so much better to be able to remain in the den and not have to face the unknown menace of being exposed to the storm.

Ailsa realised she had better get out from the underhanging rock face before the water reached her. She abandoned the remains of her lunch and scrambled up the loose stony surface at the side. Once at the summit of the rock face she lay on her front and leaning over the edge watched the water rising up and up and up even further towards her. Her former sheltered spot was rapidly engulfed. Realising she had no higher ground to retreat to she watched in fascinated horror as the flood rose to within an arm's length of her.

The wolf pack found itself in a different dilemma. There were several hills close by above water but to reach them they had to cross gullies which had become raging torrents. They pressed on and successfully negotiated the first two of these rifts but disaster struck on the third crossing. One of the adult daughters was swept off her feet by a violent surge of wind and water. Her small charge was ripped from her mouth, instantly vanishing down and away as she struggled to regain her footing. She was hopelessly gone.

The cat had discerned an almost imperceptible decrease in the noise from the river and began to consider that an evacuation of the den may not be necessary. She couldn't be absolutely sure of their safety so continued to monitor the situation closely.

Ailsa felt a growing acceptance as she lay watching the water. It was hypnotic. The movement of the current broken by the debris captured her whole attention. The logs and branches were becoming entwined as they travelled along. Rafts were forming and becoming snagged, holding up their progress. One particularly leafy one was swirling around, bouncing from one side of the flood to the other when Ailsa saw a small bedraggled grey creature, apparently drowned, splayed over one of the branches.

Ailsa leant over precariously and snatched at one of the outer branches of the raft as it drifted towards her. The twigs came away in her hand. The clump of vegetation looked as if it was beyond reach when suddenly a large log on the far side careened into it. The raft changed course. The little grey creature passed within reach. Like lightening Ailsa scooped her out of the deathly water.

Her eyes were closed, her breathing imperceptible, her limbs lifeless. She squeezed the water from off her body, unwittingly squeezing air back into her tiny lungs. After a few coughs and splutters she was obviously alive. She tucked her freezing body right into the inside of her shift next to her heart and although both human and wolf pup were wet their hearts beat in unison and their shared warmth saved both their lives.

The flood waters ran down and down, finding its own level as water does. Ailsa's village only got the rain. That was destructive enough but the neighbouring valley bore the brunt of the flash flood.

The two youngsters slept for a couple of hours then Ailsa was able to set off for home, her small charge snuggled safely in her warmth. The wolf pack had found shelter after a long trek which took them many miles from their old territory. Later that night, travelling through the miles of darkness, the mournful howl of the wolves could be faintly heard, calling to the little lost one to return to the pack. The mother cat remained safe and dry in her perfect choice of den.

As Ailsa neared home and walked the track to her washed-out settlement she began to anticipate the reaction of her parents to her rescue of the wolf pup. She knew they would be happy to see her alive and well and safely back home again but maybe not her new friend.

The pup was tucked into a bale of straw in the animal shed that night and Ailsa said nothing about her, anyway, how could she? Her welcome home was marked by such love, relief and gratitude that her mother failed to notice the extra mug of warm milk which disappeared out to the shed that evening. Ailsa was unaware of the drama about to take place in her glen.

Four tiny mouths sought the nipple of choice in the thick fur of the mother cat's belly. Four pairs of eyes were just beginning to open, little gleaming slits in their perfectly marked striped heads. Their whiskers sent sensory messages to tell them who was next to them and the butting of their siblings' heads already had established a pattern of domination. Little squeaks and squeals communicated, 'Me first', 'No, that teat is mine,' and 'Get your claw out of my face', but once all four kittens were in position and latched on, their mother could rest her powerful head, close her watchful eyes and enjoy the unrivalled pleasure of motherhood. Shortly her babies would require cleaning and grooming then she would get little rest as the four of them used her body as a safe warm playground. Once the ground above their heads had drained somewhat of the surface flood water and the vegetation had dripped and dried she would have to hunt again.

Back in the settlement the elders called a meeting. Not only the men were involved this time but in these extreme circumstances all men, women and children were included.

'Where's Ailsa now?' her dad inquired. 'Seriously we need a rope around that child.'

Morag told him she was fine, safe, strangely settled even after the Great Storm. 'She likes nothing better than playing in the animal shed.'

'Well that beats wolves for a change.' Rob managed a faint smile in his otherwise tense concerned face.' 'I will look in on her on the way past and let her know where we will be. Bring the baby Morag,'

His wife threw him a look as if to say, 'And I would be leaving without him?' but then she saw the amused glint in Rob's eyes. She couldn't help thinking how lucky she was to have him and the children despite the troubles in the world.

When Rob joined her in the meeting shelter which served as church and village hall he had a grim look on his face. 'What is the matter Rob? You look shocked. Is Ailsa alright?' she demanded rising from the bench to head for the shed.

Rob pulled her back. 'Ailsa is fine Lass. Leave her be. I'll tell you about it after we sort out this mess we are all in.'

It was a long difficult meeting. Almost everyone in the settlement bore the name of Cameron and was connected to one another by many family ties both close and distant. They were being cleared from their rented plots, their cattle were forfeit, their growing rigs for feed for animals and people were no longer viable. They needed a plan for survival but after much discussion it was evident that no one solution could save them as a community. It had come down to every family for itself.

'Whatever the outcome Rob, I want us to be with Shona, Dougie and the children.'

'I know. I want that too. Like us they have no other option but to head for the coast and see what we can sort out there. Half of us will be doing that, if not more. We don't have family in the south that would help us so it may be the boats for us.'

Morag's eyes filled with tears, 'Well, the landlords are willing to finance these voyages to heaven knows where. Just to get rid of us! At least it is an option,' she replied bravely.

'Yes I cannot believe they expect such wealth to come from these large sheep runs that they can afford to ship so many people out of Scotland. It is a mystery to the farming clans that it has come to this. I will collect you know who from the shed if you fold down her bed.'

Minutes later Rob appeared with a sleeping Ailsa in his arms. Morag doused the lamps and the little family were all in bed in their own home for almost the last time. Rob interrupted Morag who was lying in bed listing aloud the preparations they would have to make to leave. 'We have another little problem Morag. It's Ailsa.' Morag sat bolt upright, instantly alarmed. 'No no, lie back; it's not what you think.'

'Well what is it for goodness sake?'

'She has a new pet out there. She must have rescued it in the storm. She's actually taking good care of it.'

'A pet! What kind of a pet? Not another rabbit?'

'No, not a rabbit, a wolf.' That did it. Morag leapt up with a barely controlled shriek and Rob nearly laughed out loud. He pulled her back down. 'It's a tiny little pup, just a little helpless scrap of a thing. It hardly knows night from day. At this stage it is no threat.'

'Oh thank goodness for that. You gave me such a fright,' she said slapping at her husband. 'But how is she managing to take care of it?'

'Just like her mother takes care of her little brother I think.'

'Oh right,' said Morag thoughtfully then as realisation hit her she added, 'But she can't keep it.'

'Well no, hardly, although I did hear of a wolf pup growing up with a man up north and turning into a sort of wolf-collie.'

'Have you lost your mind Rob? There will be no tame wolf in this household. Anyway I was thinking about the boat. They will not let us on with any animals never mind a predator like a wolf. I expect they have their own wolves in Canada or wherever we end up.'

They both settled down but they were both thinking along the same lines… what further damage to their little daughter was about to be inflicted on her with the loss of her home and now her new friend?

The next morning Ailsa appeared in the cottage carrying her little treasure, now no longer a secret. Morag, normally soft hearted, pointed her finger out the door and said, 'Back to the shed.' Ailsa did an immediate about turn as she knew what was good for her. Shona arrived with the children and Calum announced he was going out to the shed to play with Ailsa and the pup. Morag said, 'Well, did everyone know about this except me?'

Shona laughed and replied, 'Don't worry, just us. Calum told us.'

Morag retorted, 'For a child who doesn't speak, our Ailsa doesn't keep a secret very well.'

'I've made a list of what we cannot part with. Somehow it will have to be packed and carried. We might get a cart or we might not,' said Shona. The two women got down to the practical plans for their exile while two children and one wolf pup cavorted, free of the cares of their changing world.

Only a few weeks had passed when the ultimatum was given. They had been fortunate to have had this time as many others had been cleared with no last minute notice. One more week and Rowan Glen would be cleared of people ready for flocks of sheep. All inhabitants were to be gone. Sheilings and byres will be torched. No exceptions.

Several times over the previous weeks Rob and Morag had discussed how to get rid of the pup. They had included their daughter in some of their talks but her distress was so evident that all ideas were shelved until later. There was so much to see to. There was no one to sell any of their meagre possessions to. Couples looked longingly at hand-crafted furniture, sheds of hay, half-grown calves. Women stuffed home-sewn quilts into cloth bags to take with them. 'My mother made this. My grandmother gave me this.' How can you part with what has made you who you are?

Time was running out. Morag told her husband, 'You have to deal with that animal now. We can't put it off any longer.' That was exactly what Rob had been doing, putting it off, putting off hurting his beloved little girl. 'What are you going to do Rob?'

'I can't kill it Morag. She would never forgive me and it might be one trauma too much for her', he replied through gritted teeth. 'I'm going to set it free.'

'I see, so you are going to kill it but just not in front of Ailsa. Let nature do the job for you.' Rob shrugged miserably. 'I don't know what else to do.' Morag nodded.

Rob spent a lot of time in the shed explaining to Ailsa how the best thing for her wolf would be to set her free in her own environment. Ailsa also spent a lot of time waving her arms in disagreement with her father. At seven, now nearly eight, she was extraordinarily intelligent. It was as if her inability to speak had imbued her with abilities and sensitivities unique to her. Suddenly a light came into her eyes and she jumped up and down with enthusiasm. Rob was delighted to see she had understood what was best for her little animal and he told he would take the wolf away in the morning. That did not go down well with Ailsa and after much pointing at herself, the pup and her father he was forced to agree that they would both take the wolf to set it free although he did have misgivings. As time was of the essence, action was all that left to them.

Ailsa knew the little female wolf was not weaned and would die alone in the wild. There was no way she was going to allow that to happen, no way at all. She had an idea. It was a risk but worth a try.

Most of the village's preparations were well under way. A couple of families had already left for Glasgow. They had been a simple people. They had lived their lives without excess and luxury; a pan for oatmeal, a spurtle to stir it, homemade broth thickened with barley from the rigs, soft cheeses from their milk, home spun clothing. Yes a simple hard industrious life.

Rob and Ailsa were ready to make the trek, the goal being to put the pup beyond the hands of man. A meal was packed. The baby wolf was struggling to get comfortable inside Ailsa's jacket. Rob was starting to doubt what he was doing but Morag reassured him. She did add a worried comment, 'You will be straight back, won't you?'

Rob kissed her forehead and said,' Just as fast as I can.'

Morag watched her husband and daughter go off on their mission of mercy if that is what it was. She knew it was all for her daughter's state of mind as that pup didn't stand a chance. It still needed a mother.

Not long after Rob and Ailsa's departure into the hills the much -feared Tacksmen arrived. The people were given two hours to leave. Morag's legs went weak under her. When she could breathe again she picked up baby Ian and went to Shona's cottage. Shona had turned pale at the news that Morag and the baby were on their own at a moment like this. 'I can't leave without them,' Morag sobbed.

Dougie replied, 'You can't stay Morag. It is more than your life's worth. She looked up at him in utter dismay. 'Listen, I am going to tell you this in order to save your life. These same Tacksmen cleared a valley in the East. There was an old woman over one hundred years old who was unable to flee. Knowing she was in the cottage they burned it around her. Some of the villagers tried to rescue her but even though they got her out she still died from her injuries.' Morag's eyes widened in complete horror. 'Now listen to me Girl. Your man is one of the smartest most resourceful men I have ever met. When he and Ailsa return and see the village torched and all of us gone they will follow on safely. He knows our plans. He knows where we'll be. Meanwhile take what you can. We will help you. We'll put off leaving until we have to go then we will travel slowly. They'll catch us up, you'll see.'

Morag left in a daze to do what she could. Within the two hours their little party, made up of Morag and her baby Ian, Shona, Dougie, Calum and their baby girl, had mounted the track and were heading west to wend their slow way towards the coast without a backwards glance. But Morag was praying.

Rob and Ailsa trekked for several hours up and away from the inhabited glens. The pup whimpered for its milk. Rob tried to ignore the pathetic sounds. He suggested that a copse ahead might be a good place for the pup to hide at which she vigorously shook her head pointing beyond these trees. Rob knew he had committed himself to this for his child's sake so despite his misgivings he continued on. Ailsa led the way. It became obvious to her dad that this was not aimless wandering. Ailsa had a destination in mind.

When they arrived at the river bank she forged ahead, Rob striding along to keep up. When they came to her play spot she sat down and pulled him down too. She started opening the lunch sack. As they ate Rob considered the situation. He knew the wolf pack had moved on. They were long gone so there was no hope of the pup joining her family. It didn't really matter to Rob now what would happen to the pup as long as Ailsa was safe and he could get his family to the coast. There the next round of decisions would be made.

Ailsa was watching the cliff face intently. Finally as if giving up on whatever it was she was looking for she stood up and pointed to the other side of the river. 'You want to go up there?' Rob asked. Ailsa gave a definite nod. 'You're sure? Here would be fine', he suggested. A shake of Ailsa's head and more pointing which was more like finger stabbing. 'Well', said her father, 'follow me. We will not be swimming the river then climbing those rocks. I know a better way.' He was hopeful that this was the end of the quest for a place for the wolf to live or die.

He led now. They worked their way above the waterfall. Further up there was a rocky causeway across the river and as the flood had long passed and the rainfall had been scant the water level was low enough to hop across the rocks. They crossed and walked back to the top of Ailsa's cliff. She peered over and Rob had to stop her when she appeared to be intending to climb down. She shook her head then lifted her small charge from her jacket, kissed the top of his little head, stared meaningfully into his brown eyes and lodged him in a grassy clump over the edge of the cliff. Rob was too anxious to get back to the settlement to tell Ailsa that her choice of place to abandon the pup to his fate was about the worst he could possibly imagine. The deed was done.

'Let's go sweetheart.' He gently led her away back upriver to retrace their steps home, if they still had a home that was. She skipped happily along beside him. He was puzzled. This was not the reaction he had been expecting at the parting.

Ailsa paused at the other side of the river facing the cliff. The pup was barely visible where she had left her. As she and her father walked away downstream she looked back just in time to see a tawny shape disappear into the cat den. It had something hanging limply in its jaws. Ailsa smiled.

The pall of smoke still hung over the village that night when Rob and Ailsa descended into the glen. They smelled the foul burnt scent of destruction before they saw it. In the half light they could see that the settlement was no more. Rowan Glen was deserted. The odour of burnt flesh from dead cattle stuck in their nostrils. Rob took hold of Ailsa and hoisted her onto his shoulders. Cutting through the destroyed rigs he headed up and away from yet another trauma in his daughter's life. They did not stop until the salt breeze from the sea cleansed the sad images from their minds and the sun was rising over a grey horizon. Families were spread out along the shore line in both directions as far as the eye could see. The lilting sound of their native Gaelic was carried in the wind. All were in the same situation. Ailsa thought it reminded her of the clan gatherings at the cattle markets but now minus the cattle. The shipping agents were setting up temporary offices, stalls actually. They were listing families who wished to sail and sorting out eligibility for the prepaid tickets provided by the various landlords. Dougie was dealing with the business but Morag was completely distracted. 'I left the glen without them but I won't be leaving Scotland without them!'

'Shush Morag,' Shona comforted her cousin. 'None of us are going anywhere until we are all together.' Morag had paced to the point of exhaustion and finally had slumped down leaning against some rocks.

'The agent says it will take at least a week to make all the arrangements so we are in no hurry now.' Morag held her baby close but as soon as her eyelids began to close they shot open again in panic. 'Will I be left to die on this shore I wonder?'

When the cat entered the den four kittens looked in wonder. There was a mutual wrinkling of noses at the strange smell. The cat dropped the tiny pup on the floor beside her even tinier kittens. The wolf pup attempted a hoarse little howl and the kittens fled behind their mother. She stared at the hungry pup and with a mother's sigh lay down beside him. After a little while the kittens advanced cautiously. They sensed it must be safe but there was much inspection; sniffing, pawing, and snuffling. If Ailsa could have looked into the den later she would have been overjoyed to see five baby animals nursing together in total contentment, but somehow, she knew.

Morag heard her name called. She thought she was dreaming at first. It was her Rob and her Ailsa back safely. She asked, 'What happened?' but Rob just gave her a look as if to say 'I'll tell you later'.

Rob told her he must find out what was going on there. He needed to talk to Dougie.

A week later the families were rowed out of the sea loch to the waiting ship 'Lochiel', named for their own chieftain of the Cameron Clan. This was the ship which was headed across the Atlantic Ocean to Nova Scotia, a new Scotland on the eastern seaboard of Canada.

High up in the hills a cat stood on the crest of a rocky hilltop which afforded a view all the way to the coast and out to the Western Isles. She could smell the sea on the wind. In the far distance a flotilla of small sailing ships was beating out to sea. The sails filled in the stiff breeze and the prows cut through the water with barely a heave.

On deck a little girl came running along with her cousin. She called 'Mummy, Mummy, look at the sun on the water. Look how it sparkles like stars!' Morag opened her arms and embraced her child, her Ailsa with a voice of her own once more, and also embraced the new life that awaited them in a new land.

Before the winter set in to the Scottish hills and glens a young female wolf was living in a variety of scrapes and hollows close to the top of a cliff near a waterfall. A young golden wolf came upon her one day and their approval of one another was self-evident. With much yipping and rolling and play-biting the two wolves ran off together into the woodland. A new alpha-pair had formed and with their offspring would form a new wolf pack. They would hunt the deer in this area permitting the new young trees to grow, the river bank to strengthen and a myriad of other plants and wildlife to thrive in the restored natural habitat.

The wildcat, now several years older but just as wise, could hear a new sound coming from where the humans lived and worked. She saw a different kind of wolf which lived under the leadership of men. They looked smaller to her than the wolves. They barked but did not howl. They lived with the men in their communities and worked alongside them.

Another strange creature was seen more and more by the cat. She felt disquiet at the proliferation of this malformed creature. She could see that it was covered in ugly matted wool which it never groomed and its bleating cries were an affront to a wildcat's sensitive ears. Their numbers were horrendous. She watched swelling flocks of sheep trample and eat their way over the lower slopes leaving nothing but coarse inedible plants behind. Still these grass-eating machines munched their way through the landscape. The cat had to flee the fires lit by the men to destroy the rejected plants and allow new sweet grass to regenerate the next spring. And still the sheep grazed on.

As she lay on her favourite lookout, stretching her muscled body in the morning sunlight, she was now familiar with the changes in the land below her. Gone were the bellowing, belching Highland cattle. For generations of wildcats, humans had fought one another in these lands; fought for domination of the best spots to settle, grow crops, breed both cattle and more humans. The clans, as they called themselves, meant families and they had been seldom at peace.

But now she heard the familiar scampering of padded feet approaching through the forest in pursuit of some deer. She climbed with her usual agility into the safety of the old oak tree and watched the scene replay before her eyes.

After the satiated wolves returned through her section of forest, the golden alpha male and his soft eyed alpha female turned their faces upwards and without enmity their eyes met the cat's stare. The female gave a short acknowledging yip as she passed beneath her bough. The wildcat mother remained impassively perched in the tree and listened to the howls of the wolves until they had vanished from the forest.

The ancient rock beneath her continued its slow and seemingly eternal journey across the surface of the planet, caught relentlessly in the continental drift. The land above was changed forever by the hand of man but her offspring and their offspring continued, a remnant, still silent, still illusive but still there.

From the Wildcat to Ziri

Imagine you are a bird of prey with a full-feathered wing span, floating on the thermals high above the ancient desert. All of Africa is spread below you. The Mediterranean Sea and Europe lie beyond you to the north and to the south the Sahara Desert bakes in the dry relentless heat. Movement below catches your constant watchful eye. Slowly, in ever-decreasing circles, you descend in search of carrion or prey.

The movement you spotted was around the tent of a Tuareg man of the Bedouin nation, head swathed in an intricate turban of blue cloth and loose flowing clothing. The Tuareg had inhabited this inhospitable world since prehistoric times. A similarly clad child burst from the round shelter made of skins and woven mats of fibre.

You hover unnoticed above the surface of the earth. You hear the unfamiliar sounds of the human habitation but the Tuareg language means nothing to you. You do share something in common with these people, these two-legged creatures, and that is the concept of complete freedom. You are a free bird of the air but these people are the free men of the desert. Neither of you are governed by boundaries of geography or of state. You fly where the wind takes you, a nomad of the skies. They sail the desert sands on the backs of their white camels, perched above the sands of time, as they have done for uncountable generations. You both struggle in search of food for yourself and for your young in an inhospitable environment but after all, isn't that life as it is known on this our planet Earth?

Each cat on his ledge strived with varying degrees of success to become the bird of prey and all the felines sank into the reverie of the unfamiliar sensations of height and flight while a tiny little female cat stepped forward to have her life reviewed before the others.

The Desert Sand Cat

1900

My name is Tiritziri, Ziri for short. I was named for the moonlight in which I was born and in which I lived my life. I am a sand cat of the African desert.

The scene unfolded and, as one, the observing cats found themselves stalking the stony desert floor surrounded by slowly shifting dunes, grain of sand by grain of sand, in the hot desert wind. It was dusk and the relief of the rapidly setting sun was the cue for small creatures to leave their dens and burrows in search of food. They hoped for some form of moisture, even if only condensation on the few plants able to survive the extremes of temperature.

A tiny black nose was barely visible sniffing the air above the entrance to the burrow and, satisfied that all was well, Ziri emerged quickly. She immediately ran, her belly close to the sand, away from her home. She did not want to attract unwanted attention to her carefully excavated shelter beneath the burning desert sands. She also wanted to keep moving as although the night-time chill was in sharp contrast to the heat of the day the sand took a long time to cool. She paused in the shadow of a crumbling rock formation and carefully groomed the tufts of fur between the pads of her feet. These clumps of fur were the protection her feet needed from being scorched and without them she would have been marooned in the furnace of the desert.

She lived a solitary life as sand cats do. Ziri had not yet mated and was still developing her independence from her mother and her litter-mates. She crouched in total stillness until an unsuspecting rodent passed in front of her and before the tiny creature could discern her presence its life was over. The warm blood of the spiny mouse was her sole drink for the night.

Ziri noticed that it was becoming less frequent that her razor-sharp front claws were finding the mammals she preferred. Cold-blooded lizards and snakes were more often her supper. They did make a change from the mice and jerboas, the gerbils and the jirds but she was roaming further and further afield each night in search of nourishment. Only once had she caught one of the desert birds. That lark had been a delicacy to Ziri but sadly its silence was a loss to that dry and dusty world.

The residents of Central Sahara in the country known by humans as Algeria tended to congregate in small areas made habitable by a water source and where sparse vegetation grew. There they found shelter also. The presence of certain species encouraged the arrival of others and so the cycle of life continued. This was what brought the boy and the sand cat into contact.

'Father, father, I saw a kitten behind the tent! Come and see. Over by the camels. Hurry.' Amalu's father was a marabout in the tribe. He was a leader and a teacher of the Koran to the children. His role was to be an example of his Islamic beliefs and an elder of the Tuareg people. Izem followed his excited son but as he expected there was nothing to be seen.

He laughed and explained to the disappointed boy that what he had seen was something very illusive, 'You are truly a shadow my son. You are well-named Amalu for the dark shapes that inhabit the night. You have been granted a special experience. Not many boys of your age have had the privilege of seeing the nocturnal desert sand cat. I too saw one as a boy around your age but have only rarely seen another. Treasure this night and remember it.' Izem returned to his work leaving the boy staring into the darkness. Amalu hung about for a while afterwards but he could not see any further movement, however, just outside his range of vision, a small creature sat watching. She had been enticed by a new and heady scent, meat cooking in a North African tagine, the stew pot of the Berbers.

It had been a long and very hot day. She had sheltered in an abandoned rodent burrow most of the time, still and motionless. Her scales blended with the colour of the sand. Her eyes remained closed but her body remained alert to any vibrations indicating an intruder to her place of rest. Her time had come. At sunset she left behind in the burrow a clutch of eggs, safe and cool in the dark of the tunnel. She needed to feed. Her nourishment had been used in the production of her many eggs and in the development of the young inside.

Her broad flat head pushed silently out into the cool night. Her round snout swayed as it tested the air. Above her eyes stood a pair of horns, the unmistakable mark of Cerestes, the desert horned viper. Carefully she slid out into the soft sand and, in her peculiar fashion, glided sideways without effort across the surface in search of a meal. More than one small mammal would meet its end that night as it crossed the path of this swift killer.

We do not know the workings of the mind of a venomous snake such as Cerestes. It travels where it will and eats whatever it can catch. It thrives in the difficult world of the Sahara and knows few enemies. It rules by fear, it procreates, it predates and it dominates. It does have one enemy however and soon there will be a confrontation as she has never before known.

In the meanwhile it had been a few days since Amalu had seen his sand cat but he could not shake the feeling that she was still nearby, too far away to see, crouched in the sand, watching, waiting, but for what? Ziri was indeed positioned outside the tented community of humans. This smell had permeated her nostrils and invaded her stomach so her gastric juices flowed copiously. How could humans turn raw flesh into this heady odour? Amalu wondered if this cat-like wild creature would like some goat meat so he had saved a scrap from his supper. Unbeknown to his parents he was at the edge of the camp throwing meat into the darkness. He had been doing this for several days now. Always it was gone when he checked but who knew what had actually eaten it? The next night he saw the movement and in a blur of feet and fur the scrap was taken. Success! Amalu was emboldened by this incident and each night it seemed as if the cat was more accepting of his presence.

Then one night as Amalu was in the act of feeding his new friend, as he considered Ziri to be, a shout startled both boy and cat. Ziri vanished instantly minus her supper and Amalu found himself caught up in his Father's arms. Izem was scolding the boy and hugging him at the same time. 'What are you doing son? What are you thinking of? You know well enough that the desert at night is a treacherous place full of deadly dangers to a boy like you.' He was still lecturing his son as he carried him into the tent and placed him at his mother's side. 'He is not to be allowed out after dark until he learns to obey and that is final'. Izem stormed out leaving a subdued Amalu and a very concerned mother.

Days passed and Amalu appeared to be a repentant little boy so his confinement was becoming less and less restrictive. Parents often misinterpret their offspring's intentions, imbuing them with more reason than is actually merited. He had been forbidden to feed Ziri any more goat meat under threat of having none for himself in his supper dish. Ziri of course was unaware of the feeding ban and still hovered in the darkness near the tents and within smelling distance of the cooking pot. Amalu had not disobeyed his father exactly but had now worked his way to the limit of his father's orders but was afraid to push the situation any further. He had spotted a movement just at the edge of his vision and was concentrating on trying to identify Ziri. He had not noticed the slightly rasping sound of the approach of the serpent and it was sidling in his direction. What took place next happened so rapidly that it is hard to describe. Amalu's mother had spotted her son sitting cross legged at the perimeter of the camp. She approached from behind and, when almost upon him, she spotted the tell-tale movement of the approaching snake. Before she could act the viper raised its head and opened its mouth revealing its deadly fangs, poised to strike the boy. His mother screamed, a blood curdling sound. Amalu turned and saw the snake. His eyes locked onto the two horns above its eyes. He was paralysed with fear. As the snake struck with a lightening movement a small creature shot out of the darkness and a fatal bite to the back of its slim neck severed its vertebrae and stopped the viper in mid-strike. Sharp claws slashed at the snake's head ensuring its certain death. Izem had heard his wife scream and was almost upon them when he saw a small sand cat leave the scene with a snake longer than itself dangling from its jaws. Amalu saw with amazement that the snake had eyes, now lifeless but very similar to the eyes of his rescuer. 'How bizarre!' he thought.

Amalu awoke to a flurry of activity in and around his tent. He could hear his mother's voice issuing instructions as to what was to be packed where and how and loaded onto which camels and donkeys. The boy emerged into the early morning light, the atmosphere still tinged with the remnant of cool night air and the last of the dew still glistening on the fabric of the dwellings. The entire community seemed to be in total disarray. The characteristic groaning protest of a camel could be heard above the morning clamour of an encampment on the move. 'Mother, what are you doing?' Amalu had to trot behind Kella to hear her reply.

'We are going to our Drum Group Festival. Do you remember? You were there before when you were much younger.' Amalu nodded having some vague memories of it. Seeing that it seemed to be a total decampment he began to suspect something that he did not want to happen.

'Why do we have to go?'

'Annual tribute to the Tuareg Elders,' was her brief reply as she passed carrying an armful of rugs.

'We will be coming back, won't we? Amalu of course had another agenda. He was thinking about Ziri who had been uppermost in his mind for a long time now but who had become even more important since his near-death experience. At this Kella stopped in her tracks and spoke gently.

'No son, we are moving on after the meeting to a better location. We have run out of water and food here. We are going to the southern oasis for the summer.'

Seeing the expression on Amalu's face she told him how there would be more of their people there and that he would meet up with his cousins. The little boy's face dropped. He was too young to understand the challenge that a nomadic life in the

Sahara Desert posed to his people. The need for sustenance for the humans, camels, donkeys and cattle, which were essential to their survival, constantly made relocation a necessity, like it or not. It was just how it was in a climate like that. 'And where is father?'

'Do you hear that camel? Well your father is helping deliver her calf'... but before she could say more Amalu raced off to find him. Kella shook her head and got on with the business in hand.

He got to the camel-holding just as a baby camel dropped to the ground, its pure white coat streaked with blood and mucous but bleating loudly in typical camel fashion. 'He's a strong one,' Izem said, his hands and arms still soaked in birthing fluids. 'We'll let him find his feet and have his first feed then we can load him up for the journey.'

Amalu looked at the leggy little dromedary, perfectly formed and already trying to stand. For the moment he forgot what he had come to ask his father. 'Come and we'll pack the tents now Amalu. We need to set off as soon as possible.'

'Father, where are we going? Is it far?

'Far enough son. It will take us three or four days to reach the meeting ground but we will rest in the heat of the midday sun and only travel early in the morning and then again later in the day.

Arriving back at the tent Amalu blurted out, 'I'm not going! I want to stay with my friend.' Izem and Kella exchanged glances.

'Don't be ridiculous Amalu. You can't stay here alone. Your father and I have no choice. We are obliged to pay our tribute to the Elders'

Izem cut in, 'But apart from that our survival depends on a fresh source of water. You know that surely?'

Amalu, now in tears he couldn't hold back, sobbed 'But she is my friend. She will come tonight and we will be gone. I can't go Father, I can't.'

Izem, despite realising his son was in crisis, spoke harshly,' That sand cat is not your friend. She is nothing more than a wild animal, a free spirit. She is not yours to domesticate.'

'But she saved me Father! You saw her kill that snake.'

'Yes I saw it.' Izem spoke more softly. 'But she was acting on instinct. She hunted that snake for food. She didn't kill it to help you. The snake's guard was down as it was preparing to attack you. That was nothing more than an easy kill for her. The only predator Cerestes has is the sand cat. You were so very fortunate that she spotted it and took it down just in time to save your life.' Amalu looked defiantly at his parents. 'Stop this nonsense now. Go and help load the donkeys. I don't want to hear another word about this,' and his father strode off shaking his head.

What a distressed little boy tied the bundles of bedding and household goods on to the donkeys! It took all his strength to tighten the straps which helped distract him from the departure. In a surprisingly short time the entire encampment had disappeared from the desert floor onto the backs of humans and animals and a long procession straggled across the rough, parched terrain. Amalu kept his eyes on the strangest sight immediately in front of him, a pure white woolly baby camel, perched on top of its mother, rocking gently as she walked. Its thick coat of wool was dry now and was there to protect its tender new-born skin from sunburn until it grew a tougher hair-covered hide. The unusual site of a baby camel tied onto its mother's back like baggage gave Amalu something to occupy his mind as they moved en route to somewhere else. He did not care where they were going. All he knew was that he was being taken away from his best friend. To Amalu, Ziri was truly that.

All morning they travelled in a slow but steady motion over the plains of yellow-brown sand. Mounds of bare rock interrupted the peaceful flow of the landscape from time to time. They caught the light as the sun rose higher in the sky causing strange fantasy shadows to be cast in ever changing shapes on the ground.

That night Ziri watched the sand blow gently over her front paws then trickle in a stream back onto the ground. A barely detectable tremor sent a constant cascade of sand back into the wind to try its luck on another surface or simply to blow in clouds across the face of the land. Fine as salt and formed from solid rock ejected in molten form from the earth's crust, it had been heated and cooled, also wind-eroded for over fifty million years. It now tried in vain to cover a sand cat's feet.

Mammalian squeaks, reptilian hisses and grunts travelled clearly in the cooling night air as the nocturnal creatures emerged from their burrows, from under rocks and from between stony ledges, all in search of sustenance and possibly a mate.

Ziri listened intently, then shaking her paws free of the encroaching sand she darted from her burrow in a surprising burst of speed. She had found this to be an effective tactic for emerging into the night-time scene. It startled the other creatures in the vicinity shocking them into unplanned movement thereby revealing their presence and location. Tiny although she was her skills as a predator were among the best. She was a swift, alert, cunning and successful hunter, a force to be reckoned with.

Her burrow had been excavated by a family of fennec foxes who had moved on. As canines and felines tend to avoid one another she rarely sighted the foxes. Tonight her keen hearing heard them barking but they were many miles away. However she headed off in the opposite direction.

She slowed to an investigative walk through a stone filled gully when a tiny movement startled her. It was an unpleasant resident of the rocky floor. When the scorpion raised its tail an almost imperceptible amount in self-defence, Ziri's finely tuned senses propelled her upwards and away. The death-stalker scorpion's translucent body was barely visible. It looked innocuous and fragile but Ziri had sensed its venom and murderous intent. She knew it was a threat to her life.

She hurried on. As she climbed out of the valley a loud scuttling sound distracted her. A monitor lizard, twice the size of herself, was crossing her path. She struck out with her claws extended but they skidded off the scales of the creature's tail. It did not stop to investigate which was fortunate as it is another of the Sahara's extremely venomous predators. Wild cats like Ziri sometimes successfully catch and kill monitors but they are fast and expert in climbing and hiding. This one did exactly that and disappeared up into a shrub clinging to the edge of the valley. Ziri did not give chase. She was returning to Amalu's camp. It would be supper time there, the meat would be roasting on the fires, the camel milk would be warming and all the humans would be occupied with the evening meal.

Ziri headed straight for the encampment. Strangely she was unable to smell the meat cooking but as the wind was blowing away from her she was not overly concerned and continued without distraction. She had been travelling for a considerable distance but when she emerged over the last of the sprawling foothills a cold and desolate sight met her eyes. 'They have gone!' Without a moment's hesitation her mind was made up. She followed the distinct trail of the missing humans, more by scent than by sight. Within her a feeling of desire drove her on and the longing was not just for a share of Amalu's goat meat.

Amalu's tribe moved slowly but steadily in two bursts each day with rest in between for food and sleep. Their pace was unvaried. The stride of a loaded, walking camel was their pace-maker and gently the desert caravan headed towards its destination. They followed invisible trails known to generations. Loading and unloading the animals, making camp for the night, cooking on an open fire was all a normal part of Bedouin life which had been lived in this manner for aeons of time. Amalu was by nature a product of his nomadic culture. He had adjusted well to the journey, all except for one thing.

It had been three days since they had moved on. Amalu scoured the route behind them each night, searching for that familiar flash of fur but he saw nothing. His hope of ever seeing Ziri again was fading and for the first time in his young life he felt pangs of longing. Never before had he desperately wanted something this badly. Up until now his every need had been met. He had security. His family loved and cared for him. He had been carefree but not any more. The reality was that he was growing up and was no longer a little child. He was moving on with life and experiencing the challenges that reality brings to everyone and all because of one little sand cat.

Ziri caught up with the caravan as they were breaking camp on the morning of the fourth day of travel for the humans. She had taken one single night to equal three days of their migration. Unseen she circled the bustling group to ensure that the one that she searched for was there. When she saw him she backed away and blended into the early morning light, her coat matching the colour of the dawn desert floor. She waited and watched. The only tell-tale sign of her presence was restlessness in the animals as their heightened senses of smell and defensive intuition detected the interest of a predator. Ziri remained out of sight.

Kella spoke to her son in the hope of lifting his spirits. 'This is our last day of travel Amalu. We should be there by nightfall. You'll find lots to do, things to interest a boy of your age so cheer up. The journey has gone very well.' Amalu forced a weak smile for his mother's sake but couldn't bring himself to reply. It seemed a bleak prospect to the boy. He would have been reacting very differently had he been gifted with the animal's instinct. Had he known Ziri was at that moment navigating her way around them it would have been a different story.

The leaders were starting to break free of the mass of animals. All were beginning to follow, camels, donkeys, goats, cattle and a heavy-hearted Amalu. Ziri had found a shallow hole and was sheltering inside. She had no need to follow the caravan in the hot bright daylight. She knew it would not take her long to catch up with them by nightfall so she curled her tail around her body, tucked her head in, closed her eyes and relaxed after her long night of pursuit.

Daylight was fading when a set of twitching whiskers extended themselves from the hole in the ground. Only a short distance away a well camouflaged little lark was perched low down on some scrubby shrubs. Ziri froze, her eyes locked onto what could be her supper. She noticed an increase in vegetation in this area. Obviously some rainfall had enabled these hardy plants to sprout from the seeds, dormant in the sand for a very long time. Where there was vegetation there was life.

Ziri flattened her already low-slung body to the ground. She made no sudden or unnecessary movements but somehow the distance between her and the lark was melting away. Her eyes remained fixed and all her senses were focussed on the little bird. It was preening its dust coloured plumage and as it inserted its beak under one wing Ziri tensed to pounce. A split second before she covered the space between her and her meal a large bird swept over her with a rush of air. Her fur stood on end. In the blink of a cat's eye, the lark was hanging lifeless from the talons of a hawk. It soared skywards leaving a bewildered Ziri. She watched it go. She got to her feet, stretched and shook her body and head. Although frustrated by the loss of the bird she was also grateful that the hawk had taken the lark and not her. Without supper she set off briskly. She had a trail to follow. As the sun dropped below the horizon she was already in pursuit of the caravan.

'Not far to go now Amalu. We'll be there before dark. We'll not eat until nightfall. We are arriving just in time for the start of Ramadan.' Kella was glad the exhausting trip was nearing its end. 'I shall see my sisters and their children again. It's been a while.' She daydreamed for the rest of the trip. Amalu fretted.

Izem was at the front of the procession plodding along step by step towards their destination. A low lying series of hills was all that was between the caravan and the site of the gathering. Kella and Amalu were near the rear of the straggling company when shouts and some kind of commotion started at the front. Izem had rounded the last of the hills and a horrendous sight met his eyes accompanied by terrible sounds which the wind had carried away from them.

The encampment was laid waste. Fires burned where fires should not be, animals were running loose in all directions, women and children were screaming and the men were fighting off attackers from another tribe. Shots were being fired and the sacred start of the Festival of Ramadan was in ruins.

The leaders of Amalu's tribe tried to halt the caravan and turn it around but the momentum of such a large number of people and animals was impossible to stop. More and more of them emerged in full view of the assailants. It took only a little time for the realisation of the danger they were travelling into to become evident. By the time Amalu and Kella could see the chaos before them the new arrivals had been spotted.

Izem had ridden back to warn his wife to flee back into the hills but when the leaders shouted the call to fight Izem rode back to take his place with the marabouts of his tribe.

With war cries a large band had broken away from the site and were advancing at speed, scimitars drawn, multi-pronged spikes held before them, clubs, axes and maces brandished in their hands. Izem's band was sorely under-armed, outnumbered and without choice but to defend themselves the best they could.

The air was filled with the cries of the already wounded, the loud harsh calls of terrified camels and the bleating of goats. Amalu's camel panicked along with the others and he was thrown to the ground. Kella was swept away in a stampede of animals and people but she managed to turn around and shout one last thing to her son, 'Run Amalu, run and do not stop', and with that she was gone.

So Amalu picked himself up and ran as he had never run before. He left the trail they had come on and headed up into the hills. He ran and ran and ran, the sound of the tribal warfare fading behind him. Finally he could run no more so he walked but the light was fading fast. What should he do now? What could he do? He was totally alone in a dangerous desert without food, water or his parents. He was lost, unable in the dark to even retrace his steps.

At the bottom of a small precipice he sat down amongst the rocks. He told himself there was no point in crying. He had to be a man now. There was no sleep for the boy at first. He had some shelter where he was but the rocks had lost their daytime warmth. He shivered and finally dozed fitfully. He did not know how long he had been there or how long it would be until dawn when a movement on the rock in front of him caught his eye. He blinked in wonder. Was he dreaming? There perched in front of him and looking intently at him was a small animal. In the starlight he recognised her. 'Ziri, it's you! It's really you.' He was cold and sore and unable to move. Ziri's instinct told her that her friend was in trouble and with a quick leap she landed beside him. What happened next was inexplicable. Izem would never have believed it. Ziri lay down with her warm body pressed against the boy's heart and for the rest of the night their two hearts beat as one. Amalu's survival was in Ziri's care and not for the first time either.

Morning came and Amalu was awakened by his small companion who stirred and stretched. With a small leap Ziri mounted the rock behind which they had sheltered and ran off. Amalu felt a moment of panic and struggled to get to his feet, his joints aching from his cramped uncomfortable night. He limped stiffly in the direction she had taken but it wasn't long before she appeared at his side again. Ziri took up the forward position and even though she scurried from side to side investigating the ground she did maintain a fairly direct course. Amalu had no choice but to follow. His mouth and throat were dry and he felt a thirst like never before. To his amazement in a very short distance Ziri led him to a hollow at the base of the rocky outcrop. There she dipped her head into a tiny pool of condensation and drank. Amalu willingly copied her action, grateful for the cool clear water. As the sun rose higher in the sky this source of moisture would evaporate and be gone but Ziri knew when it was available and now Amalu did also. He marvelled at how she could locate water in the Sahara.

It wasn't long before Amalu adapted to the lifestyle of a sand cat. He drank when she did. He slept when she slept. When she relieved herself he did likewise. Where she travelled, he followed. Often she got so far ahead that she disappeared from view but always she came back for him. Sometimes she returned with prey dangling from her mouth. At first Amalu could not adjust to eating raw flesh and it made him sick. Ziri however continued to present him with a share of her catch. Finally he was driven by hunger and weakness to join her. He drew the line at reptiles though and left them for Ziri's enjoyment.

Many days and nights passed in this way. Amalu was unable to keep a count. He was fighting rising panic that he would never find his family again and was destined to roam the desert alone with only the cat for company. Not that he was ungrateful for Ziri, the opposite actually. His dependence on her was total. She was saving his life. He loved her as only a boy can love, totally and unreservedly. Really he had loved her from his first glimpse of her which now seemed to have been a very long time ago, belonging to a different life. He trudged endlessly onwards. Sometimes he talked to her telling Ziri how much he needed to see his mother and father again. He feared that life as he had known it with his parents, his tribe, their noisy camels and other animals had gone forever. He did not know how he could bear it. More and more he kept his feelings to himself. Talking aloud to a sand cat is not terribly rewarding although she would sit with her head to one side as if listening intently to his conversation but her replies were sadly lacking.

If only Amalu could have known that Ziri was not leading him aimlessly across this terrain despite its unfamiliarity to them both. No, she was totally committed to following the trail of Amalu's tribe, at least those who had survived and had escaped from the confrontation at the gathering. Although Amalu was unaware of the signs of the passing of the humans Ziri was experienced in tracking them. Wasn't that how she had followed and caught up with Amalu's caravan and the hope of cooked meat again?

Why was this little wild and independent animal showing such dedication and patience in remaining with this slow youngster, a helpless and dependent human? Ziri was a young female. She had not yet mated nor had offspring but her hormones were awakening in preparation for such an event. Her maternal instinct was developing and already her instinct was to care for and protect her young. It was an unlikely relationship which flourished in the hostile environment of an arid desolate landscape but it was fulfilling to them both. In Amalu's case it made the difference between life and death.

Ziri was concerned that Amalu was weakening. He did seem to be losing heart at his situation. That night, after their evening trek, the two of them sat side by side as the light faded and the sky darkened. Together they watched the moonrise, yellow as it rose above the horizon, turning bright and white as it glistened above them. One by one and then thousand by thousand the stars appeared out of the black night, a magic carpet in the sky. Amalu's heart lifted. He loved his life. He loved his companion. Soon they settled down, warm and secure, and for the first time Amalu was without fear and anxiety. Neither was aware that this would be their last night together.

As morning approached the sky in the east began to brighten. The stars were vanishing, retreating into their daytime invisibility. Ziri was up and away before Amalu even opened his eyes. When he did and found himself alone he stretched in a cat-like fashion. Out of the corner of his eye he saw a flicker of movement in the rocks beside him. He stood stock-still. assessing the situation. A tiny mouse emerged into the open right at his feet. With a sudden movement Amalu lunged at the little creature. He wasn't fast enough to grasp its body but he caught it by the tail. Ziri arrived to find Amalu with a spiny mouse swinging from his hand. 'For you my friend,' he said and threw the mouse high in the air. Ziri shot upwards and performed one of her acrobatic leaps trapping the condemned mouse in her forepaws. On landing she looked briefly at Amalu who was laughing aloud at the irony of his catching mice for Ziri. She quickly polished off her unexpected gift and Amalu wondered if he was becoming more cat than boy.

Ziri was anxious to get moving. She could smell moisture ahead. It was almost midday when they stopped to rest. That was when she spotted a cluster of clouds on the far horizon. Later in the afternoon she set off at a furious pace. Amalu struggled to keep up.

At the southern oasis the survivors of the Ramadan attack were settling in for a stay of several months. Their gathering had been postponed until later in the summer. They had been travelling with wounded and had tried to round up stray animals on the way. Kella had been distraught. She had last seen her son fleeing the scene of carnage but he had never returned. Izem had been wounded in the fight but not fatally however he had been completely unable to form a search party to look for Amalu. What pain they were both suffering but they had no option but to carry on with their own group and with their surviving tribe to their planned summer destination. Such was the way of the desert nomads. Kella prayed that Amalu, if he had survived, would remember that the southern oasis was to be their next settlement. 'If only he is still alive,' was her constant hope.

They had established as permanent a camp as they ever made. The oasis offered shade and water. Fresh dates were plentiful and the ever-present cloud of condensation washed the area with regular precipitation and dew. The vegetation was moisture laden. Their animals were content. Quite a few had tracked them to the oasis after they had been scattered.

For a considerable distance Ziri had led Amalu towards the oasis. He did not realise how close they were getting or even that they were travelling in the right direction. It was early evening and usually time to stop for the night but Ziri was determined that Amalu would keep moving. He was starting to complain that this was turning into a very long day. He did not expect an answer. Ziri scampered relentlessly on.

Before the sun dipped below the horizon Amalu spotted something unusual ahead. He couldn't hear the sounds indicating human activity but Ziri had been detecting them for some time. He couldn't decide what it was ahead and he didn't dare hope. The strange cloud which had formed over the one spot was now lit up with a fiery orange glow from the setting sun while the rest of the sky was darkening. Amalu did not yet understand what he was seeing.

Obviously there was to be no rest for Amalu now. With a quickened step he followed Ziri as she forged ahead going directly towards the golden glow in the sky. About the time that Amalu started to hear sounds that he recognised as normal evening activity in an encampment he saw what he feared was a mirage. Often he had seen the tricks of the light the sun played creating false pools of shimmering water which one could never reach.

This was different; greenery, trees, tents, camels. He felt indescribable relief but then he was convulsed with anxiety. Were they here, his parents? Were they alive? The thought of being alone without them almost made his knees buckle. Ziri led him to the top of the sand-dune closest to the camp. The light had faded and Amalu could see the reflected flames from the cooking fires flickering on the faces of the people.

Amalu skidded down the slope towards the settlement. Kella had left Izem resting in their tent and was walking towards where the desert met the oasis. A mother's instinct is a powerful force and hard to explain but she was there and saw him coming down the dune, staggering towards her, calling for her. For an instant she thought she was dreaming. They fell into one another's arms while Ziri backed cautiously down behind the top of the dune with only her ears visible.

When Amalu arrived at his father's side there was another joyful reunion as his father praised Allah for returning his son to him unscathed. Kella placed a bowl of supper in Amalu's hands and he immediately shot out of the tent and back towards the blackness of the desert night. His parent's protests went unheeded.

Ziri descended to meet Amalu. She ate the meat, he ate the rest and they both lapped the juices, a sharing just as they had done throughout their long trek.

Ziri had mothered her first unconventional young, a human boy, but now she had to return to the wild. It was time. Amalu recognised the significance of this final meal together. He watched her scramble back up through the shifting sand and disappear into the night.

Neither boy nor cat ever knew any more about one another's lives. Thanks to her, Amalu had lived. He grew to become a tribal leader who had a great compassion for all the creatures that shared his desert home although there never was another sand cat in his life. His work in conservation of his African desert environment reached international status and was the source of much information for environmental protection agencies. His relationship with Ziri had been motivated by a boy's love for an animal and then by his need for survival in a hostile environment.

Ziri traversed the great Sahara Desert travelling immeasurable distances by night. She crossed from the Algerian region all the way to the Egyptian boundary at the Red Sea. She mated many times and raised plentiful offspring. She never again ate cooked meat from the stew pots of humans nor did she have further contact with people. She was always true to her name, Tiritziri meaning moonlight.

From Ziri to Anouk

Ziri scrambled back up to take her place. Her life in the desert was unique in the group and although it had all been quite normal to her it had been a very different story to the others. The cats so far had lived in a specific time when things were changing and evolving upon the earth but Ziri's life had a timelessness about it which was strangely comforting.

The voice was heard calling cat number eight to stand before the others. ''My friends this has been a night of revelation and adventure. Seven of you have shared your past life. We have travelled over oceans and spanned continents and aeons of time but we have two more cats remaining before our night's work is done. Anouk, will you take your place for your life-story.'

From the shadows a cat of no particular colour or description emerged, her small head raised in an attitude of intelligence and interest. The scene before the cats faded while another came into view and what a beautiful tranquil scene it was, or rather, seemed to be.

The French Farmhouse Cat

Pas de Calais
1917

It was at the beginning of the year when Anouk made her early arrival onto the farm. It was cold. The farmhouse nestled in a rolling green sea of gentle fields set amidst patches of mature woodland. There was an air of permanence rather than of progress here. Modern was not a word to describe life in northern rural France. Each stone of the farmhouse walls told of its agelessness. The moss and lichen on its roof especially echoed the sense of changelessness. No one knew exactly how many cats lived on the farm. It really did not matter.

In the shed attached directly to the house new life had put in an appearance during the night along with the snow. Anouk's mother had chosen the best possible location in which a cat could give birth. There existed a farmyard hierarchy. The chosen few lived in the farmhouse itself availing themselves of the ever-warm wood burning range in the spacious kitchen. These tended to be elderly long-time residents of this farm. The busy kitchen of a working farm was no place for a litter of tiny kittens. At the opposite end of the pecking order were the stable cats and the hay barn crew all of whom had to eke out an existence in the hayloft and dine on live vermin washed down with fresh warm milk twice a day. Then there were the cats in the middle so to speak and Anouk's mother was one of them. They resided in the warm sheds and fed on a mix of kitchen scraps and local wildlife. They inhabited the best of both worlds.

The night that Anouk slipped damply into the world along with a bunch of siblings was especially unpleasant outside but deliciously comfortable inside. She was ensconced in a pile of dry sacks against the shed wall backing the kitchen range next door.

Anouk was born neither first nor last. She was not the heaviest or the lightest. The teat she first latched onto and claimed for herself was not at one end or the other but in the middle of her mother's soft warm belly. Her first few days and nights were one contented, milky, cosy, safe, unconcerned round.

Her mother knew that sadly life would not continue in this vein for a French farmhouse cat, not when it was 1917 in Arras and two armies were dug into their trenches not far away, preparing for one of the Great War's most significant offensives.

Anouk's eyes were not yet opened when the peace of the French countryside was shattered by sporadic artillery firing which went on day and night. The shelling was close by and so intense that it reverberated through the land itself. However the banging was well muffled and as it appeared to have nothing to do with the birthing shed and had no apparent effect on her mother Anouk accepted it as a normal aspect of life.

The mother cat was committed to the protection of her offspring while she was able to keep them close to her. She knew that, one day in the not too distant future, they would grow and go away because that is what children do. She was not new to this mothering. For now she barely stirred during this offensive outside. Anouk was still sightless and her little ears were well insulated by the fur of her mother's underside to which it seemed as if she was permanently attached. Her siblings bodies piled upon hers were indistinguishable from her own and acted as ear plugs while the shelling shattered the peaceful countryside. How safe she felt with her mother's tail curled protectively around her and her face buried in a tangle of little legs.

Yes, it was an accepted situation for those who knew no better and had no choice anyway. Anouk was in the middle of a war which would be called, with hindsight, the Great War but may have been more accurately termed the Dreadful War.

Several weeks passed and Anouk was weaned from mother's milk to cow's milk but her preference was for the sheep's milk with its creamy taste and fatty texture. It had a richness and provided a delicate cheese. She would eat the cheese whenever she could access the unwanted crumbs. Her mother had provided small portions of rodent flesh followed by larger still-to-be-skinned helpings and then came the day when Anouk and her siblings were introduced to and encouraged to chase live creatures. Eventually she got the hang of the cornering manoeuvre followed by the crouch and pounce and caught her own prey. Although the taste was strong and bloody she quickly acquired a tolerance for it, dormice being a speciality.

The farm was in an out of the way part of the countryside. Anouk started setting out in mini-explorations. She soon had completed her inspection of the farmyard, the barn, the stables, the rooftops, proving she was an adventurous even fearless young thing. The fields, the young sprouting crops, the livestock, were all soon within her range. She noted the arrival of lambs and calves and spent a night watching the birth of a foal in the stable. She had grown effortlessly into a fully fledged farmhouse cat.

To Anouk the farmer was an old man. Truthfully he had been old for a very long time, just like his father and grandfather before him. The terrain outside his valley seemed to be in continuous flux; floods, droughts, lightening followed by fires, man-made disasters like war with its accompanying destruction of every living thing in its path. Stability and safety came and went as did his routes into Arras to market. However the war, which raged all around him, only did exactly that, it raged.

Now the time had come to discover the rest of the world. Anouk's limbs had grown sturdy, her back strong, her tail mobile, and with twitching whiskers she left home never to return. It was the way of the cat. Some stayed. Some went. A cat like Anouk could never have been one who stayed.

No through roads ran close to the farm. Really no roads at all went anywhere near it. Anouk soon discovered for herself that the farm was serviced by a handful of cart tracks, most of which were impassable at any one time due to flood and mud, fallen trees and also due to other acts of nature assisted by some farm animals and wild boar who dug and trampled their way across the farmland with no regard for cart tracks and their boundaries. They were no obstacle to Anouk who leapt, scrambled, even waded her way in any direction she chose. Unusual for a cat but she seemed to be oblivious to a wet belly.

Anouk looked in wonder at the lie of the land surrounding her place of birth. She saw that it lay in an inaccessible cul-de-sac shaped by the meeting of three rounded hills which gave pasture to sheep and cows on the lower slopes. This was a pleasant valley but Anouk was still to find out that erosion on the far side of these hills had caused steep-sided rocky slopes to form which continually broke apart and crumbled into smaller rocks. Neither man nor beast could mount these jagged piles without damage to hoof and paw and ankle. The way in to the valley, or what could have been the way in, was protected by a river which Anouk found out could not easily be forded. In some places it was deep, in others shallow, and there was no indication of which was which as it ran in spate constantly whether in flood or drought. An enthusiastic fresh water spring contributed to the run off from the three hills.

A tangled woodland straggled beside the river. Because of sporadic human neglect it was impenetrable due to a thicket of brambles, briars, nettles and ivy with stems as thick as tree trunks,

Somehow it had succeeded in making the transition to the other side of the stream in several of the narrower places making access to the farm more trouble than it was worth. Yes, the world outside was always a distance away but not for an agile, curious, determined little cat.

It was almost April but the spring weather had suffered a severe interruption. Cold winds had swept across the countryside every few days bringing flurries of snow and freezing the animals' drinking water.

Anouk had travelled in roughly a straight line from her home. She had tackled all kinds of terrain and had exited the valley up and over the top. She had descended to the outside world in a sure-footed manner down the rocky slopes. This had given her the opportunity to sample a bit of everything. However now it was snowing and this was not what she was expecting as the milder weather had already arrived and the singing of the birds had heralded the breeding season in the countryside.

Anouk felt drawn to an area west of her origins. Her curiosity was aroused. She could hear a constant buzz of activity ahead of her. The strange sounds which had accompanied her birthing had never ceased for long. They were concentrated in bursts but as they had featured all of her life she was unconcerned. Later she was to discover that many birds and animals were terrified by this type of noise while others, like herself and many dogs and horses, were stoically unmoved by the sound of gunfire.

But this was not what attracted Anouk. It was the human voices. They shouted, chattered, laughed, sobbed and murmured in a new tongue, unlike the speech of the humans on the farm. There was a gentle cadence in their tone, a lilting almost musical burr in their speech. Anouk was hearing the accents of the Scottish soldiers of the Royal Scots Regiments. She had been listening to it for many miles, letting it soak into her, strangely enjoying it.

But now was the time for action on Anouk's part. The snow grew deeper around her and she began to feel threatened by the cold taking over her body. She headed at full speed for the friendly voices ahead. Just then a piercing whistling sound came flying through the air towards her followed by the loudest bang she had ever heard. The ground shook. She threw herself down and fell headlong into her first military trench.

A muffled burst of laughter greeted Anouk's plunge to the bottom of a six foot trench manned by the British Forces in a field in France. 'That was a close one lass,' said a friendly voice while another added,

'We thought you were a chunk of shrapnel hurtling down on us there.'

'What was it?' another young man's voice inquired. The first soldier said,

'Well it seems to be another soldier's little furry friend,' and Anouk felt herself lifted from the frozen floor to the warmth inside the soldier's jacket. And so she passed her first night in relative safety and comfort although none of the boys and men trapped in a wartime stalemate in unbearable conditions would have shared her opinion.

All was quiet the next morning. The temperature was rising. The late snowfall was not going to lie and the frozen floor of the trench was becoming slick with mud again. 'There you go wee lassie', said the soldier putting her down. 'Mind how you go.' Anouk looked around her and as she set off decisively a voice called after her, 'Catch lots of rats for me.'

Anouk fluffed up her thick grey coat and set off to explore this whole new world. This was where she left her kittenhood behind. These fighting men over the years that Germany had been at war with the French, the British and the Russians, labelled the Triple Entente, had excavated a network of ditches which ran from Belgium to the border of Switzerland. The trench was a place of cover from enemy fire, a place to more safely return that fire but it could never ever be described as home. In them these soldiers lived and fought and died. For Anouk this discovery was one of wondrous curiosity, a cat's delight; roofless tunnels across the tortured countryside, starlit by night, infested with edible vermin and full of sad exhausted humans. The men seemed to be more than willing to share a bite with sweet-faced little Anouk in exchange for the touch of a warm living creature who was never meant to be a part of this soul-destroying conflict.

One of the engrossing features of the design of these trenches to a cat was that they never ran straight for more than a few feet. Then the entire system would dogleg preventing the spread of the blast of any direct hit into the trench. To Anouk, every few feet, an entire new world would open up just waiting for her to discover.

Anouk found that she could easily scramble to the top of the walls. They were firmly constructed with rudimentary materials. Roughly chopped tree trunks and strong branches were the posts and pretty well anything formed the walls, planks, sheets of wood, brush and twigs from the woodlands. Construction like this was akin to a network of ladders placed conveniently for a feline. Along the top were layers of sandbags designed to absorb and deflect any near hits. The men would create small spaces in this line of defence through which they could keep watch and insert their rifles to return fire. Anouk took to running across the top of these sandbags at full speed much to the mixed horror and amusement of the men. 'There she goes again. Well seen you cats have nine lives', was often shouted after her as she raced over the top.

Anouk was not alone in her friendly occupation of this line of defence. There were other cats which had likewise discovered the dubious attraction of trench warfare. A hierarchy similar to the one in the farmyard prevailed. There were cat fights over territory, matings, night-time conferences, some unmelodious nocturnal singing and one could say that life carried on in an almost normal fashion.

Sadly many awful sights greeted Anouk. Even sadder was that she became accustomed to death and injury. The suffering and pain of the humans was a daily presence. It was not for a cat to wonder at such behaviour or the why or the wherefore.

Anouk dispatched as many rats as she could and her contribution consisted of offering the rodent corpses to selected personnel who through them by the tail up and over the top for the enemy. Anouk sometimes participated in this game and retrieved them for the soldiers to throw again much to everyone's slight horror but it gave the men a laugh too.

This was not her only contribution to their shared life. She would curl up in the dugouts next to lonely lads and watch with interest while they did what they did to pass the long uncomfortable hours, days, weeks, months and years of this war. They read and wrote letters, scoured any newspapers that were sent to them. They smoked, laughed, cried, played cards, sang songs from their faraway homes all closely observed by Anouk. They were all in it together and had befriended one another in a way that would never be equalled again in their lives and Anouk was a part of it. Anouk was not ready to settle down in one corner yet. Little did she know that she had a massive journey ahead of her before that time would come.

It was almost sunset the night that Anouk went up and over the top. She sure-footedly ran out into what was called no man's land. It formed the separation zone between the opposing armies' lines. It was a desolate, blackened strip, a no-go area for neither man nor beast, not if you wanted to survive that is. Both sides kept a vigilant watch in case the enemy crept up on them for a surprise attack. Two of the British sentries saw her go and watched through one of the rifles with a telescopic sight and the other through his binoculars in concern for what might happen. No man's land at that point was not terribly wide, the enemy being too close for comfort. Even to fearless capable Anouk it can seem a very long way when you are navigating around stakes with barbed wire, shell craters, mud and sludge. One of her guardian soldier friends muttered that if some loony Hun took a pot shot at her he would personally go over there and annihilate him.

The tension increased. Facing out across no man's land were two German sentries, the counterpart of the two Scots lads on the British side. All four saw the grey shape tracking across the divide and the Germans were immediately on the alert. One of the Germans said. ''I bet I can hit that!' and levelled his rifle in Anouk's direction. When the other soldier realised what his comrade intended to do he lunged at him just as he pulled the trigger. The shot went wild and harmlessly added to the scrap metal collecting amongst the wire. A vicious exchange ensued. 'What did you do that for?' demanded the furious soldier. 'It's only a poxy French farmhouse cat.'

His comrade hissed in return, 'And I'm only a poxy German farmhouse boy'. The first soldier backed down when he saw the determined gleam in the other's eyes and anyway there may have been issues over wasting ammunition on harmless animals. The British soldiers held their fire in fear of hitting Anouk who had disappeared in the failing light. Meanwhile Anouk slipped safely into their defences and explored down the line.

The Germans held the high ground. This was why the Entente forces had been unable to move the German line back. Neither side had been able to break through. Behind a row of small hillocks the German command had set up a tent as a base. The following morning the German officer in charge stared in amazement as a little grey cat emerged from his dress Picklehause pointed helmet, stretched her limbs and trotted off as carefree as ever.

It did not take Anouk long to realise that the rats, the food, the conditions, even the friendly soldiers were just the same as she was accustomed to on the other side so she skittered back across to the British side in pursuit of a big tabby she had encountered at the edge of the German side of no man's land.

It was the first week in April. Anouk and the many other cats occupying the trenches were unfazed by the concentrated artillery bombardment. Anouk knew about these large weapons which were spread out some distance behind the lines. When it was sunny and all was quiet she would stretch along the warm gun metal and absorb the rays of the sun from above and below. She had learned not to approach when the guns were discharging but as with all the war-zone cats she was oblivious to the thunderous noise and showed only caution, not fear.

Anouk had noticed the build up of soldiers as more and more Scotsmen arrived on the scene, lorry loads of them. She made a point of greeting the newcomers.

For four days and four nights the Entente artillery slammed the German line along its length. They suffered great losses and what made matters even worse for the enemy was the loss of their wire, their line of communication. Their commanders were unable to control the remaining troops.

Anouk's main interest at this point was in developing routes which kept her out of the mud. The soldiers threw their hearts, bodies and minds into conquering the other side while the cats concentrated on staying clear of the cloying mud and on intensive grooming when spattered.

By April ninth the advance was announced. Anouk was happy to move on with her soldier friends. Where they went, she went. By bad luck the weather changed overnight. Anouk had to literally dig in to avoid the late spring snowstorm. It was a heavy one and the big guns were snowed in too far back to follow the attack of the foot soldiers and give them added support.

Anouk was not able to follow all the way as she ran out of mud protection. There were too many shell craters filled with muddy, slimy, blood-tinged water with nothing to climb up on. She turned back which was just as well. The German snipers seemed to be indefatigable also the gunners with machine-guns. Both took a huge number of men's lives but somehow the Scots pressed on in their strategically planned lines of attack. Soldiers were briefly relieved and rotated into Arras, or rather into what was still standing of the town. Anouk was happy to go with the men into town where they were given tea and biscuits and sometimes eggs and bacon which were a life-saving luxury. While advancing through this deathly battle they had subsisted only on a handful of biscuits.

Anouk discovered her old trench home was deserted and her army friends were a distance away. After the four days of fighting she and many other battle-ground cats traversed the scene of death and destruction to rejoin the men five miles ahead.

Perhaps because Anouk was feline through and through and perhaps because by nature she was a carnivore, killing was an essential for life itself so this bloody war did not distress her. Blood and entrails, whether from a man or a mouse, were in the grand scheme of things. As long as her little grey body remained intact she was unable to either mourn or sympathise. It was unlikely that many men were able to deal with it in such a fashion.

Acceptance was what she could offer. Her role was as friend of man. Food was shared, rodents were offered even if unwanted but it maintained a balance which enabled fighting men to find a small measure of comfort from a warm living creature which was not a part of this carnage. These soldiers lived in mud, breathed it, ate it, coughed it, spat it. Their world was all one colour. Or rather the world had become colourless but for the blue of the sky and the white of the clouds. There was not much opportunity for gazing skywards so the touch of a warm body was often the only comfort in a bleak and often hopeless and terminal situation.

Incidentally Anouk had no prejudice and fraternised freely with the German prisoners of war who numbered in the thousands. The Scots had won the battle but had lost so many thousands of their own. Anouk couldn't count. She spent her time with the living so her war experience was unlike anything any of the humans were going through, an enviable position.

Despite these murderous losses the Scots held onto their newly won ground but were unable to go any further. They had lost most of their officers and then the bad weather and bogged-down artillery all conspired to bring their advance to a grinding halt. All of this was commonplace opposition on the battlefields of France.

As the weather cleared and the mud solidified somewhat Anouk saw lorries taking men away. She watched with interest. There was an air of relief, even of joviality as they piled into the canvas covered vehicles. Her feline curiosity was going into high gear. As she peered up into one of the lorries she heard a familiar voice. She took one of her famous flying leaps and, unnoticed by the sergeant, landed aboard. She crouched down under the bench behind a soldier's feet. 'Hello cat', he said. 'You survived then. Me too. Let's get out of here while we can.' He was the man who had shared his jacket and his bodily warmth with a little gray French farmhouse cat during her first night in a trench in France.

And so the long journey began. It was to be a rough ride. Not just in the bone-shaking lorry from Arras to the coast of France but to their final destination.

The men of the Royal Scots Battalions were a sadly depleted group but this now was a journey of hope for these survivors. Many were sick from the unsanitary conditions in the trenches or mercifully recovering from these ailments. Trench fever and influenza had killed as many, if not more, than the battles. Anouk was impervious to these lice carrying illnesses and she brooked no lice in her clean fur. She also was spared the organ failure and bleeding of Weil 's disease caused by bacteria from the widespread rat infestation. This made the presence of Anouk and her kind worth their weight in gold. Many men were in a state of mild shell shock as if any such condition could ever be described as mild. They looked fit enough but inside these worn uniforms were the walking wounded, suffering indescribable horror from life-threatening shelling, another state that cats did not suffer from. Still, the sensation of relief that each mile of rough ill-used roadway was put between the soldiers and the front line induced nothing short of an exhausted euphoria.

Anouk could be said to have matured. She had undergone the transition from innocence to awareness, schooled in a blood-stained and disastrous war zone. She was no wildcat, never destined for a feral existence, although the next few months of her life were not exactly settled and domesticated. Now she had attached herself to an individual, a relationship by mutual consent.

'Heh Edward, that cat of yours is smart to get out of that hell-hole.' Edward smiled in his quiet way.

Another voice joined in, 'Yes we are all smart to be leaving that behind,' and a chorus of other young voices agreed. No one wanted to add that although travelling in relative safety now the war was far from over.

Edward had reached into his inside pocket and withdrawn a battered little photograph. He liked to look at it as he often did in less threatening moments. One of the very young lads asked, 'Is that your family?'

Edward nodded. 'My wife, Elizabeth, and my daughter, Jean, back in Glasgow.'

'It must be tough for you older blokes to leave your family behind like that.' There was a slight chuckle at the boy's tactless comment about Edward's obvious older age but it was true. He must have been 20 years older than many of them. He was obviously different from the rough and ready bunch. Anouk sensed that. 'How old is your little girl then?' the lad persisted.

'She is ten now'.

'So what made you join up?'

Another soldier gave the reply, 'Haven't you heard of the Military Service Act? It's been rounding up all types since last year.

Someone else said, 'From spring this year married men up to forty-one years are now conscripted.'

A strongly accented Glasgow voice commented. 'Aye, it's bad enough for oor mithers at hame without they lassies hame alone noo wi' nae menfolk.'

And still another voice was heard, 'But a harder time for us,' and a burst of laughter rose up from the lorry like sparks from a fire lighting up the sky with a fleeting flash of merriment.

The lad went on, 'Edward, not all that many older blokes are here. How come you got roped in?'

At this point, Anouk, who had been resting on the floor, oblivious to the jolts and shuddering, climbed onto the bench and inserted herself between Edward and a young soldier. Edward had a small smile playing about his mouth. 'Well, it was like this Tom. If you were physically fit but of little use to society the selection board chose you.'

'So?' Tom interjected.

Edward laughed and said, 'It was the golf that did it. '

'The golf?' asked Tom.

'Yes, the golf. I really haven't done much else.' Edward mused.

'So golf qualified you to carry a rifle, did it?' Another short burst of laughter was heard and Edward joined in. Anouk looked from face to face unable to understand what was funny but enjoying the light-hearted moment.

A little later a voice asked, 'Where are we going to now?'

The reply came, 'Does it really matter as long as it is away…'

The men and boys settled into companionable silence except for young Tom who stroked Anouk and made a final comment that she really was the most beautiful cat he had ever seen.

The Front Line lay to the north of the supply route that Anouk and Edward were following, heading towards the coast of the English Channel. It was a long, rough ride for battered men with battered minds and battered bodies. Anouk stretched her long lean body luxuriously and took the journey in her feline stride. She was a source of entertainment to some as she leapt from lap to lap, using the men as safe landing spots while she did the tour of the lorry. To others she was a source of comfort, men who just liked the soft warmth of her as she circled the group, a non-threatening silent contact with life itself. She was a friendly symbol of a better world away from the trenches and she represented their very survival.

Edward said very little but it was always to him that Anouk returned. Tom contributed the information that there was a cat in one of the other lorries also. Naturally, Anouk was well aware of this fact. The presence of another travelling feline was no surprise as it was estimated that over five hundred cats inhabited the front line over the course of the war. Anouk could not count but her estimate was, a lot. And they were fearless survival experts.

Anouk was continually aware of the direction in which they were heading. Inside her head was the equivalent of a little cat's compass; west now, turning south, generally travelling towards the unknown. Had it been required she could have retraced the journey on foot back to Arras and not by following the worn down roadways. Her senses would have taken her a much shorter and faster route, as the crow flies. However she had no interest in going back.

Now she could sense a change in the atmosphere. Perhaps a cat has a barometer built in as well as a compass. What it has taken millennia for man to invent the cat has always already had. The changes were not sudden but gently carried on the breeze, almost imperceptible, barely noticeable until a gust of wind would blast Anouk's highly developed senses into awareness.

Can you say that freshness has a smell or is it more of a feeling, a sensation? For Anouk this was followed by identifiable smells; salt water, fish, rotting seaweed, guano. The soldiers were unaware of the arrival of these new scents until they were almost at the coast. Anouk's sensitive whiskers could detect moisture in the air now. It wasn't rain. It felt to her as if minute droplets of salt water were suspended in the atmosphere and were being blown across the landscape on the onshore breeze. It was not an unpleasant sensation but when her fur began to feel a bit damp, even sticky; she had to indulge in a good shake.

Her keen hearing detected the screech of the seabirds from quite some distance. These sounds also rode the currents of air, enlivening the landscape with many voices calling 'We are here. You are not alone. Hear us as we fly.'

April showers gave way to mild May days. Edward's assignments took him gradually further south into the heart of France. Convoys of men and goods, weapons and ammunition, boots and uniforms, food and drink, all were constantly on the move. It was as if the countryside had come alive and the surface was a seething mass of ants on an anthill of wartime activity.

Summer advanced as if a war was nothing to even notice. The weather grew warmer then almost unpleasantly hot and when not on the move Anouk spent glorious afternoons sleeping in the sun. Lance Corporal Edward Macauley was never surprised when, without fail, Anouk would appear when they were loading up to move on. Edward was actually enjoying the varied work away from the horrors of the Front Line. He began to feel at home in the fertile countryside with its vineyards and olive groves while he marvelled at the soft cheeses made even from goat and sheep milk. This was a shared pleasure for Edward and Anouk who now could only vaguely associate it with her early farm life. He wondered aloud to Anouk that back in Scotland only the lambs got the ewe's milk.

As autumn reached south through the forests and fields of France Edward and Anouk were working in Marseille at the loading docks. Edward was responsible for the loading and unloading and onward transport of medical supplies and medical personnel. That was when Anouk developed a taste for a seafront French tomcat with which she was seen frequenting the docks at night.

News from the North trickled down. Sometimes it flowed like a river. Some of it was fresh, some stale, some rumour and some mere wishful thinking. Edward's fellow soldiers at the front line battled their way through that summer, driving the enemy further east beyond Ypres. Their goal was the Passchendaele Ridge from where there was hope of reaching the Belgian ports used by the Germans as a submarine base. Sadly it was easy for a cat to cross the lines but not an army. Anouk was unaware of the accounts of the strength of the German Fourth Army followed by the horror stories of weeks of relentless rain creating impassable mud. Then came the worst news of all, the terrible toll on the British Expeditionary Forces. Even the trench cats had evacuated the scene long before the end which left 300,000 British casualties. This news was not conjecture. The pressure on the medical supplies and personnel caused Edward's unit in Marseille to work around the clock.

It was into December before they got any leave but it wasn't possible to leave France. The war was everywhere. Edward hiked up away from the Cote d'Azur into the white hills beyond and lost himself in the peaceful mild winter wilderness. Of course he was not alone and a certain cat rediscovered her wildness where only goats climbed. Goatherd's huts provided shelter. Widows, not realising yet that they were, offered cheese, bread and milk desperately hoping that their counterparts in the North of France were doing the same for their husbands, brothers and sons. Anouk hunted.

Time passed unnoticed. Edward looked out from the rustic hillside hut in which he and Anouk had spent the night. They were surrounded by trees, a little green woodland on a rocky slope falling away towards the Mediterranean, and the war. 'Anouk, what day is it?' Anouk stood up and shook herself in reply. 'You have let me lose track of time. I have completely forgotten my return day!' Anouk who had been blissfully content in the hills looked up at Edward. He knew that he and Anouk had felt the same and probably Anouk knew also. With a sigh he packed his white canvas kit bag and the two of them headed reluctantly downhill.

As Edward entered the yard a sergeant–major's voice boomed out at him. Anouk fled. 'Lance-corporal Macauley, where the blazes do you think you've been? You are AWOL. Your unit was sent north to the front line the day before yesterday and they had to leave without you. What sort of example to your men do you think you are? You deserve to be demoted and locked up.' Edward said nothing. He wished he had stayed in the hills with Anouk. 'Soldier, get your kit. You are not hanging about here. How would you like to join the Bedfords and go fight the Ottoman Empire? Your ship docks tonight,' and with that he strode off leaving Edward feeling, well, he did not know exactly what he was feeling. Numb might be the best description; alone also.

Edward found Anouk curled up on his bed in the empty barracks. 'I need to talk to you young lady. I don't think you will like it in Palestine fighting the

Turks. You are, after all, a French cat. Maybe it will be for the best if you stay here.' Edward looked so sad, as sad as Anouk had ever seen him. 'I don't know what I will have to face out there. If something happens to me you will be all alone. You will not like it.' Anouk looked intently at Edward as if contemplating his every word. Then she washed. A couple of hours later she was seen standing on the dockside right beside Edward's kitbag. Her decision had been made.

The *Aragon* had been anchored off Marseille for a couple of weeks as she awaited her full complement of crew, soldiers and nurses. The quay had become a hive of activity. Anouk was dwarfed as the ship steamed ever so slowly into the quay and was nudged gently alongside by the pilot boat. Anouk's eyes widened in amazement. She had never been this close to an ocean liner before. She seemed so vast and solid with her huge hull and single funnel amidships. She had a comforting quality of solidity and permanence about her, an unsinkable aura. As Anouk scanned the *Aragon* from bow to stern, seeing things as only a cat can and process them, her little paws itched to go exploring.

The *Aragon* was no stranger to wartime manoeuvres. She had been to Gallipoli. In her civilian days she had plied the Atlantic between the UK and South America for many years. She had been hostess to many different ship's cats and seemed to welcome any feline who dared to board her.

There ensued a period of what seemed to be complete chaos but in reality was simply the normal hubbub of the crew of two hundred men loading her cargo and supplies, not to mention the troops themselves. Having been designed as a passenger liner it had not been difficult to convert the *Aragon* to a troopship and Edward was one of two thousand two hundred troops to board that evening along with one hundred and fifty officers, one hundred and sixty nurses plus one small cat of course. Anouk bounded up the steep gangplank one step ahead of Edward. Nobody noticed or if they did nobody cared.

Anouk could not hold still. When bag after bag of Christmas mail bound for the troops in the Middle East was swung aboard in huge nets and deposited in a vast hold Anouk was perched at the edge peering into the giant dark space below. That was earmarked for further investigation. Then as she was checking another hold she was covered in coal dust as the cranes dropped two thousand tons of fuel for the steam engines. She didn't stay long watching that operation. Next she supervised the gushing of seemingly endless gallons of water being pumped into the ship's water tanks. Anouk slunk back out of the path of the endless crew members who performed their tasks with practised precision. Finally with a blast of her horn the Aragon edged away from the quay and exited the Marseille docks, bound for her first stop on the Island Of Malta.

To this steam ship named for the Spanish Kingdom of Aragon, now known as *His Majesty's*

Troopship Aragon, the Mediterranean Sea was almost calm in comparison with the rolling Atlantic Ocean. Anouk peered between the guard rails and watched the foaming bow waves and observed the destroyers and one other troop ship travelling in convoy.

Anouk's world, instead of shrinking to the confines of one ship, proved to be a wondrous expansion. She had not generally strayed far from the port and the barracks in Marseille. Her strolls had covered a regular terrain which she had considered to be hers. Her path had crossed and overlapped with other cats, some friendly, some impassive, some antagonistic but it had been a fairly small cat's world. She had liked to return to Edward's bunk and not just for food as she had hunted aggressively and successfully. Wherever Edward lived was where Anouk lived also.

Edward and Anouk arrived in Malta in time for Christmas. The Port of Valetta was bustling with naval activity but the air was charged with something other than wartime activity. It was December 1917 and three years into the Great War. It was time for long-overdue festivities for weary soldiers, sailors and casualties. Apart from this Anouk was greeted by a horde of feral harbour cats. They made a good living around the docked ships. Further round the vast harbour were the feral fishing-boat cats. They preferred their fish freshly caught rather than cooked and the remains discarded in the bins. Neither man nor beast paid the slightest attention to the grey tabby that blatantly sat amidst the others and dived at the available food. Anouk felt a strange measure of satisfaction after such a meal.

That first night in Valetta the servicemen were drunk not only on beer and wine but on relief to be ashore, on being safe and on a general feeling that life was not so bad after all. Edward, not being a drinker, walked along the harbour front taking in the mild air, still balmy despite the season. In the darkness the island spread out to the north and west. To the east and south lay their final destination, Alexandria in Egypt. Edward thought he could enjoy a traveller's life. Pity about the war though. He wondered if Anouk might set up home here in this Mediterranean cat world. He thought if he were Anouk he might just do that.

Around midnight, as the celebrations were continuing noisily, further tumult arose at the invisible boundary between the harbour cats and the fishing-boat cats. The screeching and yowling could be heard over and above the singing. Anouk watched from the sidelines and then thought the feline equivalent of 'So what!' and joined in enthusiastically. Edward would not have believed that his little friend could muster such animalistic sounds but she had been a wartime, trench-cat after all. Much hissing and spitting ensued with an occasional raised claw but it was over rapidly and both gangs sat on the quay, in their own space of course, and proceeded to wash.

Anouk returned to the *Aragon.* She found Edward up on deck with some of the Bedfordshire

Regiment and the nurses of the Voluntary Aid Detachments. One of the nurses, Sophie, had taken a special liking to Anouk who was happy to be petted and cuddled but only by her. After a while they all became quiet and thoughtful and gazed up into the myriad of stars, each one thinking their own thoughts. Anouk was less concerned with the future and went to sleep at Edward's feet.

Christmas preparations were underway. The intention was that everyone should have a happy and relaxing time. For many this would be their last Christmas but no one knew that then. They maybe feared it but put the thought to the back of their minds for now.

Anouk had her own plans which didn't involve Christmas. She set off into the countryside. Her background was of course the French farmland and after all she was a French farm cat at heart. However it was a relief to find herself in a different landscape from war-torn France and to be away from the explosions and mud of the trenches. She discovered the cultivated land outside of the city. The undergrowth was coarse. Anouk followed small animal tracks. Thyme and rosemary brushed their herbal fragrance onto her coat as she pushed through the foliage. Stunted olive and tamarind trees peppered the hillsides.

As she explored she became aware of some almost imperceptible tremors in the soil beneath her feet. But where were the rivers and creeks? None. However fresh water seeped up from below ground in several places and she drank copiously. She detected the patter of tiny feet below her in the hollows and cracks in the bare limestone rocks which surfaced in increasing quantity from the thin soil. A quick scrape and a pounce and another Maltese shrew was dispensed.

A rat suddenly shot out from beneath a shrub at her feet and disappeared as if by magic right in front of her. But what was this? Anouk came to an abrupt halt. She was confronted by a tunnel. It wasn't big but it led alluringly downwards. It seemed to be some kind of underground sanctuary. This was too much temptation and down she went with her claws extended. Her keen eyes adjusted rapidly to the gloom. As a cat Anouk could not be expected to appreciate the fact that she was now on an expedition into the only known prehistoric necropolis containing the remains of thousands of individuals from 3,600 BC. Anouk's only concern was that the rat had totally vanished.

Being curious she proceeded down one of a series of tunnels. It was deliciously cool inside. The tunnel opened out into a hall. She was unable to see the roof but she could feel the space looming high above her. It was obvious that this had not been created by any shrew. She could hear and smell a substantial rat population in residence here but as Anouk did not fancy any encounters where she would certainly be outnumbered she turned tail and fled out the way she had come. She did wonder why such a vast underground place would have been constructed but the answer to that remains a mystery to man and beast to this day.

Christmas Day found Anouk sitting in the early morning sun amidst the tumbled ruins of a Megalithic temple. She was perched on top of one of the vast stones and was concentrating on washing her paws. She didn't like the dust accumulating between her pads. This was to be her last day on the Island of Malta.

Edward wondered if this would be the place Anouk would choose to settle. She was gone from dawn to after dusk every day. The next day the *Aragon* made ready to sail. All servicemen and nurses were accounted for but a grey cat was present also.

It was Sunday morning and the coast of Egypt lay visible in a thin line across the horizon. There was a sense of relief aboard that they had crossed the Mediterranean safely in the care of the destroyer, *HMS Attack.* They had already entered the channel to the Port of Alexandria but had been ordered out to await escort as the channel had been mined. They were now adrift eight miles off Alexandria. Edward was on deck. It was idyllic. The sun was shining on a sparkling sea. He was relaxed on a deck chair reading despite being only a short distance from the war against the Ottoman Empire in the Palestinian conflict. Anouk was gazing at the scene as if hypnotised. Suddenly she noticed what looked like a silver fish cutting through the still waters, its wake streaming out behind. It was heading directly for the ship. A horrendous crash ensued. The entire ship shuddered. Instinctively all of Anouk's claws shot out and she clung to the deck as the ship listed to starboard. A torpedo from a German submarine had penetrated the hull and travelled via the empty aft hold deeply into the ship. The shaft was fractured behind the engine room.

Well trained officers and crew leapt into instant action. It was all happening so fast but strangely as if in slow motion. The crew set to work launching the lifeboats. The officers mustered the troops on deck. Anouk found herself swept along towards the boats. The port lifeboats were hanging uselessly against the hull of the listing ship unable to be launched from that angle. The starboard boats were filling up with the women. There were over two and a half thousand souls aboard the *Aragon*. How could they possibly all be saved?

Nurses were piling into the boats which were slung as fast as gravity would take them down into the sea which was now covered in a slick of oil and flames. Anouk heard her name called out but before she could react Sophie had scooped her up then they tumbled together headlong into a boat just beginning its descent.

Anouk looked up, realised what was happening and scrambled free of Sophie's grasp. As the boat swung out over the water she performed another of her spectacular leaps. She was back on board the sinking ship. She did not quite make it onto the deck but managed to cling to the guard rail. A sailor grabbed her by the scruff of the neck and as he was about to pitch her back into the lifeboat she struggled free and took off back up the deck to the sound of the crewman shouting, 'You stupid animal.

You were nearly saved!' Anouk had one thought in her head, 'Where is he?'

She found the troops lined up under orders from their platoon officers. Edward's said, 'No one moves until I give the order', and drew his pistol. The crew were now waist deep in the encroaching sea water trying desperately to free more boats but it was hopeless. The men knew the available boats were gone, filled to capacity with the nurses. Some of them had already overturned. There were no lifeboats for any of them. There was only one last chance. Anouk could feel the boat sinking by the stern below her feet.

At that moment there was another tremendous blast and shudder. The cold seawater had reached the ship's boilers causing them to explode. Next moment an Indian Lascar from the engine room burst out on deck, scalded from head to toe, and dropped down dead at their feet. One of the Bedfords panicked and ran for the rail. The officer shot him dead before he reached it.

Somehow Edward was able to think rationally. He knew he was in deep trouble as he could not swim a stroke. He had never learned. He had never had to. He looked down at his heavy army boots. This was disastrous. He would be pulled under by their weight. He carefully bent down. There at his feet was a cowering Anouk. He untied his laces and straightened up with a terrified cat inside his jacket.

It didn't seem possible that very little time had passed since the torpedo struck but it had only been fifteen long panicked minutes before Captain

Bateman gave the order, 'Abandon ship and God go with you!' Edward's officer echoed this command with 'Over the side men and good luck to you all.'

Edward stepped out of his boots and joined the swarm of men scrambling over the rail. The next thing he knew the deathly cold waters were surging up past his neck and he and Anouk were in the sea with scores of his comrades. The destroyer had come alongside and was fishing men both dead and alive from the water. The air was foul with the oil and fumes coating the surface. Ropes were lowered and men were being hauled aboard to be laid out on the deck, the injured, the half-drowned, the dead.

Only five minutes after the order was given to go over the side the *SS Aragon* disappeared below the waves. She had gone, taking with her, troops, their officers, her crew and her captain. In her wake many more men struggling in the sea were sucked to their deaths.

Only another five minutes later the courageous *HMS Attack* was torpedoed amidships and blown clean in half. The survivors aboard from the *Aragon* were either blown apart or jettisoned into the water to live once more or to die.

Edward was learning about drowning. He had gone under once but somehow had struggled back to the surface. His thoughts were of his parents, his wife, his child and of the cat trustingly fastened against his chest. A second wave of suction took Edward back under. He had been breathing oil and fumes but now was inhaling polluted seawater. He surfaced once more. He knew when he went under once more that it would be for the last time. He could feel the end coming. The pull of the deep had him in its icy grasp. He was slipping away, down and away. Then a voice called out, 'Hold on mate!' and an oar was thrust within his reach by a sailor in a lifeboat. He grasped the edge of it with the tips of his fingers... an oar between him, Anouk, and eternity.

On board a nurse loosened the now unconscious Edward's sodden jacket and a little cat's head appeared with a plaintive meow. Edward regained consciousness in hospital in Alexandria suffering from pneumonia but Anouk was curled up on his pallet at his feet. She had become the ward pet but she barely left Edward's side. They were alive. They had been rescued, pulled from the brink.

After his convalescence Edward said, 'Well Anouk, it's home for us. I wonder how you will like Glasgow.' Edward was invalided out, awarded two medals and repatriated without firing a shot. The *SS Aragon* had gone down taking six hundred and ten men to the bottom of the sea. She lies there to this day in one hundred and thirty five feet of shimmering, crystal, Mediterranean water.

Edward arrived home unannounced and unexpected. Jean saw him coming along the road and was speechless with delight. When they got indoors she was curious about the basket he carried. 'What's that Dada?' she asked. He opened the lid and the sweetest little face Jean had ever seen looked up at her. Jean looked into Anouk's green eyes. Her heart skipped a beat and then it raced. It was mutual love at first sight. Edward said nothing. It was hard to believe they had come through the war alive and that they had managed to stay together. This war, the fear, the deprivation, the absence of a father had all left the child in a single instant. Anouk the French farmhouse cat had arrived home at last. Now she was Anouk the Glasgow tenement cat but she didn't mind as she could hear a mouse under the sink and set off to explore.

From Anouk to George

Anouk was left to her new contented life in the post-war Glasgow tenement and slid gently back onto her ledge. A general sigh of contentment rippled through the group. Now eight cats had been reviewed and only one remained.

From high up on the rock face a stocky ginger leapt to the forefront before he was even called. He landed squarely and confidently faced the others. 'As I am last to be reviewed I will get started. It has been a long night for us all and I am sure you are all anxious to get on with this process.'

There was a certain amount of shuffling on the ledges as the cats repositioned themselves and once this was over the voice simply commanded, 'Proceed'.

'My name is George Washington but everyone calls me George. I am a New York tomcat from a Brownstone on Manhattan Island.' The eight cats settled to watch the modern scene before their eyes as 21st Century America appeared and there was George stalking a rat in an alley. There was no doubt the entire group was gripped by curiosity and George had a rapt audience.

The New York Brownstone Cat

September 2001

I peer into the shadows of the back alley. In the roadway there are apartment blocks and shops. Many are fast food establishments. The bins at the rear are high with the odour of both fresh and rotting food. The smell can be intoxicating. My head positively spins with the joy of it. At this time of the day the vast army of the New York rats appear from the sewers, the cellars and the dark corners behind the countless bins. The atmosphere is saturated with the ordure of vermin and even from cats like me.

I am not alone in this world of plenty. We tomcats have settled many scores over a long period of time and I have the scars to prove it. Like all societies there is a pecking order, a phrase for which I pay homage to the humble duck. I am proud to identify myself as one of the back alley's top-cats having fought myself up from weak kittenhood to battle-scarred predator. I may appear to be wandering aimlessly through this darkened lane but you could not be more wrong. This is a well-worn beat; respecting areas won by other dominant cats, making detours around the danger spots, checking out the females in attendance that may be seeking a mate and watching out for the rat swarm. All aspects of feline and rodent life belong in the fetid atmosphere of a city like this. These alleys have been the scene of the conception of uncountable kittens and also the slaughter of innumerable rodents.

The rats of Manhattan are a notorious bunch; organised, fool-hardy, fearless, pugnacious and vicious. The swarms which emerge from hiding in the evenings are not a random bunch. They move in columns, running over everything in sight. They climb, leap and dive but manage to stay in formation as they occupy their territories. Bin lids are prised open, food is dragged from half empty fast food containers, drain pipes are scaled, the contents of dumpsters are tossed but the worst aspect of this is the noise. It is not just the scampering of tiny claws on hard surfaces but the relentless squeaking and squealing. It can be deafening to the sensitive ears of a cat but worse still are the ultrasonic cries which nearly unhinge my mind. I stand at a well chosen vantage point and survey the scene before me. Some of the senior male rats know me by sight and we have a mutual understanding which is 'steer clear of one another'. There are the experienced females with almost independent pups. These mothers cast their eye upon me and I see and understand their warning: 'Touch not my young', and I comply. You have to be careful not to become mesmerised by the swirl of the rat tails which flow past like a river in spate or you will never trap anything but be left gawking. No your only hope of a fresh rodent for supper is one of the young inexperienced stragglers. They don't put up much of a fight and when caught they go into a catatonic state of shock. Once I catch one I hurry out of the alley away from the swarm, the creature dangling from my jaws, while my fellow felines barely spare me a backward look.

But this is not the sum total of my life in New York City. No, not at all. I am a cat of many talents and I live a varied lifestyle. And of course New York is a microcosm of the world's population. Its ethnic diversity, its languages, its culture, are reflected in the myriad of restaurants and cafes serving all manner of international cuisine. Likewise the cats of New York represent all manner of felines in size and stature with coats of many hues. Like the human residents, all live under the one umbrella and become one thing, American. By the way my name is George Washington after a famous president but my friends just call me George.

Even after multiple generations when tastes and accents have changed, an exciting and varied gene pool gives rise to cats like George. His lineage stretches back to the persecution of the Russian Jewry. He is the descendent of a tiny kitten brought to the land of the free in the basket of a little girl. These are the embedded memories in this not quite all-American creature.

George is next seen ambling along a street in trendy Greenwich Village. In contrast to the stinking back alley it is charming and quaint. He strolls past a row of brownstone apartments. Lovely greenery sprouts from window boxes and half barrels on every available spot. The evening social crowd of humans pay no attention to this bold ginger cat on the sidewalk. George siits obediently at the crosswalk and waits for the flashing command to 'WALK'. He cannot read but knows when the crowd surges forward it is also safe for him to do so. He turns into a leafy courtyard and finds a comfy spot on top of a garden urn to survey the scene. Jazz music blares from a first floor window while a crowd of late-night revellers sits at outdoor tables. It is hot and muggy in New York in August even when the sun has set. It makes George feel he is breathing through a hot wet blanket. Although George has already consumed one rat snack he is hoping for some food scraps to fall to the ground which he will scavenge. He considers his actions to be of service to the city, a sort of social clean-up which includes rat removal of course.

'Georgio, buona sera my friend, hello!' A strongly accented voice greets George and a rotund Italian chef appears from the restaurant carefully carrying a small dish of leftovers. George leaps down to ground level, stretches, purrs and butts his head against Siriano's arm as he places the dish in front of him. George is not unappreciative of his good fortune to live in a city inhabited by many cat lovers. Can this docile, polite creature be the same one that hunted ferociously in the back alley? George is emerging as a cat of multiple personalities.

Feeling pleasantly replete, George settles down for a nap. In typical cat fashion he sleeps away approximately two thirds of his life. He may be nine years old but actually he has only been awake for three of those years but this is not a matter of concern to him. Later having been nourished and rested, George stretches first his front legs then arches his back and extends his back legs to their full length and moves on.

After only a few blocks he arrives at Washington Square. The attraction here is not solely because he believes it has been named after him but the night time activity there pulls him like a magnet. He pauses at the entrance to the wide open space to refresh himself at a puddle which is always available below the water fountain.

George's highly developed senses perceive more in this land than any human could possibly do. As he walks across the grass he feels the faint vibration of the brook which once flowed across the surface prior to being rerouted underground. The land, although now dry, still has the memory of marshland under the pads of his feet and to his delight the bones of the dead still call from their original resting place despite the exhumation of thousands of bodies by the city. George loves the timelessness of this place.

He is never drawn to Washington Park in the daylight when visitors find a refuge from the burning city streets in summer and residents bring their dogs and children to run free. By night a very different population takes possession of the space, both human and feline. These particular humans are of little interest to the cats as they are intent on a certain illegal trade. The substances available hold no allure for a cat. No, George is pulled by more than a hundred vocal sounds, cat voices raised in chorus in the dark; females in heat, answering toms establishing their dominance, high pitched attempts by the young, older youngsters asserting their coming of age, cracked and feeble calls of the aged, all asserting their right to be present there. George raises his own voice to swell the strain, revelling in the chance to demonstrate his vocal capabilities. And so George's night passes in this exhilarating manner. With satisfaction he sees the spread of the dull grey light preceding dawn and knows it is time to return to his other life, a very different one from what we have seen up to now.

He turns south along the streets which have not yet come to life. He likes to get home before rush hour. After several blocks of purposeful travel he arrives at a small street with a row of brownstone apartments. There is something comforting to George in the unchanging stability of these traditional New York dwellings. Skyscrapers abound but when he looks up through the tightly developed Manhattan streets, the sky is reduced to a sliver of blue which seems terribly far away. As tempting as it may be to scale the glass and concrete exteriors of these towering business blocks no cat in his right mind would do so. But brownstone, that feels more natural. George is unaware of the ancient Triassic history of this reddish sandstone. He simply feels the comfort of the unchanging in the midst of the modern frantic rush to develop and redevelop seemingly unceasingly.

He passes the stone stoop leading up to the front door and instead drops down the metal flight of steps leading to the basement. An onlooker at street level would think he had magically disappeared but he has simply ducked through the small cat-door into the downstairs apartment where he lives, well some of the time.

'George, there you are!' He is greeted by a husky man in the uniform of a New York fire-fighter. 'How was your night? Here have some milk. I am only home a few minutes before you. My night? Well, Busy and eventful as usual. Now I need to sleep. You too?' After a shower and breakfast Ben sleeps and at his feet George sleeps also.

The oppressive heat has relented. The New York streets are less sweltering, less dusty, less crowded and a hint of autumn is in the early morning air. September has arrived with its promise of cooler days, even cooler nights. The entire city seems to be holding its breath in anticipation of the fall colours. Ben is in a rush to depart. It's 07.00am. He is in his dress uniform. George is in no rush at all. 'I'm off to Randalls Island,' he announces to George. 'I am teaching the trainees at the Fire Department Academy this week. See you tonight rascal,' and he is gone.

George blinks in the morning light, wanders around the kitchen and laps up the last of his milk. The fresh scent from outdoors lures him through the cat-flap and up the steps. He often follows Ben to his fire station where he has become a bit of a feature but not today as Randalls Island does not sound terribly appealing to a Manhattan street cat.

'Battery Park,' George thinks. 'I'll wander down there and see what's what.' He heads south at a leisurely pace taking in the familiar sights and scents. Manhattan is where two worlds collide, the old and the new. George likes this. The Algonquian Indians had sold the island to a Dutchman over three hundred and fifty years earlier for goods worth $24 then one hundred and fifty years later George's name sake had been sworn in as the first president of the United States of America. Now lower Manhattan, seen from the Hudson River, showcases a world famous modern skyline. This is where George belongs. Battery Park is at the tip of the island facing the emblematic Statue of Liberty holding aloft the torch which welcomes all to the New World.

The first warning that all is not what it should be is when great shadows are cast at George's feet where no shadows ought to be. He looks up. The sight that meets his eyes is very strange indeed. Countless birds are fleeing north. The sky between the tall buildings is obliterated by them. Flocks of pigeons, crows forming black clouds, smaller random species, all flying flat out in an unnatural exodus. George has never seen anything like it. What can be happening? In typical curious-cat fashion, instead of turning around and heeding the warning of the birds, George sets off at a smart pace in the direction they have come from.

George realises that something exciting must be going on. He rounds a corner and there in front of him are the Twin Towers of the World Trade Center. These two skyscrapers have defined the skyline for twenty-six years and are the tallest buildings in the world. They are home to great international commerce and are renowned and visited by people from all over... and the North Tower is on fire!

George stops in his tracks. This was not expected. Never has he seen humans in such confusion. What is wrong with these people he wonders as he watches the scene? Some are moving forwards towards the burning building, their phone cameras held in front of them recording the incident while others are backing away in horror. Traffic backs up as drivers are unsure whether to proceed then finding they are unable to reverse or turn around. The stench of burning aviation fuel is travelling in an invisible cloud into George's nostrils.

Within minutes the news is being broadcast worldwide that on this day, September 11th 2001, American Airlines Flight 11, bound for Los Angeles, has, at 8.47am, crashed into Manhattan's World Trade Center North Tower. The aircraft seems to have penetrated the building near the top. George sees a vast plume of dense black smoke being carried away in the breeze. He joins the crowd still surging forward to get a better view when he sees another plane flying into view around the South Tower. It is three minutes past nine when it slams into the skyscraper only a little lower than in the North Tower. It explodes on impact turning the upper building into a catastrophic blaze. The building is immediately engulfed in a horrendous fireball which is shedding burning fuel in a torrent into the street.

This changes everything. For sixteen minutes people believe they are witnessing a tragic accident but, when Flight 175 plunges into the South Tower, panic erupts. They realise that they are under attack. At this point the sirens of the emergency services are heard screaming their way through the streets of Manhattan. George knows that Ben is on his way. Curiosity is still his predominant reaction. George's association with Ben and his time spent at the fire house have caused him to lose his protective fear of fire, a necessary instinct in the wild and one that should serve George better in this situation.

George forgets all thoughts of Battery Park. He scrambles up a trellis onto the canopy roof of the porch of a restaurant. From here he can see all that happens but is unseen by others. For the next hour George watches firefighters pour into lower Manhattan in a never-ending stream. Routes are cleared for the fire trucks which converge from all over New York and beyond. He is watching for Ben and his crew but he recognises no one in the trucks which race past. He can hear the shouts from the fire-chiefs who have set up their command post at the base of the buildings. He watches more and more people streaming out from the towers and more and more firefighters pour in. Ambulances are lining up in convoy as the injured are helped into the waiting arms of the paramedics, away from this appalling scene of disaster.

Without warning George is transfixed by a roar the likes of which he has never heard before. The ground shakes as if it is an earthquake and a great draft of air blows George off his perch. He picks himself up and is immediately swept away from the scene by four unanticipated waves. First of all George finds himself caught up in a rush of feline terror as all the cats of lower Manhattan stream north with a speed reserved only for a life threatening situation. George has no option but to go with the flow but in bewilderment he sees that they are not alone. What is even more shocking is the mass exit of the alley rats which appear to be in pursuit of the cats. Fleetingly George thinks this is a reversal of the usual situation between cat and rat but there is no time to dwell on such matters now. There is no squeaking or squealing as all energy is directed into their escape and the only reason the cats are in front is because their legs are longer than the rats'. Then come the people, civilians, running, limping, hobbling, dragging one another ahead of an unimaginable cloud of dust which appears to be in pursuit of all the others.

The South Tower has collapsed, not sideways as you may expect but vertically downwards into itself creating a cloud of powdered concrete and pulverised glass. It is blowing like a tornado through and over the streets consuming all in its path. Without a mask no one can breathe so George runs without stopping.

Several blocks north of the chaos George sees more fire trucks heading for the scene. One of the last of them is trying to navigate its way through the blockage at an intersection with cars trying to get away and emergency services trying to get through. This crew has been held up due to being on a training course at Randalls Island that morning.

They are determined to join their fellow firefighters and nothing is going to stop them. George's keen cat ears hear a familiar voice above the clamour and he spots the crew he knows. He has seen so many helmeted firemen this day, more than he realised existed in the whole of New York City, but here finally is the one he is looking for. He streaks across the road and with a flying leap is on the rig. He lands right at Ben's feet. Ben stares in shock at the dust-coated, bedraggled-looking creature which has appeared as if from nowhere. He doesn't recognise him until George turns his face up to him and meows. 'Good heavens cat, is that you? What the heck do you think you are doing? Go home you crazy animal! You do not want to get involved in this.' Ben bends down and scoops George up. He intends to release him back onto the street but at that moment the truck jerks forward and tears off southwards following a path which is opening up for them. Ben is going to the biggest rescue mission ever by any firefighter in any country in the world, to a fire they know they have no hope of putting out and he has his pet cat with him. No, this cannot be happening!

Ben knows he may not survive this mission, that many of his fellow firefighters will not be going home that day but that he has a job to do and an oath to honour. As one one of New York's finest he is always expected to put the lives of others before his own and so very many lives are at risk this day. He cannot be worrying about one small animal but he realises that George's life is in his hands, literally, and in his heart he knows, if he can, he will save him.

The truck arrives and joins the other emergency vehicles at the scene. What a scene it is! There is no time to stop and stare or ponder what has caused this mass destruction in the centre of an American city. The crew get their instructions: Assist the crews inside the North Tower who are helping evacuate the civilians. No hoses are required. The situation has gone long past that.

Ben propels George into the cab and slams the door shut. As he runs with the others towards the building he glances back and sees George with his hind legs on the driver's seat, his front paws on the steering wheel and his little face peering forwards out of the windscreen. To any observer that fire truck is being driven by a cat! It is the only light moment in what is to become the worst day of Ben's life.

People are still running out of the North Tower. It was struck by the first plane but is still standing after the loss of the South Tower. The plane has impacted floors ninety three to ninety nine. No one in that area has any chance of survival. The plane has sliced through the three stairways which are now blocked by rubble and fire. Ten thousand gallons of burning jet fuel has cascaded down the elevator shafts. This is what awaits Ben and his fellow rescuers.

The North Tower is now standing on borrowed time. Its fall is inevitable. The firefighters already inside the North Tower, toiling up the endless stairs to reach the upper stories hear the terrible roar and feel the building shake when the South Tower goes down but they have no view of it and do not know what is happening. Communications are cut off. The word from the command post is spread upwards to the rescuers: Evacuate the building. Not realising the imminent danger, the firefighters begin an unhurried descent, floor by floor, helping those still on their way down.

The twelve men from Ben's rig are instructed not to climb up into the North Tower but to assist those already exiting the building. Many are burned and injured and need to be taken to the ambulances. Then with a roar and a dust cloud like a nuclear explosion the last standing structure of the World Trade Center Twin Towers falls to the ground, disintegrating as if liquefied. George flees beneath the seat in the cab as the smoke and the debris roll over the fire truck. Ben and only seven of his men are far enough away when the second building collapses.

A short time later Ben's surviving uninjured crew gather at the truck to get their new instructions which are to search for survivors amidst the vast field of compressed concrete and twisted steel. When the cab door is opened a terrified cat slinks out unnoticed and goes away. Ben sees his tail disappear amidst a shower of shredded office paper falling like snow on the devastation.

The hunt is frantic. Blistering fires are burning in the rubble, hot enough to melt the shoes of the searchers. It is thirty-six hours later when a traumatised and exhausted Ben joins George at home. He collapses on the bed, unfed, unwashed, unable to even speak. George is there, licked clean, renewed, recovered and his old self once more, something that Ben will never be able to be. Ben is unaware as he sleeps that he is not alone because George is there sleeping beside him.

Sadly Ben and the surviving firefighters' duties at the site are not over. In the first thirty-six hours only another eighteen people are found alive. They are the last. Ben spends the following five months in the gruelling clean up during which time New York mourns. He loses three hundred and seventy three of his fellows. Those who survive are hailed as heroes. Ben does not feel like a hero.

George's life however goes on almost as before. He never does go back down to Ground Zero as the site is now called. He stays a bit closer to home. There is no record of any cats having been killed in the 9/11 disaster and George knows nothing about terrorists or why these planes brought down those tall buildings that day.

Onwards to the New Beginning

Present Time

It was dark in the den with only the faintest glimmer of light seeping into the cave from the entrance a long way off. Only a cat could make sense of it; the dry floor, the soaring walls with cracks and hollows, the shelter it offered and the safety within. Inside a hollow a mother cat breathed heavily as she laboured alone in the gloom. Her distended belly had reduced her mobility to almost nothing and she had used the last of her strength to climb up into her safe place. Never before had she experienced a weight in her womb like this. It was time to lighten her load and her contractions confirmed it.

One after another the tiny new beings made their way into a world they could neither see nor hear, their eyes firmly shut, their ears folded down. However the tantalising smell of their mother's milk and the warm feel of her fur covered belly was all they sought. They pushed and squealed from the moment the mother licked them free of the birth sac to claim their unique feeding spot. Happily she had two rows of five teats unlike the general two rows of four because this little brood was exceptional and she had given birth to nine baby cats.

From the moment they were born she could identify each one. As the next few weeks passed she saw not only their different physical characteristics but their personality traits as clearly as the markings on their coats. Her first born was unmistakably large, large at birth and consistently bigger than all the others. A little sandy coloured female had surprisingly short legs but was as agile as her siblings. One male with a shaggy coat seemed at home amongst the rocks in the cave and was first to scamper over the boulders as if this rocky world was already familiar. A shy stocky female was first to show the characteristic coat stripes of the tabby and she was proving to be a secretive creature. One male was a dedicated explorer and he managed to reach places in the cave the others never got to. A sleek smooth-coated boy seemed to have charmed his sisters and two of them in particular were his dedicated followers. Only one was a ginger tom and a more relaxed animal you could not find. The large one was male but not aggressive. He was the one who led the little troop to the mouth of the cave to view the world for the first time, a natural leader. The other eight happily followed after him.

Sunset that evening found the mother cat basking contentedly in the golden glow of the dying light while nine infant felines played at her feet. The light was reflected on the surface of Lake Van which was a considerable distance below them while the lakeside cherry blossom scented the evening air. Above them the Turkish mountain top still had a covering of snow but spring was in the air and without doubt all nine kittens were content to remain together high above the foothills and the shimmering lake. Descent to the shore-line and the plain below would wait for another day. For now, it was simply enough to live again.

A Message from One of the Cats

I lived and then life ended.
You live, time suspended.
Loved and known
My life has flown
...and now I am remembered

My name you know
My song did flow
Surfing through time
Your life touched mine
...and so I am remembered.

Poverty or fame
Your life may claim
But my wish for you
When life is through
...that you also are remembered.

Made in the USA
Middletown, DE
23 September 2017